This is a work of
events are entirely

WITHOUT REDEMPTION

First edition. November 20, 2017.

Copyright © 2017 David Griffith.

Written by David Griffith.

Prologue

I'd been pinned in that wet, mosquito-infested hole for a good part of the day. The bullets still splattered on the rocks behind me, which meant the cartel gunmen had no intention of leaving. I tucked the battered pistol under my injured arm while I fumbled to the bottom of my *mochila*. A couple clips remained. When those shells were gone, I'd join the fifty thousand other casualties of this south-of-the-border drug war.

This had been pitched as strictly a reconnaissance mission, a holiday actually. I should have known better. Where the company sent me, everything was dangerous. This trip hadn't been any different.

I peeked around the side of the mossy rock to see if any of those killers were trying to creep in close and finish me off. That was a mistake. A bullet sliced a neat hole through my tourist hat. I ducked back behind the boulder, snatched it off and surveyed the damage. I'd paid a goodly sum for that hat because Clarissa had said it made me especially handsome, which I knew wasn't true, but I'd have given more just to hear that from her. I should have been glad the shot only ruined my hat. What few brains I could boast of had only been two inches below that bullet hole and though they weren't Harvard quality, if I got out of here, I would have need of them.

Chapter 1

Though low in the sky, the west Texas sun had lost none of its scorching heat. The chunky bay mare, unruffled by the noise and excitement, stood in chute number five. She cocked one ear as I slipped the halter over her nose. Gentle as falling rain, I eased the cinches tight, then measured off the rein. A win tonight would power me back into the top fifteen and give me at least an even chance at the National Finals in Las Vegas. This horse could be my ticket. The clock for me was running out, and deep down I knew this would be my last shot at a world championship.

Every bronc requires a set amount of rein, each one different, unique. For a small horse, Brown Betty took plenty: a hand with thumb extended plus three fingers behind the swells.

With the easy confidence gained from a thousand broncs, I slipped over the chute bars and into the worn saddle, watchful, ready for the unforeseen, even though today there would be little danger. I'd drawn this mare at least twice before. Brown Betty was always a money horse, sometimes nervous in the chute, but never bad or dangerous.

When I reached down for my stirrup, my eyes left her flickering ears, those telltale harbingers of trouble. Suddenly, she violently reared. I grabbed at the top bar, struggling to stay above the eleven hundred pounds of flailing horseflesh.

WITHOUT REDEMPTION

As quickly as she'd come up, she dropped and stood quiet, her four unshod hooves solidly planted in the Texas sand as if nothing had happened. Her case of nerves now over, I clambered out onto the catwalk to reset my saddle. I'd not cinched as tight as I would have liked. She bucked better with a looser cinch, just one of those little pieces of information we bronc riders pass back and forth to each other.

The arena director paced in front of the chute, snapping his program against his leg like a riding crop. "Come on, Lonnie. Hurry."

I glared at him, the familiar danger and need to win an adrenaline rush in every muscle as I stepped over the chute again. He had two thousand Texas fans to send home knowing they'd seen an exceptional performance, but it wasn't my fault his horse had gone crazy and held up the show.

This time, I got scrunched down into my saddle long enough to nod my head. The moment I tucked my chin and braced for that first powerful jump into the arena, everything else faded, no crowd or noise, nothing but Brown Betty's tossing black mane and powerful surging shoulders. She kicked high in the air, doing her best to send me into the dirt while my feet searched for new holds. Each jump, her head disappeared between her front legs, and my dull-roweled spurs traced an invisible arc from her shoulders to the cantle of my saddle. They were natural reactions gleaned from a legion of wild horses in dusty arenas from Calgary, Alberta to the Mexican border. Somewhere in the background a horn signaled the end of the ride. Neither the mare nor I needed it. Either of us would have known from long experience the exact moment the eight seconds ended. The pickup men closed in. Brown Betty still bucked, but now only half-heartedly. She'd done this long enough to know when her job was finished. I handed the braided buck rein off to the pickup man on my left. He slowed the mare with a half-turn on his saddle horn. We were closing in on the fence, the bunting draped grandstand directly in front of us. I stood out in my right stirrup and reached for the cantle of the other pickup man's saddle to vault over the other side of his big gelding, safely away from Brown Betty's dangerous back feet.

A loud crack, like the distinctive bark of a colt .38 broke my concentration. Without thinking, I swiveled toward the sound. A kid in the stands with a silly grin and a newly popped balloon leaned over the rail. Brown Betty slammed on the brakes at the crucial moment, which splatted me right under that pickup horse's steel shod feet. One of them came down with a good portion of thirteen hundred pounds directly on my left arm. The pain was instant, and I didn't have to look down at the ripped sleeve of my green shirt to know that at least one bone had snapped. The too-familiar queasiness associated with bone injury roiled through my stomach, but I gritted my teeth and pushed to my feet. Holding the injured limb next to my body, I stumbled toward the chutes as I listened to the announcer's excited spiel. Brown Betty had done it for me. We'd gone to the lead and would probably win, but what good would that do me now? Behind the chutes, I leaned against one of the stock holding pens, then slid to the ground while I waited for the nausea to subside. It would, long before the disappointment of a failed shot at the National Finals. I stared at the twisted limb on my lap. This had been my last chance. There would be no more.

WITHOUT REDEMPTION 5

A paramedic made her way through the assorted saddles and other rodeo cowboy rigging.

"Let's have a look at it." She set her bag on the ground and gently reached for my arm.

"It's broke," I grated through clenched teeth.

The lady didn't even glance up. She just peeled back my sleeve to inspect the bowed limb and did her best to stabilize it. Likely this wasn't her first experience patching up a rodeo cowboy. Ambulance rides cost money. If I could walk, I'd make my own way to the hospital.

"Better get to the hospital, cowboy. I'll call and tell them you're coming. This one's not going to be a quick fix."

"Ya' think?" My attempt to be flippant sounded strained even to me. The arm was really beginning to throb, but despite all the pain, I grinned at her, but the increasing nausea forced me to turn and study the row of now empty chutes to mask the agony.

After the paramedic had splinted my arm, I pushed away from the fence, cradling my arm while I shuffled toward the parking lot. Every step hurt, but not nearly as much as the knowledge that I'd now be sidelined during the most critical part of the rodeo season. Once, I glanced down at the rapid swelling. The injured limb was my riding arm, the one that held the buck rein. An early comeback would risk even more damage. Not a good thought.

Clarissa had seen it all from the stands. When she met me in the parking lot, worry lines tugged at the corners of her eyes. Six-month-old Conor peered up at me from the stroller as he tried to shove his toe into his dirt-smeared mouth.

David Griffith

"What happened?" Clarissa's worried gaze rested on the stabilizing splints.

"Some kid popped a balloon in front of us. The mare put the brakes on and dumped me under the pickup horse." I shrugged and stared at my splinted arm. "It just snapped."

"Come on. No, wait here. I'll get the pickup."

"There's nothing wrong with my legs," I growled. I led the way through the trailers, pickups and every kind of camper any road warrior could wish for. When we arrived at our pickup, she fumbled Conor into his car seat, her fingers clumsy as she rushed.

"You should have let them take you in the ambulance."

"Naw, it hurts, but we'll make out okay. Just get us there as quick as you can."

She nodded, the rising panic plain to see as I maneuvered my frame into the passenger side seat.

A few minutes later, we pulled up to the emergency entrance of Northside Memorial. When I pushed through the front door, the lobby brought back the same memories of a host of other medical facilities I'd had the misfortune to visit. While I signed the necessary forms guaranteeing somebody would pay handsomely for the provided services, I drew in shallow breaths of the bland institutional air with faint scents of whatever concoctions hospitals use to keep germs at bay. The paperwork over, I followed a nurse down the hall to curtained-off cubbyhole next to an operating room. Another injury, more twisted, broken bones and time off to do absolutely nothing. And, if this was anything like the last break, it would take months to heal.

WITHOUT REDEMPTION 7

They helped me into one of those skimpy gowns that would have embarrassed even my breechclout-clad ancestors, then knocked me out in order to add more pins and plates to the ones I already had. My final thought was that cremation would create financial difficulties for Clarissa. She'd have to hire a dump truck to cart off all the steel in my banged-up carcass.

Sometime later, consciousness returned, and so did the questions. When it had only been the two of us, Clarissa had her insurance adjuster job. Then, it hadn't mattered as much whether I won. Now, an injury meant Walmart wieners and oatmeal. For the foreseeable future, I wouldn't be winning anything, and we had only a small cushion in the bank. I stared at the ceiling as I considered what to do. We'd moved to Texas to make this last big run at a world championship. Today, that dream had gone up the stovepipe. I'd gambled, and it hadn't worked. How would I support my family? Presently, I had no answer to that question.

The squeaky wheel on Conor's garage sale stroller alerted me to Clarissa's presence before she ever turned the corner into my room. Despite the worrisome thoughts, I forced a smile. "I'm sure they'll kick me out of here first thing in the morning. Just go back to the hotel and put Conor to bed."

She leaned over and touched my forehead with her lips. "Conor's fine for a while. I'm a lot more worried about you."

"I'm okay."

Her eyes said she didn't believe my glib response.

David Griffith

"Alright, I guess I'm not." I stared at the cast on my arm. "After a few days, I'll be able to face it, I suppose, but it's tough when we were this close to a championship—and now it's over."

Clarissa's jaw set in that so familiar stubborn angle. "Lon, neither of us can see why this happened. It's a huge disappointment, but I believe there's a reason for everything." She stroked my good arm while she spoke. There wasn't anything she or anybody else *could* say. The career loss hurt, and like the arm, would take time to heal.

Clarissa bent down and kissed my forehead while her fingers riffled through my hair. "I love you, and we'll get through this." She picked Conor up out of his stroller and sat him beside me on the bed. He stared at my cast, then with a worried scowl, he reached down with his pudgy hands and patted my face.

I hugged him close. "Hey, little guy. Daddy's going to be fine. You take care of Mommy tonight for me."

Conor seemed to understand enough that he decided not to cry. I kissed him before Clarissa picked him up and set him back in his stroller. "I'll be here in the morning as soon as I get us ready. Is there anything you need?"

"No, and don't rush. I'm sure they won't turn me loose until the doctor has another look at this arm."

Clarissa's lips met mine as she smoothed the hair away from my forehead. "I love you."

"Love you too, hon, and thanks for . . . for your support, and just being you."

Before long, I fell asleep. The long night hours seemed fragmented by fitful periods of rest interspersed with more

WITHOUT REDEMPTION

worry. Three months with no income, and with a broken arm, other job options were limited. In the early dawn I dozed off, only to be jarred awake by the soft click of a turning doorknob. Instantly wary, I scrambled for a non-existent weapon. I'd gathered plenty of enemies, ones who absolutely hated me enough to do a hospital assassination. But when the light from the hallway fell onto the bulky figure entering my room, the silhouette brought a sigh of relief.

"Hi, Frederick."

He nodded in the gloom as he advanced toward the bed. "I happened to be in the stands. Thought I'd slip in for a bit before I leave town."

Frederick had always been a fan, absolutely rabid about the sport, the same way folks get goofy over football or golf. If a rodeo happened to be within driving distance, he was there.

"Good to see you." I held out my hand. He took it, and must have felt a momentary sense of compassion because he didn't maul it the way I'd come to expect. In some circles I was considered tough, but when that big bear grabbed my hand, I always breathed a sigh of relief after he returned it uninjured.

"How bad is your arm broke?"

"Bad enough. Both bones—radius and ulna."

He nodded. "Call me after they let you out of here. I'm sure we can arrange something to tide you over."

I stared suspiciously at him, but he didn't add anything further. We talked for a few minutes about rodeo, and then he turned to leave. At the door he paused, and I struggled to a sitting position. "What did you mean about work? There's not much I'm good for with a broken arm."

His lips flattened as he inspected me. I'm sure in a hospital gown with my tousled black Indian hair shooting every which way, I didn't look like one of his star agents. Though I didn't really care what I looked like, I was worried about supporting my family. However, Frederick's offer of a job to tide me over sent warning signals up my spine. Anywhere he sent me, a whole body in tip-top shape was a prerequisite to staying alive. Whatever screwball idea Frederick might have had—he could keep it.

Chapter 2

Clarissa rescued me later that morning. With a couple heavy-duty pain pills, we made the hundred and fifty miles to our rundown rented acreage outside of Uvalde in record time. As we bounced up the potholed driveway, I scanned the property we called home. The '70's vintage twelve-wide trailer house we lived in sat at a cockeyed angle, like the previous owners had dragged it that far and then abandoned it, which maybe they had. The inside had seen better days. We reminded ourselves the place was temporary, and cheap. Plus, we had the best neighbors ever. Many times on the road, I'd been comforted by the thought that if Clarissa had any problems, Holger and Betty would be instantly there to help. Both in their seventies, they were as retired as either of them would ever be. Most days, Holger still cowboyed for one of the nearby ranches, and lived life as near as he could get to when he'd worked for the massive Spanish Fork outfit. To Betty's exasperation, he still figured if work couldn't be done from the back of a horse, it probably didn't need doing. Whatever their issues, they were special people who kept an eye out for the woman and little guy I loved dearly. My calling in life meant I had little time at home, and though I often wished things had turned out different, I had to make do with what the Good Lord had dealt. I was a rodeo cowboy, at least that's what I'd been until Frederick Roseman

David Griffith

came along. He changed everything, because other than an uncommon knack for staying in the middle of a bucking horse, making life miserable for drug cartel bad guys was about the only other skill I possessed.

We pulled into the yard and I scooped up little Conor with my one good arm. I studied his mussed-up, dark curly hair as I packed him into the house. He had my high cheekbones and facial features, but his mother had put her stamp on the rest of him, which made me even more proud of him.

The following days were marked by pacing the floor and gritting my teeth against the throbbing in my arm. But the respite from traveling gave Clarissa and I time together, and we'd had precious little of that in the past six months. I told her Frederick had come by my room in the hospital and indicated he might have some work for me to do. Her response was mixed, and like my initial reaction, mostly suspicious.

"Lon, I don't trust him. He's always sending you to some crazy place where it's a miracle you return home alive. And now—"

"But sweetheart, we need the money. Hey, it might be a job in Albuquerque, probably some office work, or a contract out at the agent training facility."

"Oh sure. You're going to teach other agents how to kill more efficiently when you have a broken arm?" Her left eyebrow arched. "And another question I've wondered about for a while. When you're on one of those missions, how do you justify killing people?"

Clarissa had skirted around this question before, and my answer carried a big defensive 'no.' "We have commando types who do that. My work is intelligence."

WITHOUT REDEMPTION 13

"So would you kill a man if you had to?"

I shrugged, and tried to brush her off. "What do you mean, 'if I had to?' That takes in a lot of territory. Hon' that's not my job, so I've never had to make that decision."

As usual, she refused to leave the subject alone. "But really, if you had to pull the trigger, what would you do?"

"Whatever the situation requires," I hedged. This was not a new argument, and though at times I had reservations about actions our people took, I had little professional desire to concede. "A soldier has no choice, and really, that's what I am. At Stirling Associates, I follow orders."

Clarissa dropped her eyes, her face flushed with emotion. "How can you use that excuse if you have even a shred of belief in the sanctity of life?"

I leaned forward. "Okay, so your argument is Biblical? If you want to cut into that carcass, then you better figure out what to do with old King David and Saul and all those other guys in the Bible that slaughtered their way to fame. Every one of them killed hundreds, usually because God told them to."

Clarissa sighed as she likely marshalled more arguments, but I had no intention of capitulating.

"You're telling me I'm wrong to protect my family and my country from the ravages of drugs? In a war, people die. That's reality." I did give her more arguments, some of them less than kind. By the time I'd finished my rant, the volume had increased considerably.

"Settle down, and get off your soapbox. I will always stand behind you. It's just, I don't think it's right, and . . ."

14   *David Griffith*

The sound of a vehicle stopped our heavy discussion. I peered through the living room curtain. A nondescript, mid-size rental car pulled up to the railroad ties that defined our more-dirt-than-gravel driveway. Probably a salesman, or somebody from the government. Either would only add more misery to my already pain-filled day.

The driver's door opened, and a figure uncoiled from the seat. He stood on our desolate prairie road like he owned it. His immaculate sports jacket should have been out of place in this tumbleweed backwater. It wasn't. Frederick always made an impression.

I stepped out on the veranda. I had expected him. I just didn't figure he'd show up this soon, which made me more than usually suspicious. Anytime Frederick Roseman showed up in my vicinity, trouble trailed behind him like a junkyard dog, and I resented his presence. I used to welcome the turmoil he brought, or at least tolerate it. Now, even though we did need money, I wanted to be at home, think about my future, and, most of all, just heal up.

He took the stairs two at a time to our plywood deck. I stood at the top and greeted him with the minimum of politeness, then waved him to one of our rickety patio chairs. I eased into another across from him. Whatever he had in mind held little interest. I leaned back and crossed my arms, or as close to that as one can get with a cast.

Frederick was without a doubt one of the top ten intelligence operatives in America. He read people like a first grade primer, but apparently he'd failed college psychology. Crossed arms are an overt, antagonistic body language, signaling rejection. He ignored my pose and started his pitch.

WITHOUT REDEMPTION 15

"You look healthier already. That's the thing about being in superb condition. One heals faster. However, it'd be better if you don't have any stress or duties for a while." He reached into the breast pocket of his gray blazer and held out an envelope. "Here."

I leaned back in the chair to the point where I might have succumbed to gravity if I'd tried to get any further away. I wanted none of whatever he was selling.

Frederick shrugged, then chucked the envelope on the table. "A little bonus. You've done some stellar work. Take a holiday—on the company."

I uncrossed my arms and warily picked up the envelope, my eyes shifting between the man and his supposed endowment. A no-strings gift? I had my doubts as I slit the top with my pocket knife. Inside, a typewritten sheet of paper listed the itinerary for two adults and an infant. Plane reservations from San Antonio via Houston to San Jose, Costa Rica. A three-week stay, split between an all-inclusive hotel at a beach resort and some dude ranch deal called *Rancho Curada*. I peered under my eyebrows at Frederick, but as usual, his face remained expressionless and unreadable.

"You've had some tough missions. Call this a gift of appreciation for a job well done. We like to take care of our people."

I cautiously nodded, but the instant stench of a rat was overpowering.

"Actually, Lonnie." Frederick crossed a leg and started tapping on the deck railing with his index finger.

When he did that, it meant the heavy sales pitch came next. Frederick's drumming meant that steel trap mind was

16   David Griffith

engaged, and right now I suspected it might be stuck in overdrive. He waved a hand at the ticket vouchers I still held. "All legitimate, and you can use them any time . . . but, the sooner the better."

"Why's that?"

"Well . . . it's just that I need you to do a little—"

"No! Forget it! I'm not doing anything down there, and besides, what is there to do? It's Costa Rica. Thanks for the tickets, but if they're contingent on any involvement with cartels or drug dealers, you can keep them." I stuffed everything into the envelope and tossed it into his lap.

"You misunderstand."

His hurt look skewered my resistance.

"This is nothing." He again laid the envelope on the white, plastic table between us. "A little reconnaissance while you're on the beach. Maybe a short meeting. All you have to do is retrieve some papers." He waved a hand. "We could get anyone to do that. But you're already going to be there." He leaned back and spread his hands innocently. "Doesn't Clarissa deserve a holiday?"

At that moment, the woman in question made an appearance, bearing coffee for me and black tea for our guest. She set the cups between us. "What's this about a holiday?"

Without a trace of a smile, Frederick contemptuously waved a hand at the envelope he'd laid on the table. "We had some tickets lying around the office, and I thought perhaps Lonnie might want them. He doesn't think it would be possible for you to go. I understand. This may not be the best time of year to visit Costa Rica."

WITHOUT REDEMPTION 17

"Costa Rica?" Her eyebrows hit the only cloud on this sunny Texas day.

Out of the corner of my eye I observed my wife giving me the 'why-did-I-marry-this-idiot' look. Frederick busied himself with stirring sugar into his cup, purposely avoiding my glare, and probably trying not to laugh. I was beat. He knew it, and I knew it, but I wouldn't back down without a fight.

I held up my good arm, palm forward to ward off the accusations and arguments. "Hon, we were just discussing the issue. Wouldn't it be better if we planned to go next year? I'll probably have to see a doctor again. They might have to do more x-rays or something. Besides, how much fun would it be when I have a broken arm? Swimming would be out, and—" I clamped my jaw shut when I saw the building excitement in her eyes.

"I could swim. You'd build sandcastles with Conor. How about we call this father and son bonding time?"

"He isn't old enough to build . . ." My voice trailed away. Did it matter? A trip together might make up for all those months I'd been on the road. And nobody deserved some downtime more than Clarissa. But deep inside, the arguments for *not* going mounted higher. Frederick had never offered any holiday before, so why now? What was this really about?

Minutes later, the man in front of me inspected his watch as if it had just suddenly appeared on his wrist. He stood, nodded respectfully at Clarissa and reached across the table for my hand. "I must be going. Call me when you are ready to leave." Both corners of his mouth twitched upward. For him, that qualified as the equivalent of a regular typhoon of hi-

David Griffith

larity. He'd enjoyed my discomfort. My only consolation was that he couldn't ask me to do much beyond a meeting because of my useless left arm. Could he?

Frederick turned his car in the driveway and gave us a cheery wave. We waved back, mine somewhat less enthusiastic than Clarissa's. He disappeared over the hill on the county road and we sat quietly, the white envelope between us soaking up a coffee stain. Coffee? Yeah, Costa Rica was supposed to have some of the best. I tried to drum up everything I knew about the country. Good beaches, at least a couple awesome volcanos, and if the literature was right, a monkey for every tourist. I shrugged. Why not? Too often I'd been on dangerous missions where I'd been out of touch for weeks at a time. My wife deserved something for putting up with all that. Costa Rica was a great idea. She would love it.

Chapter 3

Call him Paolo. It wasn't the name his Italian immigrant mama gave him, but his real name is unimportant. You see, Paolo is a *sicario,* a hitman for the Sinaloa cartel. They have a long arm. You can't run and you can't hide, and if for some reason you are foolish enough to divulge any cartel details, you will wish for death long before oblivion takes away the excruciating pain. The best is to know nothing about the cartel. It's what Paolo would want, and cannot have. A *sicario* can never leave. If he tries to quit, the sole person he will talk to is the Devil.

Paolo's career started on Benito Juarez Street in Mazatlan. Tourists. The sea. *Olas altas,* big waves, and drugs—mostly cocaine. His earliest memories were of a home far to the south where there was never enough to eat. But there was always *cocaina,* because the father who appeared at irregular intervals to beat Paolo, his sister and mother was a smuggler for the Gulf cartel—or so his mama said. At the age of twelve, Paolo packed the few clothes he possessed and walked away from the mountainside hovel where he'd survived. Far to the north, in the sea port of Mazatlan he begged on the street, mostly from tourists. It wasn't long before he graduated to petty theft. One day, in front of the Blue Bay Hotel, he slipped the wallet from a stranger's pocket. His sharp eyes had missed the two bodyguards who followed the Sinaloa cartel lieutenant. They didn't miss him. They offered to cut his skinny little throat. If he wanted to live, he could work as a *halcone*. That didn't seem like much of a choice. He reported for work.

Halcones are the eyes and ears on the street, the ones who let the cartel people know when there are armed troops or federal police in the vicinity. Paolo never let the bosses down, and soon, finding enough to eat wasn't a problem. A *halcone* was paid the princely sum of twenty U.S. dollars a day. His cousin worked long hours washing dishes at the Hotel La Siesta for less than half of that.

Every day, *taxistas* lined up in the Zona Dorada, the Golden Zone, to ferry tourists around the city. But two of the little white *pulmonias* were not taxis—at least not real taxis. Their job was to deliver cocaine to rich Americanos for Carlos Cuevas. Carlos was the *jefe,* the plaza boss for the cartel. Nobody crossed Carlos and lived. One day, Paolo watched him shoot a man who did not show enough respect. It was the first time he'd seen anyone die—and the beginning of the nightmares. It was also the first night he used the white powder, the only escape from what he saw on the street.

At fifteen, Carlos promoted Paolo to the next level, well on his way to becoming a full-fledged *sicario*. Now, his job was to collect protection money. Officially, the Sinaloa cartel didn't charge shopkeepers for protection, so Paolo was sent to accept donations. The amount set by Carlos was whatever he felt the shopkeeper could afford. If the merchant refused to pay, an older *sicario* in training was sent to give a gentle warning. If there was a second offense, Carlos would send two full-fledged *sicarios* to deliver a stronger message—or kill

WITHOUT REDEMPTION

the offender. That only happened a few times. The tax was very low. Unlike *Los Zetas*, if a merchant had problems, they would often be forgiven, or the tariff would be deferred unless it was determined that they were disloyal or holding out. If that was the case, there was no forgiveness.

About six months after Paolo had been assigned to collect protection money for the cartel, he stopped at a shoe store on Benito Juarez Street. The owner, Enrique, was old, maybe fifty. He'd never been trouble. He always paid. Now he refused. Paolo swore at him and tried to bully him into paying, but in the end, he backed out of the store, unsure of how to deal with such insubordination. Besides, the old guy suddenly looked tough; not the usual pushover. That afternoon, Paolo reported him to Carlos.

Carlos nodded, seemingly unconcerned. "Leave him alone."

For two weeks, Paolo never went near Enrique's shoe store. Then one day Carlos summoned him to a little bar on Juan Carranza Street. He entered and peered into the dark interior. A drug ballad blasted from the juke box. At a corner table, Carlos beckoned him forward. The plaza boss reached across and shook Paolo's hand.

"You are doing a good job."

Paolo's face flushed with pride. "Thank you, *jefe*," he stammered.

Suddenly, Carlos pulled a .45 caliber pistol out of his jacket pocket and laid it in the middle of the table.

Paolo's heart stopped beating.

His boss leaned forward, his sooty eyes hard, calculating. "Can you do it, *niño*?"

22 *David Griffith*

Paolo leaned as far away from the gun as the chair would allow, his emotions ricocheting between fear of what Carlos might mean, and chagrin at being called a child. He stuttered, "Do what, *jefe*? What do you want me to do?"

"It is time for you to graduate. Are you man enough to now do what is necessary?" His eyes burned with a hellish intensity.

"My life is yours, *jefe*. You want something, it will be done."

Carlos threw a loaded clip into his lap. "Tomorrow, you walk into the store of Enrique Sanchez and kill him. He cannot disregard the authority of the cartel. He must be punished as an example to others."

Paolo's head bobbed too far up and down. He tried to slow it, to appear more professional, but it seemed to have a life of its own.

Carlos watched closely as Paolo reached for the gun. The instant the young man's hand touched the pistol, he nodded and strode out the door.

Early the next morning, Paolo sat at the corner of Benito Juarez and Zaragoza. He peered down the pavement toward the offending shop. Usually deserted at this hour, the street seemed clogged with traffic and people. Why? The fear that had denied him any sleep rolled into a bigger ball inside his belly. He needed to be alone. After he shot the man, how would he escape through these throngs of shoppers? A pickup idled by. Six federal police stared from the back. Paolo's heart double-timed, attempting to hammer a crater through his skinny chest. Did they know? Was this all a trap? He clenched his fists to stop the trembling in his hands. To fail

WITHOUT REDEMPTION

23

was unthinkable, because if he did, his work with the cartel would be over . . . and Carlos probably would kill him as well.

The target approached his store from the other end of the street. Paolo walked up behind him as the man slid the long steel security apron against the wall. Enrique stepped inside and when he turned, Paolo again faced the hard eyes and drooping mustache. The minute he saw the kid, the old man seemed to know. It did him no good. Swiftly, Paolo kicked the safety off with his thumb and shot him in the chest. The man's face contorted with pain as he staggered backward. His left arm caught the counter, and for a long moment he held Paolo's eyes. Paolo wanted to scream at him to die, but the man wouldn't. Finally, he slipped to the floor, but still no anger clouded the dark visage in front of Paolo's eyes—only sadness.

Paolo turned and stumbled blindly toward the door, wanting to be gone, away from the accusation in the old man's eyes. Inside, he felt he had done a great evil, crossed a divide from which he could never return.

Twenty minutes later, he opened the door that led into the back room of the bar.

Carlos glanced up. "Did you—?"

Paolo nodded.

Carlos rose and shook his hand. Immediately he flicked out his cell phone and gave rapid instructions. Within minutes, they'd whisked Paolo to a safe house filled with all the rewards the Sinaloa cartel lavished on those fortunate enough to be called *sicario*. He had graduated. The drugs and sex took away the guilt . . . at least until morning. From that moment, he was supplied with every pleasure. But it didn't

David Griffith

take him long to realize he would never go far if cocaine became his master.

Within a few months of that first killing, he did two more, one a businessman who refused to pay, the other a snitch. Both killings bothered him, but not as much as the first. As time went on, he became more skillful, and the terror of his victims no longer disturbed his sleep.

About six months after he had gunned down the snitch outside his home in *El Centro*, Carlos called him to a meeting at a small bar on *Calle Carnaval*. When Paolo pushed through the doors, Carlos hadn't arrived, which was normal. He seldom showed anywhere at the appointed time. Paolo knew the routine. He would wait. After fifteen minutes or so, two of Carlos's bodyguards would quietly enter and examine every customer. They would move to where he sat, give him the evil eye, sometimes even frisk him. Then one of them would go to the door and nod for Carlos to enter. Almost vaudeville, the setup achieved its desired result. Paolo was properly awed—and scared.

When Carlos's short powerful figure swept through the door, Paolo stood and respectfully waited for him to cross the floor. Any other response would be dangerous to his career. A hundred others roamed the street with more brains and talent than he had, just waiting for a chance to prove what they could do. If he expected to survive, he'd better make no mistakes.

Paolo nervously held out his hand. Carlos ignored the overture. Quickly, he shoved his hands in his pockets and cursed himself. He should have waited for Carlos to establish the correct protocol.

WITHOUT REDEMPTION 25

A fleeting, sardonic grin creased Carlos's face, then instantly hardened. "Sit." He nodded at the chair Paolo had vacated to stand in obeisance.

Paolo scrambled into the seat. He never took his eyes off Carlos and the two goons who now stood at a respectful distance while they monitored the entrance and the rest of the bar. While Paolo waited for Carlos to speak, his mind flipped to the same combat survival zone he'd developed as a little kid. No human is to be trusted, and certainly not Carlos. He would only survive if he was useful to the cartel. When that ceased, a bullet would find him.

The waiter scurried up to the table. Carlos waved him away then turned and smiled, or at least as close to a smile as a rabid coyote can get. "We have decided to give you a very important assignment. I think you are too inexperienced, but . . . perhaps it is the best way." He sat back and folded his arms while he studied the young man's face. "There is a traitor who must be eliminated."

Paolo swallowed, then did it again in a futile attempt to keep the lump of excitement and fear in the bottom of his belly. "I can kill him. Trust me."

Carlos eyed him. "Perhaps you might. Then again . . ."

Paolo leaned forward and clenched his jaw. "Tell me his name. I will find a way." His voice rang with false bravado.

Carlos snickered. "This will be the toughest assignment you have been given. Nothing—"

"I can do it!"

Paolo's voice was too loud, and Carlos's lips firmed into a hard line, the only other movement his obsidian pupils as they searched Paolo's face. "Then you shall have the opportunity, *niño*."

It was the second time Carlos had called Paolo a child, and though his anger flared, discretion prevailed. He bit his lower lip to hold back the angry retort on the tip of his tongue. At the age of sixteen, he'd been made a *Sicario*. Whatever childhood he'd had was long in the past. A sad voice, faraway in his head said possibly he'd never been a child, but he pushed the thought away. That didn't matter anymore. Behind the curtain of gall, he understood that Carlos was baiting him, trying to make him angry, but why? He hadn't long to wait. The cartel plaza boss uncrossed his thick, hairless arms and placed them on the table. He leaned forward and spat out the order. "Katrina Lopez is a traitor. You will kill her."

The blood slowly drained from Paolo's temples, down through his cheeks to somewhere below his heart. In his world, he trusted only one person—Katrina. They had met on the street. She, one of the multitudes of homeless ones had touched something deep in his soul. Dumped with a distant relative at birth, her story was a parallel to his own. She'd left the Mexico City slum-shanty to escape the abuse. Not that the street was better, but like Paolo, she'd fought to survive. Often, they would talk. They became friends—then lovers.

When Carlos dropped the bombshell that Katrina was a traitor, that she worked for the Gulf cartel, something died inside him. Never again would he trust. Two days later, he walked up to the girl he'd loved, pulled out the nine-millime-

WITHOUT REDEMPTION 27

ter Glock and squeezed the trigger. The bullet blew her face and a huge part of himself into another world.

When word got back to Carlos, he once more called Paolo to a meeting, this time at an exclusive restaurant in the Plaza Machado. Tuxedoed waiters brought them rich wines and the very best steaks, meat usually reserved for the gringo tourists, or at least very rich Mexicanos. After they'd eaten, Carlos laid out the reward. His usually insolent condescension had been replaced by a reserved, almost respectful deference.

"Paolo, you have talent. I am sending you to an old friend. His name is Lorenzo Estrada. He will teach you much. Learn well. When you return, you will be given bigger and more important assignments. *El Chapo* himself has noticed you. You have a great future."

Paolo walked out of the restaurant. From that night, his life changed in a way he never could have imagined.

Chapter 4

The day after Frederick's visit, Clarissa started packing. That started after she informed me the first thing a woman needs on an exotic holiday is a new bathing suit. I reminded her she'd bought one last year, but that didn't seem to carry any weight. This trip required another, and it seemed an entire beach wardrobe to complement it. After she'd plunked our son in my arms, she pulled out of the driveway to go shopping. Conor and I did a passable imitation of the rodeo queen wave.

Conor and I were bonding, or so Clarissa had informed me. That went well until he messed his diaper. I could handle a wet one, but I had a weak stomach for those others. They did me in. I'd tried, but after I'd retched and gagged for twenty minutes, Clarissa rescued me. We made a deal that I would spend more time with Conor, do the dishes, anything, as long as she dealt with those stinky diapers. Clarissa agreed, albeit with a healthy dose of skepticism, convinced I was shirking my job as a father.

The bathing suit excursion must have been a success. Clarissa drove into the yard with bags of beachwear she'd found in town. She modeled the results of her shopping trip which caused . . . well, never mind, but after that the holiday sounded better. To spend lazy days on a beach with this

WITHOUT REDEMPTION 29

scantily clad woman who had condescended to tie her future to mine sounded downright heavenly.

In the meantime, Conor sucked on his soother, cooed, drooled, and did everything contrary to his usual demanding nature, to the point that it gave both of us a false hope that a holiday for adults could still be a good time, even with a kid.

Four days later, I met Frederick outside a downtown hotel in San Antonio. We strolled along the city's River Walk while he talked.

"It's a simple pickup of documents. It could be one sheet of paper."

"And then?"

"You will take a duffle bag fitted with a special lining. Carrying it in your regular luggage would probably be fine, but this isn't a time to take chances. If this were viewed by the wrong people, it could set off some fireworks we don't' want or need."

I stopped and leaned against a lamp post. "This sounds risky. Maybe I should just go alone, without Clarissa and Conor. Then, when I get home we would take the holiday. Besides, you're saying the meeting is in Nicaragua. That means I'd have to cross the border from Costa Rica. How dangerous is that?"

Frederick stared at me as if I'd backhanded him. "Listen, this is already a done deal. The negotiations have been completed. What I'm proposing is a simple courier job."

I made no comment. Obviously, whatever he wanted me to spirit out of Nicaragua had tremendous importance, enough that it would be dangerous for somebody—which meant me. Usually, that wasn't a problem, but with Clarissa and Conor along? That didn't sound wise. I made one more protest.

"I just don't want my family around if—"

"Lonnie, this is the biggest scoop on any of the Mexican cartels in the last ten years. You're the only one I can trust with this. Besides, your family won't be anywhere near where you'll pick up the package. As you've pointed out, they won't even be in the same country."

The River Walk followed a gentle bend, then ended at the bottom of a set of stairs. Frederick was right. This should be an easy assignment. A quick meeting with some bad guys who really wanted to cooperate. I would pick up the papers, and then we'd carry on with our holiday. Nevertheless, to do any intelligence work when my family was in the same vicinity gave me instant ulcers.

"Who's the contact, and in a general way, what's in the package?"

Before he answered, Frederick scanned the surrounding area. "A month ago, a man named Arturo Reyes called me."

"An informant?"

"No, I wouldn't call him that. He's Joaquín Guzmán's cousin, and a high-ranking enforcer in Guzmán's Sinaloa cartel. Arturo would never sell out El Chapo, but he's a very crafty politician."

"And he wanted a deal?"

"Yes—for Guzmán. Everybody wants El Chapo's head, but he's still the undisputed drug lord over a vast chunk of Mexico. Nobody's going to walk in and take him down. They've tried a dozen times with nothing to show for it but

WITHOUT REDEMPTION

dead bodies, most of those the good guys. But the Mexicans are putting a lot of pressure on him. We are as well."

"So, what did this Reyes guy have to offer?"

"Lots. Enough for me to take the deal directly to the Drug Enforcement Administration."

"Why didn't Reyes go directly to them?"

Frederick shrugged. "He's one of Chapo's high-level lieutenants. He carries multiple U.S. indictments. Like the rest of them, he's got a lot of blood on his hands. I have some history with him that have no bearing on the present matter, so it's a trust thing. He's afraid the DEA will decide his head is worth more than the *supposed* bonanza he has to offer."

"Which is . . .?"

Frederick smiled and stared into the nearby water. "Chapo offered to trade twenty high-level names along with the address of every safe house Los Zetas has in Reynosa and Nuevo Laredo."

I pushed away from the lamp post. "How could he know that?" I scoffed. "They're at war. And even if what he's saying is true, what's he trading for?"

Frederick chewed his lower lip while he paced back and forth. "Immunity."

I jammed my thumbs into my pockets and waited while a young couple, their arms draped around each other, walked by and out of earshot. "Immunity from who? No one's been able to apprehend him."

"So far, that's been the unfortunate truth. But this administration in Mexico has made his capture a priority. They are working very closely with ICE and the DEA. Chapo knows the net is closing, and he wants to make a deal."

32   *David Griffith*

"Politics. He should have been at the top of the list a long time ago."

Frederick sighed. "I won't argue, but that's not for us to decide. Our business is to follow orders and do the best with the information we have."

I held up a hand, the one without the cast. "I understand, but this makes so little sense. Chapo swaggered around Culiacan. Occasionally, he'd slip in and out of Guadalajara, but now, he seems to go wherever he wants, and he's dangerous everywhere—even here." I leaned against the low wall. Both of us remained silent while more tourists sauntered by. After they were out of hearing range, we climbed the stairs and strolled through a deserted avenue of classical Georgian mansions. I had no doubt their heavily draped windows and silent grandeur cosseted their own historical secrets, not so much different than ours.

Frederick turned toward the side street that led to his hotel. "Lonnie, I'm convinced this deal is the real thing. Chapo's demanding that we sign a no-extradition guarantee. He's sure that if he is prosecuted in Mexico, everything will go his way. They'll give him a thirty-year sentence, he'll be in some jail cell that soon turns into a high-end hotel room, and he will continue to run his drug empire. Business as usual. In the U.S., depending on which state gets first shot at him, he would probably get the death penalty."

I scowled. "Nobody here is going to agree to a no-extradition deal."

Frederick's words, when they came, carried all the weariness of a nation in denial. "They already have. If he turns over that much information about Los Zetas, the Feds have agreed to waive extradition, and as I understand it, the Mexican government has guaranteed the same."

I shook my head in bewilderment. "How can they do that? The man is responsible for ten times what he's been indicted for. The death penalty is too good for him, and now he's going to get away? Where's the justice in that?"

"This isn't our call, Lonnie."

"So... Chapo turns over his bitterest enemies to the Feds so he can then take over their drug corridors."

"Maybe. But in Mexico the killing might slow. If the Mexicans break Los Zetas and incarcerate Chapo, it will be a big win for them." He shrugged. "And—it may be. The Mexican government is turning up the heat. They've captured some of Chapo's key people and he knows sometime soon, his luck will run out. He's over fifty, an old man in the drug world. You can bet he's tired of living with constant fear, always looking over his shoulder, never knowing when the bullets will come for him."

The anger in my chest faded to a simmering resignation. "So let me guess. No—forget it. Those Los Zetas names? That's the parcel, isn't it?"

Frederick nodded.

I stared at him, trying to read whatever message lurked behind those pale blue eyes. They revealed nothing. "Okay, I'll do it, but you had better be a hundred percent certain there is no danger in this. Remember, this is supposed to be a holiday—for Clarissa and Conor. A very *safe* holiday."

David Griffith

THE FOLLOWING THURSDAY, we trooped onto the plane. Having Conor and enough luggage for a small army gave us a leg up on the rest of the would-be tourists. Priority boarding meant we were well settled long before United finished jamming every available seat.

I'd likely grumbled too much at all the extra bags we had to stow. Clarissa patted my knee. "Hey, you have to remember, if Conor isn't happy, we aren't going to be happy either. And neither are the people in the ten rows around us."

I grinned, pleased and proud of her caring concern and skill with our son. "Yeah, you're right, hon—as usual."

Our flying culvert finally left the ground. Conor cooed and played during takeoff, while Clarissa fed him. Conor never complained if he could eat, which meant we, as well as our fellow travelers were content. After a while, the steady drone put him to sleep. His mother set him in his car seat between us, and we settled back to enjoy the flight.

Clarissa's eyes flashed with anticipation. No wonder. We'd never been on any kind of vacation, except for rodeo trips.

I reached over for her hand. "So, what are you really looking forward to doing?"

"Mostly, I just want to get some sun and sand—and spend time with you. You've been gone so much this year."

"Sweetheart, I wish it could have been different, but—"

"No. I'm not complaining. We decided to do this, but it's been a long, hard road."

I gently picked up Conor's car seat and shifted him to the window seat, then slid into the middle one and slipped her

WITHOUT REDEMPTION

hand into mine. "You will never know how much I appreciate the sacrifices you have made."

She laid her head on my shoulder. "Everything was different before Conor came along. I had my work. Your being gone didn't used to bother me, but now I wish you were home every night, like other husbands. It's like I'm a single mom."

There was little I could say, and maybe that wasn't a bad thing. I squeezed her hand and listened, desperately trying to make her understand how much I loved and supported her heroic efforts while I lived life on the road.

"There are times I feel like our relationship has slipped in the last year, along with everything else in my life. Probably it goes with the business of raising kids. I don't have time for all those little extras I used to take for granted."

"Yeah, and when I'm off at another rodeo, I'm not much help." I caressed her long, slim fingers. "When I'm home, I will try to look after Conor more so you can—"

"No, you are a *very* good dad. You always pitch in when you're home. I'm just complaining. I appreciate what you do, but this holiday will be a good time to unwind. I might even revisit why I made the big trade. Conor instead of a career. It's not that I'm sorry but being a mother has been a major readjustment."

We spent the five-hour plane ride in deep conversation, something married folks ought to make time for on a more regular basis than we had in the last year.

When we hit the runway in Costa Rica's capitol city, it seemed half the plane had already changed into shorts. Clarissa had as well. I saw no need. I'd refused to take any.

36   *David Griffith*

They seemed undignified, not something a cowboy would ever wear. We piled down the stairs and onto the tarmac like lost arctic ptarmigans. The tropical heat enveloped us with a damp but welcome blanket after the wind-driven sleet crystals we'd left behind. Mind you, that had been unusual for south Texas. Nevertheless, we were glad to escape.

Helpful attendants steered the lot of us through the terminal and toward Customs. Being a tourist was all new to me, but packing a screeching kid expedited the procedure. Clarissa tried to quiet Conor, but by the time they'd herded our group into ragged lines, the sparkle of excitement in her eyes had dimmed. She tried to quiet our offspring, but he'd already had his fill of being a tourist. Nothing helped.

We'd hardly cleared Customs when a gaggle of helpful folks descended on us like crows on an open lunchbox. Several offered a free ride to our hotel. The catch didn't seem too terribly bad. All we had to do was attend a small seminar the next morning, and for our trouble they would provide breakfast, plus give us a jungle tour, all with no cost. I turned to Clarissa. She looked skeptical. The last supposedly free thing she got was me, which possibly had soured her on giveaway programs.

I wasn't one to miss a deal, so I signed on right away. Sure, it just happened to be a rather busty local girl, but she seemed to feel a real concern for our welfare, so I didn't figure we could go far wrong. Clarissa raised an eyebrow, but I paid no mind. It was plain to see, these folks had a heart for visitors to their country and were trying to help us out.

The young lady tucked our luggage into a white van and drove us to our digs in some beach place called El Coco. The

WITHOUT REDEMPTION

brochures had neglected to mention that the hotel was located a long way from town. Nevertheless, it sat right on the ocean, so I guessed we'd make out fine. The nice lady deposited us in front of the spacious lobby, and even Clarissa warmed to her when she said she'd be there early the next morning to take us for breakfast.

We checked in, unpacked and hung our clothes in the closet. The room appeared a bit bedraggled and didn't seem to be anywhere near five stars; not at all like the pictures in the brochure. Our eyes met across the room. Clarissa's left eyebrow arched a bit higher than usual. I didn't have to ask what she meant. Her estimation of Stirling Associates' holiday division had taken a steep dive. Clarissa changed Conor's stinky diaper. I stood out on the veranda and marveled at the acres of warm sand. Sure, the room wasn't five stars, but I'd made the right decision. Clarissa would love this, and it was long past due. We'd never had this nice of a holiday, and I even considered asking God to bless Frederick for his generosity. I didn't, because I decided he didn't deserve any blessing, being as how it was obvious he'd had other motives. Once more, I recited the phone number he'd given me. No big deal. Call the guy, pick up the package and tuck it into the specially fitted lining of my duffel bag. Tomorrow would be soon enough to think about that. The day after would be even better. We needed to get some sun, bond as a family, and see the sights. Business could wait.

Clarissa finished with Conor and changed into some of that new beachwear while I rounded up a full bottle of formula, a spare diaper, the wet wipes, Conor's sun hat, a

38   *David Griffith*

soother, and the half-dozen other items she had instructed me one needs just to stroll down to the beach with a baby.

My beautiful wife looked like a million bucks times ten in her fancy coral and white cover-up, which was a bit of a misnomer. The "cover-up" did conceal more than what some of the bodies along the stretch of white sand obscured, but she looked the best of them all.

The stroller wheels bogged down and refused to turn in that soft sand, so I packed Conor and the stroller until we found a piece of beach with only a scattering of walrus look-alikes. We spread out all our baby gear and plunked down like we did this for a living. Probably, I looked somewhat out of place. Nobody else wore a straw cowboy hat and jeans. Apparently, my everyday rig didn't cut it as fashionable beach-wear, but the woman beside me didn't seem to mind, and that was all that mattered to me.

Clarissa stripped down to that gorgeous bathing suit she'd bought and laughed with delight as she held her hands up toward the heat that streamed down on our bleached northern bodies. "How about I go for a swim?"

"Certainly hon; this vacation's for you. All you have to do is say what you want." I waved a hand in the air like I was Houdini the magician. "Consider it done."

She reached over and hugged me. "I love you. Thanks."

And that made it worth anything I had to do, or whatever sacrifices I had to make for this holiday. I grimaced at the green cast on my arm, trying not to think of the fun we might have had together.

Conor cooed happily when I plopped him down. We had a whole town of sandcastles to construct, so I figured we

WITHOUT REDEMPTION 39

might as well start. As it turned out, I built the castles. He smashed them—with great glee.

A half-hour later, Clarissa walked out of the surf, dripping water with a grin as big as a quarter-moon. She sat down beside us. "Lon, the water's so warm, it's unbelievable. You've got to go in and try it. Oh, I wish you were able to swim. It would be so much fun together."

"Yeah, and who would look after this guy?"

"Yes, I know . . . but someday."

I leaned forward and kissed her. "You're on. Consider it a deal."

She took Conor's hands and helped him to fashion a sort of castle while I wandered down to the edge of the water. A swim wasn't going to happen, at least not on this trip.

The waves surged lazily onto the sand at my feet. I strolled down the beach, avoiding kids and dogs while attempting to not focus on the bikini-clad female bodies stretched out in seductive rows. They were a distraction from what I was really looking for—which was what? I didn't know, but the intelligence business had been part of me for enough years that I had an eye for the unusual, or out of place. Sometimes it was only a casual glance that rested a second too long. A hundred feet from where we'd parked with Conor, a muscled local with close-cropped hair as black as mine lounged on an oversize beach towel. Beside him, a skinny, dark woman snapped a photo of the picturesque offshore island. They'd arrived after us, and though my beachwear was a little unorthodox, his sharp glance seemed out of place. And the picture of the island? I had to have been in the middle of the photo. Coincidence? Maybe, but it still bothered me.

I tried to ignore the danger signals that skittered against every nerve ending in my chest, but they were warnings I'd long ago learned not to disregard.

Chapter 5

The morning after he'd met with Carlos at the restaurant in the Plaza Machado, Paolo caught the bus north to Los Mochis. From there, the *Barranca del Cobre* train wound northwest through two hundred miles of one of the deepest canyons on earth. Every switch-backed inch was territory held by the Sinaloa cartel. At the mountain village of Creel, he hoisted his backpack, descended to the concrete apron, and squinted into the slanting sunlight. At the far end of the station, a swarthy face stared disinterestedly at the disembarking tourists and travelers. Paolo walked toward him, simply because there was no one else in sight. "Are you Lorenzo?"

The wooden visage in front of Paolo never changed, nor did the man answer as his disinterested gaze flickered over Paolo's frame. His expressionless eyes burnt like charcoal orbs above cheeks as parched and weathered as the Sonoran Desert. Finally, the man spoke, his tone tinged with disgust. "That might be my name." The voice rumbled clear and deep from the bottom of his chest.

"I am Paolo."

The man's thin lips flattened, as if the words angered him. He turned to stare at the other passengers. "Why did they send you? I see nothing special in you."

42   *David Griffith*

Paolo dropped the backpack and straightened to his full height. Not that five feet seven was impressive, but the cocky old desert rooster should be taught never to insult a *sicario*. His voice cut across the silent void. "I have killed better men than you."

The hard visage instantly turned from the other disembarking passengers to Paolo's face. Neither his lips nor his eyes smiled.

"So, the puppy barks. I wonder if he can do anything else." Suddenly, he reached down and picked up the dropped pack. "Follow me, *perrito*."

Paolo scowled. His gun lay in the bottom of that pack. If it would have been within reach, he would have taught the old man a final lesson on respecting his betters. For disrespecting him . . . he should—and would—die. However, the straight frame and square shoulders had already disappeared down the steps at the end of the concrete.

Paolo swore under his breath. Later would have to do. He couldn't shoot somebody he couldn't see, especially when the cocky rooster had just walked off with his gun. Seething inside, he trotted to catch up. He didn't need whatever knowledge Carlos thought this man possessed. However, he did need the pistol.

By the time they'd reached the street, Paolo scurried at the old man's heels, who disconcertingly seemed not to notice. The man in front of him plodded forward in a deceptively fast shuffle, which appeared to be his normal gait.

After they'd passed the last house, the trail split. Lorenzo took the less travelled fork along the edge of the same massive canyon the train had followed. Paolo felt naked without the

WITHOUT REDEMPTION

43

ever-present handgun. For two years that pistol had never been beyond his reach. When you are a *sicario*, it is necessary to be armed. You watch your back, because somebody is always looking for you. Those people he'd killed? They had brothers, sisters, cousins, friends. His life was always in danger, and now the gun had been taken from him like a bone from a butt-wriggling puppy. Embarrassment suffused his face with a crimson tide of anger. This had gone far enough. The old man picked his way over the rocky trail. Paolo stepped forward, grabbed his shoulder, and spun him around, or at least he tried. Lorenzo stood as solid as one of the boulders. He turned and glared.

"Give me my pack."

A slow smile lit the old man's seamed features. Slowly, he slipped the blue backpack off his shoulder. Paolo reached for it. Lorenzo never took his eyes off the young man's face. He stepped back and flung the packsack out over the rim of the canyon. Paolo watched as it sailed out of sight. Somewhere, two thousand feet below, what few possessions he'd brought, disappeared into a forest of pine. Blinding anger activated every muscle in his chest. Whatever Carlos had wanted him to learn here was not going to happen. His hands clawed at the old man's scrawny, corded neck. Only his neck disappeared, and Paolo was on the ground. Over top of him, the man's eyes burned like pinpoints of burnt-out coal. A huge blade at Paolo's throat drew a pencil line of blood just under his chin. Words dripped like molten metal from the thin white lips. "You should not have done that, puppy. Carlos said you were smart. He lied."

David Griffith

Paolo felt the slow trickle down the side of his neck. Death lay seconds away, and he thought of his mother and father. They hadn't been much as parents, but they were all he had. Today, he would meet God—or so that old priest Father Miguel would say. That scared him worse than this crazy man. He would not even be granted purgatory. He felt a sudden overwhelming desire to cross himself or say a prayer, but he didn't dare move.

Suddenly, the knife disappeared, and Lorenzo stepped away. Paolo struggled to his knees and rubbed his sweaty palms on his pants. How had this happened? How had this man made such a fool of *him*, a seasoned *sicario*? Humiliation flooded from his belly up into his face. Revenge would come, but it would be at the right moment, in his own way. Clearly, he had underestimated this wizened desert rat. He would not make that mistake again.

He studied his adversary for several long seconds before the old man turned and jerked his head in the direction of the trail. "Follow me. Never do anything like that again, because the next time I will kill you. You have the impression you are tough. You are not, but if you have an ounce of intelligence you will perhaps reconsider the folly of your ways and come to understand that I can teach you skills that will truly make you a force to be reckoned with." His slow, almost musical tones dampened the burning humiliation, enough to make Paolo realize that Carlos had sent him here for a reason, which probably didn't include being killed by this man. The first seed of a growing respect, along with a niggling doubt whether he *could* kill him, made him nod in acquiescence. He

WITHOUT REDEMPTION

struggled to his feet and again wiped at the oozing blood on his neck. "Who are you?"

> The old man's expression never softened. "For you, I am only Lorenzo. That is enough." Paolo shrugged. "Yes. Perhaps I should not have acted so hastily."

Lorenzo abruptly walked away, unresponsive to the young man's faltering attempt to make peace. Paolo fell in behind him, careful to stay at least fifteen steps in the rear. The raw line on his still bleeding neck remained enough incentive to avoid more confrontation.

As Paolo followed, he became more aware of their surroundings. Lorenzo led them up a long slope along the edge of a steep escarpment. He moved fast, skirting fallen logs and underbrush. Sometimes, Paolo had to trot to keep up, and often he stumbled over the unfamiliar terrain. Never did he take his eyes off the broad shoulders in front of him. There was no doubt in his mind that if he placed one foot off the trail or made any aggressive move, that big knife would this time be buried in his chest. The old man had shown mercy once. He'd not do so again.

The trail switch backed along the canyon rim in a westerly direction, then ran south for another mile. Though he gasped for breath, Paolo would have died before asking for a rest. He would not be left behind.

Finally, Lorenzo stopped and stared over the edge of the massive crater. Paolo stayed a respectful distance from him—and his knife.

46   *David Griffith*

A grim smile flickered across Lorenzo's face. "Now *perrito*, we will see what you are made of. Follow me."

Anger again exploded inside Paolo at the derogatory term. But before he could answer, the old man disappeared. He shuffled warily to the edge of the canyon wall. Twenty feet below him, Lorenzo stood on the trail and taunted him. Only, it wasn't a trail. A narrow ledge dropped precipitously toward the floor of the canyon, probably navigated by only the most daring mountain sheep. Paolo's jaw set. He took a deep breath. Now he would die. However, his smoldering anger and unreasoning pride gave him the courage to place his right foot over the edge. Somehow, his left followed, and he tried to focus on the narrow ribbon of rock at his feet. Once, he looked far down to the forest floor, mesmerized by the jumble of rocks hundreds of feet below. Immediately, he had to turn his face to the wall, his breathing ragged and shallow as he waited for the dizziness to go away.

After his original taunting laugh, Lorenzo had only glanced back once. His derisive scowl added all the clarity needed as to what he thought of his recruit. Paolo glared back at him, but his jaw clamped shut as he slid his right foot forward. The old man would not have the pleasure of watching him fall. Whatever Carlos had intended for him to learn would happen.

Anger drove most of the fear away, or at least kept it at bay. Step by step he descended, though he dared not look up to see whether Lorenzo remained ahead of him. If the old man decided to shoot him for being too slow, then so be it. That would be a better death than cartwheeling through the

WITHOUT REDEMPTION   47

air until he smashed into a quivering blob of jelly on the granite boulders far below.

Paolo crept forward, each step an agony of fear. Later, he could never have told how long he'd crept down that precipitous decline, but when a hand reached out and touched his arm, the sun had already slipped below the western horizon.

"You survived." Lorenzo stood in an indentation in the rock wall, his feet spread wide on a pile of broken shale. He eyed Paolo then inclined his head and gestured for him to follow. There didn't seem to be any place to go other than along the narrow trail that must lead to the bottom of the canyon, but suddenly Lorenzo again disappeared. Paolo stepped ahead and to the left, to where the old man had stood, and immediately saw the opening in the wall. In front of him, a thousand years of rain, wind, and erosion had carved a semicircular room-sized opening in the rock. The floor, though mostly flat, was pebbled in the corners. At the far end, a shallow but wide cave appeared to provide a reasonable shelter from the infrequent rain. A wall of mesquite wood closed off the entrance. Paolo followed Lorenzo inside. The cave was more spacious than it had appeared from the outside. A comfortable room contained living quarters furnished with a cobbled-together fire-pit, rough-plank table, a couple of chairs carved from pine saplings, and a bed of the same material.

Lorenzo turned and faced his less than eager guest. Paolo still truculent, but intensely relieved to have not died on the rocks far below, waited for whatever the old man had to say.

David Griffith

"You have passed the first test." Lorenzo shrugged noncommittally, as if he'd just informed his new apprentice that it had rained yesterday. "The last puppy fell over the edge."

Paolo shuddered, but kept his eyes riveted on the old man's face in an attempt to mask the horror that surged through his chest.

"Sit if you like." Lorenzo gestured to one of the chairs that hugged the sides of a large axe-hewn plank that served as a table.

Warily, Paolo lowered himself into the seat. The rawhide-bound joints muttered a squeaky warning as his weight settled into the woven leather bottom and he wondered if Lorenzo had invited him to sit there on purpose. Any movement he made was well-advertised by the creaking leather seat.

The old man lit a single candle and placed it on the table. The flickering light cast shadows over his solid figure while his gnarled hands patted tortillas into paper-thin patties. He worked over a small open stovetop on a raised platform. Occasionally, he would poke at the burning mesquite fire. Once, he went to the doorway and peered out over the chasm below. He seemed to have forgotten his unwilling recruit's belligerence as he stared in silence into the darkness.

Paolo studied Lorenzo's movements, wondering at the man's age. Forty? Sixty? Possibly even older though other than his deeply lined face, his body showed few signs of decay. Never once did Lorenzo glance in Paolo's direction. Neither did he speak. Minutes later, he placed two well-filled plates on opposite ends of the plank table and gestured for the young man to eat. Paolo needed no second invitation.

WITHOUT REDEMPTION

49

Whatever Carlos had sent him for, it wasn't to starve, and he found the food more than adequate. The old man's well-seasoned offering was superbly done.

When they'd emptied their plates, Lorenzo pointed to a large pan beside a bucket of water. "That is your job."

Paolo grudgingly nodded. Scouring a couple of plates was not something to die over, but he would not forgive the old man's rude insolence.

A small pail of sand doubled for soap, and Paolo used it liberally to scour the plates and silverware. The single candle provided little light, but he needed no more. Lorenzo watched from the shadows, or at least Paolo thought he did, for his back was turned. Several times he wondered if the blade of that big knife would be the last thing he felt. He must have telegraphed some of his uneasiness because before he'd finished, the old man cleared his throat.

"Carlos is my friend. I owe him much, which is why I allow you to come to this place." He shifted in the chair and placed his left leg over his right one. "You can be safe here—and you can learn."

Paolo continued scrubbing sand and water over the last plate and waited to see what would come next.

"If you are one of Carlos's chosen, it means he thinks highly of you. I doubt you deserve that, but if you cooperate, then I will try to teach you the skills he sent you to acquire. It is up to you whether you learn them."

"I wish to do that." The words left his mouth before he'd even thought. Paolo hated the old man, but Carlos had sent him here for a reason. It would be wise to find out why.

Possibilities paraded one by one as he carried the plates and forks back into the cooking area. What if Carlos had set him up? Did he *want* Lorenzo to kill him? That was possible, but then why hadn't the old man sliced his throat and thrown him off the cliff? Did this desert hyena really have something to teach that would increase his worthiness to the cartel? It wouldn't hurt to bide his time. A few days here would tell him whether he should stay longer. That much, he could do.

Lorenzo pointed toward a mat in the far corner of the room. "Sleep there. Tomorrow we talk about what you must learn." With that, he disappeared. Paolo didn't see where he'd gone, but he had no intention of following. He'd had more than enough of that old man. Tonight . . . he would sleep. And tomorrow? A certainty grew within him that he would be doing exactly what Lorenzo wanted.

Hours later, he rolled over for what seemed the thousandth time, trying to find a comfortable spot on the thin mat. Nothing softened the hard rock underneath his hips and shoulders, but eventually, the thrumming chirp of the crickets lulled him into a restless oblivion.

Chapter 6

Despite my misgivings, we had a great time at the beach. Spending the evening at a seafood restaurant would have wonderfully capped the afternoon, but Conor was past ready for bed. Dinner out would have consisted of dirty looks from the other diners because of our howling kid. We sat cross-legged on the bed, ate pepperoni pizza and whispered back and forth so we didn't wake the screecher. At least we got to tiptoe out to the veranda and watch the sun sink into the ocean. I stroked Clarissa's hair as we talked.

She turned, her gray-green eyes luminous in the near darkness. "What do you see us doing now? Are you really done riding bucking horses and trying for a world championship?"

"Wow, heavy questions. Aren't we supposed to leave all those big decisions at home?"

She chuckled softly. "If you want, but it does seem a good time to talk about our future." The musical sound of her voice fit so well with the dusky silence of the night.

"Yeah, you're right. That's what this holiday should be about. We never take time to discuss those big-ticket items at home."

Clarissa propped her feet up on the low table in front of her chair. "It's where we're at with our too often crazy lives." She slipped her arm across my shoulder, her fingernails caressing my neck. Her voice, when she spoke remained pensive and thoughtful. "In the last while, I've thought a lot about where we want to be a year or two from now. And what does our faith in God have to do with it? How much does He control our future?"

I sat up straight, while I tried to formulate a well-thought-out-response, which would have been mostly a lie, because I hadn't spent time considering that question—ever.

Clarissa chuckled and squeezed my knee. "No, don't answer. It's just something to think about. I guess I mull it over, especially when our finances are in a mess, and we can't pay the credit card bills. Then I wonder if we're supposed to be going a different direction." She leaned over and laid her head on my shoulder.

"Different direction? Like what?" I asked.

"I haven't a clue. You and God need to have a powwow."

"A powwow—with God?" I propped my bare feet up on the little table in front of us. "You might be a racist."

Clarissa chuckled, and entwined her fingers in mine. "Yep, I'm guilty. I have a definite bias toward a certain man who just happens to have a whole bunch of Indian under his skin."

I pulled Clarissa close and kissed her beautiful lips, all the time thanking God for this woman whose beauty went so far beyond skin deep. Our marriage had survived, not because of me—or even her. We were still an item because Jesus Christ was first in her life, and though I'd been late to the party, he was becoming first in mine. We had other problems, some of them financial, which made Clarissa's next comment ring true.

WITHOUT REDEMPTION

"Then we always had enough money to pay the bills, go out for dinner, or whatever else we wanted. Now, it's not as easy, and what savings we had are long gone."

I sighed, the familiar tension building in my chest. Everything Clarissa had said was right. This had been a hard year, and though I'd won lots, the road expenses ate up too much of it. I did need to think about a career change, but hey, that could be addressed tomorrow.

When the pale, yellow moon slipped over the top of the distant jungle, we stepped inside and latched the sliding door. Clarissa's lithe body melded into mine. A volcano of passion electrified every nerve. My hands caressed her shoulders and moved down her back as our lips met. Each curve was familiar, exotic, still, and always exciting. Suddenly, a piercing scream filled the room, followed by an angry torrent of wailing tears. Clarissa sighed in exasperation, broke away, and rushed to pick Conor out of his makeshift bed. So much for romance. This was not exactly how either of us had pictured our Costa Rica holiday.

Later, we lay side by side. The moonlight streamed through the patio doors, bathing her pale skin in a translucent bath of diamonds while I ran my fingers through her sandy hair. We chuckled quietly at our rocky start. Baby or not, we were determined to have fun.

Tomorrow afternoon, we would drive out to *Rancho Curada* for a week of solitude, or so said my wife. She'd enthusiastically pointed out the website that gave a glowing report of the lucky tourists who rode around the countryside gazing at the wonders of Costa Rican flora. Apparently, the ranch had a first-class program for looking after kids, so the parents

54 *David Griffith*

could participate in all the fun activities. Clarissa was skeptical about leaving Conor with anybody. I hoped she'd feel comfortable enough with whatever arrangement they had that she would agree to at least one or two short excursions.

The following morning, we departed with the busty local lady to her breakfast presentation—which turned out to be a fruit plate. After a tour of a dolled-up condo and several hours of hard sell, she determined we were beyond help and let us escape. We gladly gave up the promised jungle excursion in exchange for our freedom.

Later, we rented a car, loaded the boy and all his gear, then followed the hilly, winding road into the north-central part of the country. The ranch nestled a few miles from the Nicaragua border, which would make my job for Frederick much easier. This family time was important, and I didn't want to leave Clarissa and Conor any longer than necessary. What I had planned could be done quickly from there with little disruption to our holiday plans.

Two hours later, we turned off a badly graveled road and pulled up to the ranch gates. Though I would rather have stayed at the beach, baked in the sun and sampled first-class seafood, I tried my best to match Clarissa's excitement.

"Well, I guess this is it," My attempted enthusiasm for Clarissa's choice sagged further as we surveyed the cobbled-together gate posts and rain-faded welcome sign. The only item that resembled the internet pictures was the rich, purple bougainvillea that graced the lime-green façade of the building directly in front of us.

"Isn't that gorgeous?" Clarissa snapped a photo.

WITHOUT REDEMPTION

"Yeah . . . nice flowers." I did my best to sound enthusiastic. "You're sure we're at the right place?"

She glanced at me with a wry grin. "This must not be the right place."

"I'll find out." I stepped out of the car and walked inside. This over-advertised farm adjacent to a snake-infested jungle was exactly the dismal setting I'd dreaded.

A heavyset man lounging over a cup of coffee advised me that, indeed, this was Rancho Curada. He pointed out the building where we needed to check in.

At the main ranch house, a woman who introduced herself as Conchita welcomed Frederick's Visa card like it was her beloved second cousin. After she'd taken a firm imprint of that gold mine she led us to our abode for the week, an upstairs cabin about fifty paces from what smelled suspiciously like the cow barn. The inside of our cozy shelter consisted of a bedroom and bathroom. An oversized, square purple bathtub seemed to be the pièce de résistance. It sprawled majestically over most of the bathroom, but the miserly trickle of water dribbling from the tap would have taken most of the night to fill it. We looked at each other and chuckled. It would take more than that to wreck our holiday.

Clarissa unpacked Conor, and we ambled over to the ranch restaurant in time for supper. There was no menu. We got what they served—like it or not. Mostly we did. The food, though heavy on the local staple of rice and beans, was superb.

Later, we settled our little guy into his crib, then crawled into the queen-sized bed. Both of us tossed through the night trying to get comfortable on the slab of a mattress. At four-

56 David Griffith

thirty, when the first bird chirped a good morning, I growled an unprintable answer. The fancy bedspread had been excellent camouflage. We'd not oversleep here.

For the next week, in a whodunit lineup you couldn't have picked us from any other tourist. We played it to the hilt—and enjoyed every minute. The first day we hiked. The second, Clarissa wandered out to the corrals where Arturo had started training a colt. That skill, thanks to old Bob Besser at the Blackwater Ranch, was an area where my wife excelled. When Arturo asked if she would like to help, she naturally jumped at the opportunity to exchange training wisdom. Most of what they did we would of the southern *vaqueros*, with the goal being submission. I rocked Conor and watched, proud of her skill with making the young horse want to work; eager to be a partner. Though I knew much of broncs and the wild ones, it was Clarissa who understood how horses thought, why they reacted the way they did, and how to change their response to gentleness and obedience. By the end of the day she rode a colt that was willing and comfortable with her on his back. Arturo grudgingly admitted it would have taken him much longer to gentle the horse, with less pleasing results.

All in all, we had a great day. The next was every bit as memorable, though for a different reason. When we'd left the hotel room on El Coco Beach, we'd forgotten to pack the big bag of disposable diapers Clarissa had bought. Conor had disposed of the last ones she'd stashed in her kid bag, but Conchita said not to worry. In Costa Rica, rural people still did it the old way. They used cloth diapers, much cheaper than buying disposables from the store. We could just borrow

WITHOUT REDEMPTION 57

some from her daughter Dora and we'd be in business. Clarissa was game. Neither of us wanted to spend half a day driving to the nearest town. She borrowed a dozen from Conchita, and Conor filled them. Then she swished them around in the toilet before throwing them into Conchita's decrepit washing machine. Everything was good—until I had to do it.

I'd hesitantly informed Clarissa I would have to leave to attend to some company business the next day, so she'd asked whether I'd look after Conor so she could go shopping with Conchita, get some munchies, and of first importance—disposable diapers. I reminded her I had no ability to half-sanitize a stinky diaper in a toilet. Clarissa guaranteed she would be back by three. Worst case, Conor might have a wet one, but that would be all. My stomach handled that with reasonably well, so I kissed her goodbye and picked up my little son. What an awesome kid. I held him up and gazed into his face. He stared back, his dark eyes close to mine, filled with the trust and curiosity of a baby.

I nuzzled his soft skin. "I'll take care of you, bud. Whatever it takes, I'm here for you." Right then, I heard the sound I dreaded, Conor filling his pants. Panicked, I held him at arm's length and glanced at the clock. Clarissa wouldn't be home for at least two hours. I laid him in his makeshift crib. Maybe he would go to sleep. He fussed, then started to cry. I picked him up again, eyeing the offending diaper. He smelled terrible. I swallowed and turned my head away. I couldn't do this. After Conor's volume rose twenty decibels, I decided I had no choice.

"Easy guy. Dad's going to take care of everything." I laid him on the bathroom floor next to the toilet and grabbed the

58 **David Griffith**

last clean diaper from the bag on the table. The big safety pins on both sides of his fat little tummy released easy enough. I undid them and kind of scraped the contents together without looking, because I knew if I did, there would be another mess on the floor, and that wouldn't do either of us any good. Hastily I dropped the well-soiled diaper in the toilet, then leaned back and gagged. Conor kicked his legs, cooed, and played with his toes. Obviously, he was happy to be rid of the stinky garment. I found a wet cloth, cleaned him up, and shoved a fresh diaper under him. I only stuck my hand once with the sharp pins which drew a little blood, but at least I didn't poke him. Then, I put him down for a nap, proud of my fatherly skills. I'd done it. Mind you, lunch was out of the question, but I had really changed a dirty diaper. Clarissa would be *so* impressed.

A half-hour later, nature called, and I walked over to the toilet. The forgotten diaper lay right on top. Until somebody did something with that mess, these facilities were out of order. I stared. My stomach again did flip-flops. I couldn't stick my hand in there. It wasn't possible. With only one bathroom in the cabin, and three cups of morning coffee weighing heavy, I didn't have a choice. I reached toward the now brown-colored water. The smell hit me full in the face and I retched. This wouldn't work. I staggered away, my eyes watering while I swallowed the bile in my throat. What could I do? Again, I glanced at my watch. Not a chance. Clarissa wouldn't rescue me. How did she do this? What made her different from me? She swished those things around like they were ice cubes in a martini. I tried again with no better re-

WITHOUT REDEMPTION

sults. This time, I nearly added my breakfast to the mess in the toilet bowl.

After another attempt, I decided I wasn't going to win. Nevertheless, the morning's coffee still weighed heavy. I walked into the kitchen. In the silverware drawer, I found a pair of pliers. Why they were there was anybody's guess, but I needed them. I found some leather gloves, grabbed the diaper with the pliers and sluiced it up and down as I flushed. There, I'd done it. I held the offending piece of cotton cloth as far away from my nose as I could manage while it dripped into the toilet bowl. A sudden noise distracted me. Clarissa stood in the door with her hand over her mouth. When our eyes met, she couldn't hold it back. Peals of laughter rang through the cabin. Every time she looked at me with my sleeves rolled up and my gloved hands holding the diaper at the end of a set of pliers, she howled even louder. "Don't move. I have to take a picture."

"That isn't going to happen," I growled.

"Oh, please." She giggled. "This is so classic. I'll never forget you standing there with that look…" Another peal of laughter.

Sheepishly, I dropped the stinking piece of cloth back in the toilet and peeled off my gloves. Clarissa swished it around, wrung it out and put it in a bucket to be washed.

Later, while we stood out on the veranda, she slipped into my arms. Her voice broke through the barely held laughter. "You may not do the diaper thing too well, but you're still the best dad ever. Conor's a lucky little guy."

I hugged her close. "I'm so glad you're his mom, and hey—thanks."

Chapter 7

Paolo's hand automatically clawed under the pillow for the pistol, a first conscious movement, the reflex action of survival. His fingers searched every corner, then frantically moved back and forth. It wasn't there. Why? Terror shot through every artery. Los Zetas had caught him alone. He had no weapon. Now he would die.

The last scrap of sleep fled from his brain. His eyes focused on the camouflage breeches across the room. He followed them upward to the corded torso and wrinkled arms of the old man from the night before. The smell of frying venison brought everything rushing back. Relief sucked the breath from his chest like sewer water swirling down an overactive toilet. He didn't care. At least he wouldn't die at the hand of Heriberto Lazcano, or any other of the Los Zetas pigs. He pulled the blanket higher around his shoulders, but Lorenzo had apparently noticed.

"Get up. We have much to do."

Paolo fingered the tender, bloody line Lorenzo's knife had left on his neck. It didn't seem wise to argue, so he sat up. The instant his feet touched the cold stone floor, goosebumps exploded over his bare legs. Hurriedly, he scrambled into his clothes then turned to roll up the blanket—and froze. His pack lay against the woven saplings that defined the outside wall. The old man had thrown it from the top

WITHOUT REDEMPTION 61

of the cliff. How had he retrieved it? Paolo scowled. Was his gun still inside? Gingerly, he fumbled across the bedroll for one of the straps, his eyes glued to the back of the wrinkled neck above the tan t-shirt in front of the fire. Lorenzo poked a fork into the meat frying on the makeshift grill. A low whistle escaped his lips, a tune unfamiliar and haunting. Quietly, Paolo rummaged through the middle compartment of the bag, as if searching for a clean pair of socks. When his hand slipped over the checkered grip of the Glock, he smiled. The weight of the gun told him the loaded clip remained in place.

The old man's whistling picked up volume for a moment, then dropped as he spooned the venison, fried eggs, and chilies onto two plates.

Paolo pulled the semi-automatic out of the bag and clicked off the safety, waiting for Lorenzo to freeze, to show some fear. He did neither as he set the plates on the table, never once looking at the young man.

"Are you going to shoot, or eat?" His calm question on one level was humiliating, but deep inside, Paolo marveled at the old man's complete lack of fear. He shook his head, again wondering why he had been sent here. What had Carlos wanted him to learn from this throwback mountain man? Never once did Lorenzo so much as glance up from his food.

After the last bite had disappeared, Lorenzo leaned back in his chair, crossed one leg over the other and studied his newest recruit. "You have decided not to shoot?"

Paolo shrugged. "Carlos sent me here to learn whatever you can teach. It didn't seem wise."

Lorenzo eyed him while he moved a toothpick from one side of his mouth to the other. "It was perhaps the first smart

David Griffith

decision I've seen you make. My old friend Carlos might have made a reasonable choice after all. You may now be an ignorant puppy, but at least you are a puppy that can be taught." He leaned forward. "I will teach you as much as you are capable of learning."

Paolo's face colored, but he staunched the rising anger. This was a time to walk softly, to find out exactly what skills this man would be willing to pass on.

"Clean the dishes." Lorenzo abruptly rose to his feet and strode to the low doorway built into the curtain of brush. "When you are done, come outside." With that, he left Paolo alone with a bucket full of anger, the dirty plates, and some silverware. The plates were easier to deal with than the anger, but by the time he'd finished, the indignation had been scoured along with the rest of the dishes. He stepped through the doorway, convinced his biggest challenge would be to not kill this insolent old man.

Lorenzo stood at the edge of the rock face. He inclined his head for his student to follow. Paolo set his jaw, determined to overcome the instant terror that coursed through his belly. He wasn't afraid of heights, but neither was he used to the narrow, crumbling trail that they had traversed last night where one misstep would precipitate a terrifying fall, and certain death.

He so badly wanted to refuse, but pride would not let him, so he nodded. "I am ready. Lead on."

Lorenzo's lips tightened, but underneath the disdain scrawled across his granite features, there seemed to be a fleeting approval. He turned and slipped out of sight behind the rock wall. Paolo followed. Instead of turning up the trail

WITHOUT REDEMPTION 63

that led to the canyon rim, the teacher followed the shale-littered trail downward toward the canyon floor.

Most of the narrow track to the bottom was no more than eighteen inches wide. Some places it narrowed to a foot. Every fiber of Paolo's being focused on his feet and the narrow ribbon in front of him. He dared not look down, but occasionally his eyes betrayed him, and instant vertigo threatened to send him cartwheeling over the edge. When that happened, like last night, he turned toward the cliff face and breathed into the ochre rock until his head cleared sufficiently to go on. Once he heard the old man chuckle, but this was not the time to take offense. He had enough on his hands. If fighting were needed, it could come later—on flat ground.

At one point, the trail disappeared altogether. A three-foot section had broken off, which required a jump through space to reach the other side. Lorenzo stood twenty feet farther down, eyeing him as he approached the gap. The teacher's voice floated upward. "Your first test. Perhaps you will fail and I will be spared from paying the debt I owe to Carlos." With that, he turned and picked his way toward the canyon floor.

Paolo cringed away from the gaping hole in front of him as his left hand instinctively clawed at the rock wall beside him. If he made it to the bottom, he vowed he would never cross that broken stretch of trail again. All he wanted to do was make it to the bottom. Somehow, he would find another way out of the canyon.

When his feet skidded into the shale on the other side of the gaping hole in the trail, he attempted three "Hail Mary's," for truly it must have been God's providence that had saved

64 *David Griffith*

him. Whatever Carlos had sent him for, it wasn't this. He could never find the skill to stay alive on this mountain trail. No more! He would kill the old man—and take his chances with Carlos.

As Paolo sidled warily around the last bend in the trail, he glanced down to the bottom. Like a turkey buzzard waiting for his prey to die, Lorenzo perched on a fallen log, watching each shuffling step his protégé made. When Paolo stepped off the rock face to the spongy black soil, Lorenzo spoke to him. "You did better than I expected." He motioned to the gnarled pine. "Sit."

Paolo, elated at not having died was happy to comply.

"You may be as capable as Carlos said. Then again, you might not. However, you did well today. It is time we talked."

"Go ahead, old man. I'm all ears." Though Paolo had recovered enough to be mildly confident and sarcastic, his hands still trembled.

Lorenzo picked up a twig and proceeded to mangle it into short chunks. He seemed to be thinking, because he made no response to Paolo's sneering retort. When he threw the last piece of twig onto the ground, he spoke.

"As I told you, Carlos has sent others. One of them lies over there." He pointed to a shale escarpment a hundred yards to the west.

"He fell?"

"No."

"What—?"

"I killed him."

Somehow, Paolo had known what the answer would be, but it still elicited the familiar short circuit in his gut that put

WITHOUT REDEMPTION

his brain into survival mode. This *was* the cartel. Regardless of anything else that happened, in the end, he would either kill the old man—or be killed.

"Why? What did he do wrong?"

"It doesn't matter. Your training is what is important now." Lorenzo stood and walked up to Paolo, his eyes barely a yard away from Paolo's own. "Do you have the capability to learn, or are you more concerned with projecting a tough guy image?"

"Why does it matter?"

"Because your answer is important. I will not waste my time on one who does not place the proper importance on what I can teach you."

"And why would I need these skills?"

"Only Carlos can answer that."

Paolo thought back to everything his boss had ever said about this man, which wasn't much. Apparently, Carlos had sent others here who had failed. What did that mean? And why had the cartel deemed this training so important? Was this a way to advance? *Sicarios* had short lives. Any mistake made you vulnerable. If you tried to leave, your life was on the line. Killing somebody from a rival cartel made you a target. The only sure protection a *sicario* had was what he himself provided. Nobody watched your back, and to have any chance of survival, you had to move up the ladder. This old man might be his ticket to stay alive.

Lorenzo scuffed the dirt with the toe of his moccasin. When he looked up, he stared at the far horizon.

66   *David Griffith*

"Everything depends on you." Lorenzo's voice held none of the earlier condescension. "Do you want the knowledge I can teach you? If you don't, then leave now."

"I do." Paolo's words were simple, and genuine.

"Fine. You shall learn. I know much, because many years ago, someone taught me."

"And what will you teach me?"

"Everything of the wild. Most of all, you will learn how to find and kill an enemy. Sometime in your future, that may be important."

Paolo nodded, determined to soak up every skill Lorenzo had to offer. No longer would he think about killing the old man. That was over—at least for now.

At first, Paolo learned about the desert floor and every conceivable plant that grew there. Then, the forest. And finally—tracks. For months, Lorenzo taught him the secrets required to follow every animal. They dissected and discussed every trick known to man or beast. Lorenzo taught how to find each disturbed leaf and twig, and what it meant. Then, he learned to track the old man. For weeks he followed him through every inch of that sprawling wild canyon. Often when Lorenzo disappeared into thin air he grew frustrated, and sometimes afraid. The old man had no forgiveness for incompetence. Throughout his training, Paolo was never sure that Lorenzo wouldn't one day slip up behind him with his huge blade and cut his throat. On the last day of the course, Lorenzo ramped up the stakes.

Paolo's final exam was simple—pass or fail—all at the bottom of the vast *Barranca del Cobre*. The stifling heat made the sweat pool and drip off Paolo's skin. Today would pit the

WITHOUT REDEMPTION

hunter against the hunted. Paolo, armed with all the skill the old man had taught him would be the hunter. Lorenzo, the hunted, left no doubt in the young *sicario's* mind about the results of the outcome. If Paolo passed, he would live. If he failed, Lorenzo would kill him.

After breakfast, the old man stopped honing the ten-inch blade in his hand. He wiped the black debris from the stone onto his pant-leg, then leaned back and replaced the knife in the scabbard on his belt. He crossed his arms. "You will give me a half-hour head-start. Then, you may follow. Your job is to capture me. If you fail . . ." He didn't have to finish the sentence. The .308 caliber assault rifle lay on the table. Paolo stared at the blued barrel with the stubby scope mounted on the camouflage stock. Lorenzo hoisted it to his shoulder and walked to the edge of the escarpment. He'd left no doubt as to his intentions. The smaller caliber AR-15 still rested in its place by the kitchen stove. Paolo eyed the gun Lorenzo hoisted to his shoulder. The .308 was meant to blow a good-size hole in a man. Paolo understood. There would not be a make-up exam. Whether he passed or failed, today was his last school day.

Before he disappeared around a bend in the trail, Lorenzo turned and looked back at Paolo one last time. He started to speak, then seemed to change his mind. Instead, he flashed a noncommittal salute in the young *sicario's* direction.

Paolo wiped at his face and forehead, suddenly very afraid. How could he ever track that old desert fox? Though he'd spent months with this throwback mountain man, Lorenzo had been right. He *was* still a puppy! He tried to stop the trembling in his hands. Had a half-hour passed?

No clock graced the wall in this cliff dwelling and his cell phone had long ago run out of juice. Here, only the elements marked time. When the sun shed light into his mountain stronghold, Lorenzo left his bed. He ate when he was hungry, and when darkness cloaked the mountains, he went to bed.

Paolo picked up the AR-15, stepped from the safety of the cave and onto the now familiar trail to the bottom. This was crazy. He would die. His eyes swept the forest below. Then, he glanced at the trail that led to the top of the rim. Suddenly, the answer came. He would not play Lorenzo's game. By the time the old man figured out Paolo wasn't following him, it would be too late. He would slip in to Divisadero, catch the train, and be back in Mazatlan before the old man even figured out he was gone. The weeks of camping where night found them, the running and tracking through all kinds of terrain, had hardened Paolo's body. No, Lorenzo would not catch him. He would leave.

Paolo turned right and started up the trail. He'd not taken the third step when a bullet splattered rock chips in his face. As the unmistakable crack of the rifle echoed off the canyon walls, he scrambled back into the safety of the cave mouth. Angrily, he scanned the forest far below. He saw nothing, but somewhere, Lorenzo watched. He'd known. That's why he'd taken the longer range .308. With that, he could easily pick a man off the cliff trail. Paolo squatted out of sight in the entrance. Down below his chances were limited. Up here, he had none. There would be no escape.

Five minutes later, Paolo took a deep breath and again exposed himself to the rifle. He picked his way down the narrow sheep trail to the bottom, alert, watching for the slight-

WITHOUT REDEMPTION 69

est movement ahead. Each step he looked for sign. Even on solid rock there could be a scuff mark or a misplaced pebble. When he reached the floor of the canyon, his confidence rose. Lorenzo had taught him well. Maybe . . . just maybe he had a chance.

For three days, Lorenzo eluded him. Twice, the old man doubled back and nearly killed him, but in the end, whether by Paolo's own skill or by Lorenzo's design, the *sicario* caught him resting against a small sapling in a hidden alcove in the forest. Paolo's knife was instantly at Lorenzo's throat. Paolo wanted to kill him, but deep inside he knew the old man had let him win. Nevertheless, he couldn't resist the urge to leave a thin bloody line dangerously close to the carotid artery before he stepped away.

The old man never even turned, but Paolo saw the grim smile at the corners of his mouth.

"Go, Paolo. Go now, because for that I must kill you."

By good fortune and perhaps by Lorenzo's moment of compassion, Paolo had won, but only a fool would linger. He walked away, all the time watching his back. Once, he stopped. He wanted to thank the old man, to say something. Instead, he turned and trotted the eight miles to the trail that led to the top of the canyon rim.

Paolo never saw Lorenzo again. He never wanted to see him. What he'd done at the last had been foolish, unforgivable. Though they'd spent weeks and months together, he knew the old man would kill him, with no more animosity than stepping on a spider.

Two days later, Paolo stepped off the train in Mazatlan, a different man than when he'd left. He reported to Carlos who hugged him as if he were his own son. From that moment, Paolo became a rising star in the Sinaloa cartel.

Chapter 8

Paolo now had an array of skills and experience that set him apart, and for the next four years he honed the craft Lorenzo had taught him. Sometimes, the federal police sent guerilla teams into the mountains to apprehend members of the cartel. Paolo's job was to track and ambush them. He pursued each one relentlessly. Their losses mounted, and soon they abandoned any attempts at penetrating the secret places that hid Joaquín Guzmán.

After one of his frequent trips into the Sierra Madre to kill federal police, Paolo heard about the Indian. He dismissed the story as more racial nonsense than anything of value. Some tough guy had caused havoc with the La Familia cartel. If he'd been White or Hispanic, nobody would have noticed. But apparently he was some sort of Native American which suddenly elevated him to world class *sicario* status. Paolo scoffed at the *campesino* who brought the news. This supposed aboriginal wonder-man was undoubtedly just another American federal agent. As such, he hated him and would kill him on sight.

Later, another *sicario* confirmed the story. Everyone argued over the Indian's origin. He looked, and spoke like a native. Many remained convinced he was actually Mexican. Nobody knew for sure, but on one thing, everybody agreed; he was dangerous—and needed killing.

David Griffith

Paolo carefully sorted through information and innuendo. The Indian's nationality was important. Wiping out a U.S. federal agent stirred up hornets and made you more vulnerable to extradition if you were caught. American prisons were about a hundred times better. The fringe benefits were second to none, but so was their security. Nobody wanted to go there, because unless you were a big player, you couldn't continue to run your business—and the chances of escape were nearly non-existent. If you remained in the Mexican penal system, conditions were tougher. But if you had money and connections, life could be if not good, at least reasonable. You could buy amenities, and sometimes even bribe your way out. If you couldn't do that, there was always the possibility of a massive jailbreak—after the right people were paid.

Paolo learned about the prison system the hard way. In a botched hostage taking in Los Mochis, he had been captured by the *Federales*. A judge sentenced him to fifteen years. After six months of misery, he escaped and vowed to never spend another day in a prison, Mexican or American.

On a late summer evening, Carlos summoned Paolo to a meeting. That was not unusual. Paolo still did the odd contract killing, though usually those were handed to lower level *sicarios*. His assignments had gained importance, often involving covert surveillance, or the assassination of police or politicians who had refused to be reasonable. Occasionally, Carlos sent him to track cartel members who tried to leave. If they didn't know too much they sometimes were ignored, but most of the time they were mutilated, then killed as a lesson to others. With Chapo, security always came first.

WITHOUT REDEMPTION

When Paolo stepped into the vehicle to be transported to Carlos's compound he suspected nothing other than an ordinary assignment. But when the black SUV went the opposite direction and turned onto *Calle Refugio*, he started to sweat. What was going on? Hard-eyed men loitered along the whole length of the street, each of them armed, and within yards of either late model pickups or SUV's. Even to the uninformed they looked menacing. That they were bodyguards for somebody much more important than Carlos was obvious.

The SUV stopped in front of a sprawling mauve wall. Two of the men led him through the steel gates and toward a one-story hacienda, then escorted into a room in the inner part of the building. Carlos along with two other high-level local cartel lieutenants sat hunched and nervous at a polished boardroom table. Several *sicarios* stood at attention against the back wall.

"Carlos." Paolo scrutinized every corner and door. "What's happening, man?"

Carlos only shook his head, refusing to answer, which was not a good sign.

Paolo's mind scrambled through the last few operations he'd been involved in; each acquaintance, every conversation. Had something he'd said been misconstrued? Had some jealous rival pointed the finger at him? What accusation would he have to defend against? One never knew. He'd seen more than one summoned—then executed.

Two more *sicarios* appeared behind him. Both carried assault rifles . . . the old reliable AK-47. They stood well back, quietly alert. He glanced at their faces. He didn't recognize

David Griffith

either one. They watched him intently, which gave Paolo a small measure of comfort. Even in the cartel, only the very hardest can look you in the eye with no emotion before they kill you. Usually, there is anger or disdain for the victim. As near as he could tell, these showed only curiosity.

An expansive mural of the sea filled the far wall. In the middle, huge breakers crashed into rocky cliffs that stretched to the ceiling. Paolo watched as the darkest part of the rocks suddenly parted and the wall silently slid away like a theater curtain. A group of men now stood in front of him, spread away from a central figure. Though he'd only seen pictures of the man, Joaquín Guzmán was instantly recognizable. Paolo stared, ignoring the men spread out around him. These, the hand-picked guards assigned to El Chapo were collectively and irreverently referred to as the "twelve apostles." They lounged with the careless alertness of all Special Forces soldiers. The tallest of the two soldiers behind him prodded Paolo forward. Slowly, he walked toward the diminutive figure with the nickname "Shorty". Though Chapo stood a full head shorter than Paolo, one never looked down on Joaquín Guzmán. His was the sardonic gaze of the most powerful drug lord on the planet. For thousands in Sinaloa and far beyond the borders of Mexico, he distributed the power of wealth or the degradation of abject poverty and fear. The hand that beckoned Paolo closer had been ordained—to distribute death.

Paolo stared at Chapo's face while he tried to swallow the lead weight in his throat. Somewhere, he had made a bad error. If he was very lucky, the unreadable features in front of him would be the last thing he would see. But if he'd been ac-

WITHOUT REDEMPTION 75

cused of something especially treasonous, his death might be days away, with unbearable agony between now and then. He had seen it—been part of it. There could be only one reason he'd been brought here. His life was over.

Seconds seemed like hours as he waited for Chapo to pronounce sentence. If there had been any doubt whether he was guilty, he would have stood in front of Carlos to account for his sins. He would have been questioned, allowed to state whatever case he had. Here, guilt had already been established.

Paolo tried desperately to stifle his rising panic. Would they cut out his tongue? Sever a hand? Genitals? He clenched his fists to stop the trembling in his whole body while he attempted to project his mind past the fear. If he tried to escape, they would have to shoot him. That would be the only way to assure a quick death. Slowly, he spread his feet and sidled to the left, just enough to be able see both men behind me. The tallest one he'd kill. Surprise would be his, and the man would never get his gun into play. The second? Who knew? He might neutralize him as well, but before he reached the door, the twelve against the wall would riddle his body with bullets. That was the best he could hope for, a fate much preferable to anything Chapo had in mind. Escaping the bullets of the twelve was the last thing he wanted.

A final glance at the line of armed assassins told him they were ready. Each man had been recruited because of their loyalty to Chapo, and their elite status as ex-Special Forces. They were the best, and he knew by the still, hard eyes that they'd read his body language like an open book. The sound of released safeties echoed loud in the tiled room's silence.

76 *David Griffith*

Twelve index fingers curled from the extended safety position along the barrel to the trigger guard. Special Forces soldiers never do that unless there is an immediate red alert. Within the next ten seconds, each intended to shoot. Every muscle in Paolo's body tensed, ready to explode into action. His hand stiffened and he shuffled half a step backward, a split second away from launching a lightning jab at the closest throat.

"Paolo." Chapo's voice was hardly above a whisper, but it carried across the room as if he had shouted. "Relax." He stepped forward and touched Paolo's shoulder. "You are chosen."

Paolo stuttered, the words clattering off his tongue like rusty ball bearings. *"No entiendo,"* and truly, he didn't understand.

"Can you not count?" Joaquín Guzmán half turned and swept a hand toward the apostles. "Eleven men stand behind me. It is necessary I have twelve. Are you worthy of that position?" It was as if Chapo's obsidian eyes had bayoneted the young man against the wall.

Suddenly, all the air in Paolo's chest dribbled out into the room. Strength drained from his arms and legs. He wasn't going to die. Every one of the men against the wall were ex-Special Forces, elite troops, but Chapo, the greatest man on the planet had recognized his skills, far above those eleven in front of him. Nevertheless, Paolo bowed his head in the expected obeisance as the cartel boss spoke.

"You have proven your loyalty, and I may have need of the skills you have so aptly demonstrated." Chapo again placed his hand on Paolo's shoulder. Instantly, Paolo felt a

WITHOUT REDEMPTION 77

burning heat shoot down his torso. He wondered whether that came from Chapo's overwhelming charisma, or as his enemies said, that he was truly the spawn of the devil? He didn't care. Long ago, Paolo had made a choice. Now, he made another one. He would not turn back.

"You have only to instruct me. *Señor* Joaquín, how I may be of service."

The black eyes searched Paolo's face. "Be ready to leave tomorrow morning. Tonight, we celebrate the addition of a new apostle. We will soon discover whether we have arrived at the right decision in replacing Judas."

The veiled threat made Paolo's chest muscles contract. The instant fame of being one of the chosen was tempered by the knowledge that in the world of the Sinaloa cartel, glory and notoriety often led to an early death. Whoever the previous number twelve had been, he obviously no longer resided in the land of the living, and Paolo knew; one mistake, and he would follow Judas to the grave. Paolo answered Chapo with as much tact as he could summon.

"*Señor*. You are my life and my future. I am yours to command."

The hand slipped off Paolo's shoulder. "Be here at eight tomorrow morning. Come prepared. You will not return."

Whatever not returning meant, at least it meant a chance at life. Carlos paid the rent on his apartment anyhow. Or he said he did, though Paolo suspected that the owner of the ocean-front building he lived in was required to donate that unit in exchange for protection. That common practice meant that those business owners who had a problem with the way things worked had wills, bequests to their loved ones—and they better be up-to-date.

"Go." Chapo nodded his dismissal and Paolo wasted no time in hitting the street. Outside, a light-blue Escalade waited, the engine idling. The driver beckoned him.

While the man wove through the throngs of tourists, Paolo's thoughts turned to the poverty of his childhood home in Guerrero. "You have come a long way. You are a great success." But he had to squeeze his eyes shut to block out the bloody, tortured faces of those he had killed. Paolo shook his head, trying to dismiss the savage and sordid memories. Silently he screamed at the cadavers. "I did what I had to do." They receded into the background of his mind, but Katrina, as always, refused to go away.

Chapter 9

Before the sun cast its first light over the dark hills to the east, I awoke and slipped out of the hard bed. I'd tried to be quiet. I didn't want to disturb Clarissa. She deserved to sleep in every morning, or at least as much as Conor would allow.

Her sleepy voice jarred my search for a lost sock.

"I wish this was a *normal* people vacation."

"Go to sleep. It's only one day. I'll be back tonight," I growled. Mornings had never been my best time. I didn't have it in me to be civil before two cups of coffee. Finally, I found the lost sock I was looking for, and finished dressing to the too loud sounds of the gurgling, cheap coffee maker. I kissed Clarissa's warm face before I tiptoed out of the bedroom.

In the kitchen, I poured a mug full of java, grabbed a couple Power Bars, and hit the narrow jungle road that led out to the highway. An hour later in the village of La Fortuna, I ditched the rental car in front of a restaurant, walked to the local bus station and boarded the northbound bus for Los Chiles.

I picked a seat next to the window and inspected the passengers surrounding me. I'd dressed as usual; a decent long-sleeve shirt and American cowboy jeans. Tourist shorts wouldn't have worked here. The other men on the bus had long pants, hats, and probably the same brand of "made in China" shirts as mine. My wardrobe was right. My face didn't look like a regular tourist, so neither should the rest of me. My nervous fingers twisted at the straw hat in my lap as we travelled north. A rather large lady with hair pulled back tight into a ponytail boarded at the first stop and took the seat next to me. Her world-weary eyes roved up and down my lean frame like I was a cut of prime beef. I looked down at my flat belly. Possibly, I wouldn't grade triple "A," at least not yet.

"Where are you going?" Her question caught me by surprise.

"San Carlos—to visit my uncle." It was an off-the-cuff answer, a reasonable excuse to be heading north.

"Who is your uncle? Perhaps I know him. I have lived there since childhood."

Panic flooded to the tips of my fingers. What a stupid mistake. I should have known better than to lie. Though an agent must have a cover story, I'd never been good at making up complete falsehoods. Every time I had to manufacture some wild tale, it came back to bite me. "Uh-h"—I scrambled for a name. "Victor. My uncle is Victor Rosales. He's my mother's brother," I finished lamely.

She shook her head. "I cannot place him. But there are so many new people there now. It's not like the old days where one knew all the neighbors."

I breathed a sigh of relief, instantly grateful she didn't recognize every face in town. "Yes, he has only lived there a few months," I added hastily. If I was to survive this interrogation, I'd better tread carefully.

"What part of town does he live in?"

WITHOUT REDEMPTION 81

"I'm not sure." I stuttered. "I have never actually been there, so I was going to call him when I arrived." My answer sounded phony, but it seemed to satisfy her curiosity. I tipped back in the seat and closed my eyes, hoping to suppress any further family queries. Maybe this nosy woman would go away. All I wanted to do was pick up Frederick's package, then get on with our holiday. As soon as this side tour concluded, we were moving to a beach hotel. Enough of that jungle and ranch venture. We needed to relax, get some more sunshine and sand, and most of all, not have to think about drug smugglers or international criminal organizations. Seven more days on the beach would cap what had so far been a memorable holiday. In fact, tomorrow I would drop a postcard to Frederick. A little thank you note wouldn't hurt, just to let him know I was grateful for the company picking up the tab.

The bus crawled forward the last mile to the border crossing. Eventually, everyone had to get out and go through Customs. The Nicaraguan officer stared suspiciously at me, but I reckon that had more to do with my brown face than the actual passport. I'd considered using my American one, but Frederick seemed to think in our line of work, Canadian credentials had an advantage. Today it worked well enough. After a few perfunctory questions, to which I answered with all the respect I could muster, the uniform scowled, stamped a blank page, and waved me on. I skedaddled.

Within minutes, I arrived at the river and paid the fare for the two-hour jaunt upstream to San Carlos. Other than a lot of egrets and other tropical birds, the journey was unremarkable. When we reached the town, I grabbed my genuine vacationer backpack and trudged up the street to a parked taxi. Though the right front fender had been a victim of either bad driving or the economy, it beat walking. I gave the driver the address I'd memorized. Twenty minutes later we pulled up to the gate of a walled compound.

"No Trespassing" signs would have been redundant. Barbed wire and broken glass atop the adobe walls advertised an income stratum to which few in this country could aspire, and a desire for extreme privacy. I paid the cab driver and stepped onto the sidewalk. The too-familiar tightness in my stomach was not comforting, but I shoved it aside. Get the papers. That assignment hadn't changed. In two hours I'd be out of here. By tonight, I'd be back in Costa Rica at the lodge. There might even be time to sit on the deck with Clarissa, watch the southern stars, and really start to unwind.

Chapter 10

The morning after the meeting with Chapo, Paolo packed a few personal items into a small bag. As the door on the third-floor apartment swung shut behind him, he had a fleeting premonition that wherever Chapo sent him, he would neither require furniture, nor would he return.

An hour later, he boarded a cartel jet with the other bodyguards. Nobody seemed to know where they were going, not that it mattered. Their job was to take care of the boss—wherever he went. Paolo glanced nervously at the men in the surrounding seats. The hunched figures stared straight ahead, every one alert, but disinterested in conversation. After a few halting and useless attempts that only elicited cold stares, he settled back and closed his eyes. They were not really being standoffish. They were just men who didn't talk—in any situation. He awoke, when the plane landed and bounced down a rutted and pot-holed runway.

After they'd taxied to a stop, he followed the others down the steps and onto what had once been tarmac. A squat, oriental looking guy with a broad face and pushed-up cheekbones barked orders. Paolo remembered that someone in the plane had called him Mavelio. He stood at the bottom of the steps as the men trooped onto the pavement, his thick biceps nearly the size of Paolo's waist. As Paolo passed, the man sneered at him. "Pick it up, runt!"

84   *David Griffith*

Paolo scowled back. Mavelio might be able to kill him barehanded, but the AR-15 at his side leveled the playing field. He would have no problem filling Mavelio's belly with lead. However, this was not the place to test his standing. It would be wise to bide his time, but the slur was something he would not forget.

The men loaded into three SUV's, all Cadillac Escalades or Chevy Tahoes, every one jammed with all the options money could buy. Twenty minutes later, the team pulled into a rundown set of hovels that appeared to be a leftover roadside motel from the seventies. The patched blue adobe was streaked with water stains, and the broken roof tiles obviously only warded off a percentage of moisture. The paint-peeled doors had originally been a light green, possibly matching the roof tiles. Keys were handed out by an old fellow with sad eyes and a droopy speckled mustache—two men to a room. Paolo's roommate was a tall, taciturn man with gray eyes—a color no Mexican should have, but the explosive powder behind the color warned Paolo that his parentage was not something a stranger should question, even if they were supposed to be squad buddies. "Gray eyes" entered the room first and threw his gear onto the bed closest to the door. Paolo didn't argue.

"I am Jorge."

"Paolo." He held out his hand.

"I know your name. We all do."

Whether that was good or bad, Paolo shrugged it off. Questions could be answered later.

Within minutes, a fist banged on the cheap wooden door. Paolo's roommate instantly flattened against the wall,

WITHOUT REDEMPTION 85

then tipped a curtain inward to peer outside before he strode over and jerked it open.

Mavelio stood in the twilight. "Come to the restaurant. We will eat. Orders are that we are to be ready to go—directly from there. The boss has a meeting at nineteen hundred hours."

So far, no one had given any instructions, so Paolo watched Jorge for direction. The man gathered a small amount of gear, extra clothes, and his weapons. Paolo followed suit. Whatever their assignment might be, he would be prepared.

The eating place on the other side of the courtyard could hardly have been called a restaurant. A cobbled-together group of rickety tables sat end to end in an open-air room with a crumbling concrete floor. A pock-marked man with long greasy hair stirred a steaming pot on an ancient stove and gave orders to a couple of kids who apparently doubled as waiters. The smells emanating from the slurry on the stove did not bode well. A few bites of the viscous mess was enough. Paolo pushed the food away and surreptitiously studied the men seated around the room. They were warriors, and sometimes assassins. Whatever tonight required, they appeared capable and ready.

Most had finished doing battle with the grisly fare when Chapo appeared. Three men arrived with him. They stood at ease while he walked amongst the most trusted of his considerable army. He spoke quietly to several of the twelve, then turned and faced the seated men.

"Finish eating. We leave in five minutes." He paused, his eyes roving over the group seated at the rickety square tables.

86   *David Griffith*

"As all of you know, the Americans are making it more difficult and expensive for us to operate. With the help of our own *Federales,* they have cut off some of our best supply routes." His face hardened. "The traitorous puppets who control the Palacio Nacional in Mexico City have sold their souls to Washington. So . . . tonight will see the culmination of a deal our intelligence people have worked long and hard to make possible. Some of you have been an integral part of that." Again, his eyes flickered over each man, the newest recruit last. Paolo was transfixed by his mesmerizing stare. "This, I hope, is the final battle in our war against the Los Zetas dogs."

The sharp intake of breath around the room at the mention of their biggest rival and worst enemy was testimony enough that whatever Chapo had planned for tonight had come as a surprise. Nevertheless, as "the disciples", questioning the boss was inconceivable. They would accomplish what was required, with brutal efficiency.

Paolo leaned over and asked Jorge about the three men flanking Chapo.

Jorge stared at him as if by asking, he'd committed the unforgivable sin. "They are the inner circle—Pedro, Jaime, and Juan."

Despite his total rejection of his childhood faith, Paolo cringed at the possible sacrilege of using Peter, James, and John as nicknames for El Chapo's bodyguards. The heretical inference might be bad karma. Quickly, he pushed away from the table and followed the others out to the waiting vehicles.

Twenty minutes later, they pulled up to a yellow one-story structure at the edge of town. Here, no streetlights cut

WITHOUT REDEMPTION

through the darkness. Two of the transports stopped. Men piled out and immediately fanned out to cover the perimeter. Paolo rode in the last of the three Hummers. He watched as the first group worked their way around the walled compound. Fleetingly, he wondered why the building hadn't been secured hours before, but nobody had asked him. Nor, he decided, were they likely to do so. He was the junior man, but he knew instinctively—Lorenzo would never have done it this way.

Chapter 11

I'd be a brazen liar if I said I wasn't well spooked when I dismissed the taxi and walked to the gate of that big house. My eyes darted to every hidden corner and crevice, and though there seemed nothing amiss, I remained cautious. Though I couldn't say why, there was evil here. Something bad was going to happen, but instead of listening to the warnings, I jammed a thumb at the doorbell button mounted in the wall. While I waited for some response, I turned and surveyed the slope toward town. Night would soon creep over the jungle, which meant I'd never make it back to our little *cabina* tonight, but with any luck I'd be there first thing in the morning. Somewhere in the bowels of the complex, a signal must have sent a servant my way. A tall, emaciated Nicaraguan opened the barred door in front of me. When I stepped through, he nodded politely. I was obviously expected, because he didn't ask my name and neither did I volunteer it. He beckoned me forward. I followed his stick-man figure down a short hallway. At the end, he opened a door. Four ornate wooden chairs with leather upholstery huddled around an oblong wicker table in the center of the massive room. He slid one out and motioned for me to be seated.

"*Por favor, Señor*. If you would make yourself comfortable, I will inform *el jefe* you are here."

WITHOUT REDEMPTION 89

El jefe? Inwardly I scoffed. Who was this supposed "boss?" Contrary to what Frederick had said, I doubted it would be anyone with any authority. Impatiently, I crossed one leg over the other and waited for whatever low-level cartel snitch they'd sent to make his grand entry. The list meant we would probably get unimportant drug runner names from a Nicaraguan bush-league wannabe. Ferrying information of dubious quality to whoever Frederick dealt with in the U.S. would be a wasted effort, and of no value to anyone, but if that's what he wanted, I would deliver. Then it would be back to the beach to play with that woman who remained my best friend, and that neat kid . . . and at night? Well, I'd make love to the most wonderful woman in the world.

A long twenty minutes later, the door at the far end of the room opened. Twelve men trooped in and spread out against the wall. Though none sported any kind of uniform, arm patches or chest candy, the confidence they shared, and the familiar way they handled their assault rifles didn't need any more statement. They were all *sicarios,* and if there were that many of them, they were protecting someone of huge importance.

Two of them stepped forward and searched me. They did a thorough job. If I'd had anything larger than a toothpick, they'd have found it. They moved back against the wall and I returned to my chair. A small man with light skin and intelligent darting eyes strolled into the room. Frederick had tried to prepare me, but still my jaw fell toward the floor. The man in front of me was not a low-level Nicaraguan sycophant. He was Joaquín Guzmán, El Chapo, the king of the Mexican cartels, and though I'd often scrutinized his quizzical mug in old intelligence photos, they didn't do justice to the man. He'd aged, and his frame was padded with at least twenty more pounds. But what kept my attention were the eyes. They darted nervously through the room before they rested on my face. He moved toward me, his pace measured and slow, and I couldn't decide if he looked more like the king of the lions, or the chief rooster. I wasn't about to discuss my disrespectful musings. Any show of disrespect would be my death warrant.

A sardonic grin flitted over the man's features. My mind raced. Was Chapo really finished; ready to make a deal? Was that what had drawn him so far from his impregnable security zone in the Sierra Madre of Mexico? Too many lawmen, both military and civilian had come up empty—or dead—after pursuing Chapo there. For years, he had been untouchable, despite the best efforts of two nations and a multi-million-dollar reward on his head. For him to have risked coming here meant this was a very big deal.

A niggling fear crept up from the pit of my stomach, and I gripped the cast on my left arm to keep my hand steady. When Chapo reached the table, I stood. It's what one does for kings, and though some may disagree, Joaquín Guzmán was a king, albeit an evil one. In a wide swath of Mexico, he held more power than any potentate or president. He pulled out the chair across from me, sat and crossed his arms—all five-foot-six of him. For a long time, he studied me. He must have decided not to cut off my head, because he waved me to be seated.

Once more, the door at the end of the room opened. A man walked rapidly into the room and stood on the far

WITHOUT REDEMPTION 91

side of the table. I recognized him immediately. He was the one I'd seen the first day on that El Coco beach, and in the next second, I understood. They'd tracked every movement I'd made from the moment my plane landed. Inwardly, I shrugged. I should have known. These weren't amateurs. He nodded to Chapo, then abruptly strode out of the room.

Chapo's voice broke through the silence. "You are the American cowboy?"

I tapped a finger on the table. "I have been called that."

"And you work for Stirling Associates?"

"I do." A cold dread seeped down from my brain and into my chest. He knew too much.

Chapo leaned forward. "I have found it useless to do any kind of deal with the CIA or DEA. Neither will honor their word. That is why you are here. Several times through the years I have trusted Frederick. He never let me down. But you?" Quizzically, he studied me. "Obviously, he sent you here. Does that mean I can trust *you*?"

We stared at each other. There didn't seem any right answer to that question, so I made no reply.

"Your features could be Mexican. Where do you come from?"

"Perhaps the same place as you." I crossed one leg over the other. "My people settled in the north—before the Spanish—and perhaps others. Whether they were the first on the land is questionable, but for a while, we remained strong enough to hold a large part of it."

Chapo waved a hand contemptuously. "That, I care little about. It is always the strong who win. Here is the deal. Never has it been negotiable, and nothing has changed. What I am going to put into your hands requires a guarantee on Frederick's part. Do you have it?"

I stared into his eyes, though they constantly shifted around the room, the wary distrust plain on his face.

I nodded. "I have it."

"Good. Then I will give you Heriberto." His voice rasped across the silence.

I leaned forward. "You mean Heriberto Lazcano? Los Zetas?" My disbelief must have been apparent, because his confident sneer changed to instant displeasure. My jaw clamped shut, and I squirmed in my chair, chagrined that I'd shown any emotion or disbelief. That had been unprofessional, but what he'd just stated was scarcely more believable than if the Prime Minister of Russia had offered to assassinate the current Ayatollah of Iran.

Chapo eyed me with disdain. "You heard me."

"Of course. May I ask how?"

"Never mind how. I am El Chapo. What I say, I can do."

I held up my hand attempting to ward off his anger. "I did not doubt your word."

His irritation vanished instantly, and his head thrust forward. "We must trust each other if this is to work." His eyes again darted nervously around the room. They reminded me of a wolf I'd once watched through binoculars as he warily circled a kill, searching for my hidden traps, sensing their presence.

I jammed both thumbs in my pockets, perhaps a nervous reaction to keep my one good hand from fidgeting while I studied his face. No matter what he said, I'd not trust El Chapo—ever. But this trade that had been made by people

WITHOUT REDEMPTION 93

far above my level. I cleared my throat, pulled the envelope out of my shirt pocket and set it in front of me on the table. "And you are giving us Lazcano for this, I presume?" I shoved Frederick's written promise across the table. I'd been privy to the contents, and for Chapo, it was life-changing. It guaranteed that when Chapo surrendered to the Mexican authorities, the U.S. Feds would not file for his extradition to the United States. I could not even imagine what he'd had to trade in Washington for that deal.

Chapo's left eyebrow rose as he ripped open the envelope and read the single page. "He must have great confidence in you."

"Perhaps." I didn't think his comment needed further answer, but a roiling apprehension stirred a whole nest of frogs down around my belly button. This was absurd. How could Chapo deliver the number one capo of Los Zetas, Heriberto Lazcano, a man every bit as canny as himself? For years, the two cartels had engaged in a death-struggle for the border crossings, while they scattered the grisly remains of young men and women eager to trade grinding poverty for the ephemeral promises of the drug lords. Most of those kids died in a brutal nightmare, dumped like so much excrement in the streets of a nation awash in carnage. But that was Mexico. Our meeting in the Nicaragua border country may not have been completely safe, but there wasn't a drug killing every five minutes like happened in Juarez. However, if the Sinaloa cartel had established a presence, that would likely change.

With no warning, Chapo stood, placed his hands on the table and leaned toward me. Our eyes locked in an instant struggle of mental superiority. I purposely let mine slide away as his words struck with all the force of one of his armor-plated trucks.

"I have negotiated a summit with Los Zetas. It will be at a place where you can capture or kill Heriberto Lazcano, and perhaps other top echelon Zetas as well. That will be up to you."

Instantly I froze, my mind spinning into overdrive while I tried to keep the incredulity from showing in my voice. "And this summit? This is not a thing lightly done—by the kings of the earth or by Mexican thieves."

He never answered but his face darkened at my insult, and for a moment I thought I'd gone too far. "When is this to happen?" I asked.

Chapo straightened and crossed his arms. "Soon. You will know in good time."

My eyes flickered over the line of guards against the far wall. Their inscrutable faces stared back at me. I wanted to catalogue each of them for future reference, but I couldn't because the most dangerous man in the world occupied the chair across from me. I had to focus my attention on him.

Chapo's fingers moved purposefully to an inside pocket of his tailored, leather jacket. I tensed, though with a dozen AK-47's twenty feet away, I could have done nothing if his hand had reappeared with a gun. It didn't. He handed me a sealed business envelope.

"Give this to Frederick Roseman. No one else."

I reached over and took it, then tucked it into the bottom of my *mochila*.

WITHOUT REDEMPTION 95

He leaned across the table until his face was inches from mine. "Our agreement stands. Twenty names. Every person in the top tier of Los Zetas. Where they live, their spouses, girlfriends, family, and safe houses. As we agreed—everything. I have done my part. Make sure your people do the same. Under no circumstances am I to be prosecuted in the United States. I am to be left alone." He pointed at the envelope. "Most of those names will be at the summit." He stepped back and slashed at the air with the edge of his hand. "If you cut off the head of the Los Zetas serpent, peace will return. There will be security on the American border, and stability for Mexico."

I picked up my *mochila* and balanced it on my lap. Chapo had us in his pocket—and he knew it. If everything happened according to plan, we would buy tranquility—at least for a while. Deals would be made, powerful people would be paid, and territorial power for the surviving cartels would be established. Was it right? No—but fewer people would die, and in an era where nearly seventy thousand had lost their lives in the cartel wars, that was appealing to everyone who had lived through this violence.

I pushed the chair away and stood. Whatever I privately thought about the deal, my job was to follow orders, secure in the knowledge that I'd accomplished the mission for which I'd been sent. My face betrayed none of the disdain I felt for this man. Deliberately, I reached across the table. Our hands clasped, and it was as if I'd touched a fuse. The east wall exploded in a cascade of brick and mortar. Body parts, blood, and guns scattered through the air. The blast flung me to the far side of the room. The last thing I saw was the instant rage and betrayal in Chapo's eyes.

Chapter 12

When Paolo's eyes opened, his first joyous thought was that death had somehow not claimed him. He fought to regain consciousness while his confused mind struggled to answer the murky questions he could hardly formulate. He'd entered the room with the other *sicarios*. He remembered studying the stranger seated at the ornate wooden table. Why had he risked coming here, and what had been so important that Chapo would personally meet with him?

Chapo had been nervous, and it seemed, angry at the stranger's clipped and curt responses. This foreigner was either a fool or very brave. At the end of the discussion the two had shaken hands. At that moment the east wall had disintegrated into a shotgun blast of deadly shards. A black shroud cloaked Paolo's eyes. Minutes later, he fought back the curtain and a low laugh escaped with a trickle of blood from his cut and bleeding mouth. Perhaps God had wanted to wipe him out because of all the people he'd killed. Well, He'd failed. A grimace of pain stifled his thankfulness. He did what he had to do. It was God who had made him poor. People without money have to do different things, fight harder than those who are born rich. He scrambled through the blood and bodies until he reached the middle of the room. Chapo lay on the floor, nearly covered by the upended table, but he appeared to be unharmed. Paolo put an arm around him and dragged him to the jagged hole in the wall. Several others joined them, each of them spewing blood from some body part. No enemies seemed to be close, so they staggered downhill to the jungle, a hundred paces away. They'd scrambled into the thin covering of jungle when two more rocket-propelled grenades hit the building. The first one pulverized what was left. The second did nothing. Every step, Paolo expected the rapid fire of automatic weapons to slice into them. To stay here could only mean death. Whoever had blown out the east wall would move in to finish the job. The deep jungle behind them was their only chance to escape.

In a small clearing, Chapo gathered everybody at the base of a spreading Guanacaste tree. "Friends, do you understand what has happened?"

It seemed a trick question, and every one of them stared at the three apostles. Certainly, they'd not done much of a job of protecting the most powerful drug lord in the world. But it wasn't their fault. The apostles had handled all the security details—intelligence, logistics, and negotiations.

In between surveying the surrounding jungle for hostiles, all twelve stared at their toes.

"You." Chapo stabbed a finger at Paolo. "It is time to discover your value. Can you find him?"

Paolo snapped to attention. "The man who was in the room with you?"

"Who else?"

"Certainly." Paolo hadn't really meant to say that. He had no idea who the man was, or if he would leave any trail to follow. Hastily, he tried to backtrack. "I mean—given some time, and, well . . . by morning—"

WITHOUT REDEMPTION 99

"Go. You have until daylight to find him. Do not kill him. This one will die later—but very slowly." His voice was punctuated by the last of the falling rubble from the wall behind them. Along with everybody else, Paolo instinctively hit the ground. Minutes passed with no further noise, yet every one of them were aware that somewhere in the dark perimeter, there might still be men lying in wait.

Paolo turned to Chapo. "We need to move. Now."

"I give the orders." Chapo's eyes flamed like burning sulfur in the gloomy night. "Do not forget that."

Paolo's face flushed with embarrassment and anger. He was right, and he sensed Chapo knew it as well. Why had the boss chosen to humiliate him in front of the other men? However, his resentment had no time to smolder.

"Go. Take two men with you." Chapo pointed at the first two hairy chests in line with his finger. "Radio back when you have picked up his trail."

Paolo's lips tightened with scorn as he turned and slipped into the jungle. He needed no help to track a man.

With Paolo in the lead, the three of them made a wide circle, careful to avoid any who might still hide in the darkness. If the enemy was still out there, Chapo and the others could deal with them. He didn't care how, as long as they covered his back while he searched for the man with the broken arm.

Several times, Paolo glared over his shoulder at the two who floundered behind him. Even at this slow pace, they moved through the jungle like a pair of rhinoceroses in heat. He hunched into the bole of a Eucalyptus tree as the first one slipped on a downed log and fell flat on his face. The crash-

David Griffith

ing underbrush, resounding thunk, and subsequent groaning were more than Paolo could take. He swore at the man's incompetence and sent him back. With any luck some of the other men would mistake him for the enemy and shoot him. The second muscle-man seemed a little more in tune with his surroundings, enough that Paolo decided, at least for the present, to tolerate his bumbling ways.

Still wary of whoever might be out there in the underbrush, Paolo kept the beam of his pencil flashlight low to the ground. As they approached the south side of the clearing, a dark figure slipped empty-handed through the scattered trees, hurrying toward the still smoking ruins. Paolo dropped to a knee and in one fluid motion killed the light and released the safety on his rifle. The rapid click behind him was quiet notification that his backup had attained privileged bodyguard status for a reason. They crouched as the man passed, unaware of their presence. Once, he glanced over his shoulder, then quickened his pace. Was he only a *campesino* stumbling home after a rendezvous with a woman, or perhaps a late night in a local cantina? That didn't seem likely.

With the help of the flashlight, Paolo followed the man's back trail a few yards into the jungle. The story was clear. He'd crouched behind a fallen log while he watched the building. Paolo's flashlight flicked from scuff-mark to track as he read the sign. For him, the marks were no more difficult than a first-grade reader, and he sent up a silent prayer of thanks to the Virgin of Guadalupe for Lorenzo. Somebody had slipped up behind this peasant. There hadn't been a struggle, which said to Paolo that the man had been completely unaware there had been anyone near. Whoever had

WITHOUT REDEMPTION 101

set up this ambush was a very bush wise and seasoned professional, and though he had no way to prove it, Paolo was sure he had just found the trail of Chapo's betrayer.

A shiver started at the bottom of his spine and worked upward. Sticks and leaves littered the ground. Only someone who had studied under a great master like Lorenzo could have passed through that noisy underbrush with no sound. Inwardly, he scoffed. Nobody was that good. Probably the man who watched the house had been high on drugs—or asleep? In his mind, he again followed the *campesino* across the clearing. No, the man's step had been that of someone purposeful and alert. Undoubtedly, he'd been armed, which meant whatever weapons he'd carried were now in the hands of the stranger. Paolo ticked off the possibilities. Knife—possibly. Revolver or pistol—likely. Semi-automatic rifle—almost a certainty. He squatted and stared uneasily at the tracks. If the stranger now had a rifle, it would be a short-range assault weapon, either an AK-47 or an M-16. He must be very careful. This stranger had a broken arm, but he'd not only surprised the man behind the log, he'd disarmed what very likely was a rival *sicario*, a man at home with combat. Paolo peered into the jungle ahead with a growing wariness. This bushman would watch his back trail. He might set up any number of traps. It would pay to be cautious.

A hundred yards further, Paolo squatted on the edge of a spongy creek bank and studied the first clear track the stranger had left. He sat back on his heels. They were odd prints, the soles like tire tracks . . . and then he remembered. At the bottom of the *Barranca del Cobre* the deepest canyon in the Americas, the *Rarámuri* still lived the same lives as their ancestors. They were backward folk who disdained the ways of modern Mexicans and the civilized world. The soles of their *huaraches* were often carved from discarded tires, and in a muddy depression next to a bamboo grove, the distinctive track of a *Rarámuri* man stared back at him. Was the stranger one of those ancient canyon dwellers? No—he couldn't be. His features were foreign, different, and in some way, more dangerous. A disturbing thought rocked his cool composure. What if this was the Indian, the one who had infiltrated La Familia? Momentary panic threatened to engulf him as a riptide of fear cascaded through every vein in his body. No, that wasn't possible. That was back in Mexico. He could never be here. But nothing else made sense. The man he followed could only be—the Indian.

Chapter 13

Dust still hung heavy in the room when the marbles in my head started to roll back into place. I'd struggled to my knees and wiped the blood that dripped from the side of my face. There was no pain, and I had no idea what had happened. All I knew was that if I wanted to live, I needed to get away. Hanging shreds of plaster swung lazily over the gaping holes the RPG's had punched through the adobe walls. I crawled over the bodies and swallowed the bile in my throat. Blood seeped across the floor. A head scowled at me from the corner, but it wasn't attached to anything. I pushed a disconnected arm out of the way, scuttled through a small hole in the west wall, then sprinted down the dirt road that led toward town. Two more grenades from the eastern edge of the clearing shattered the night silence. I was too exposed, so I made a sharp left and trotted into the jungle to the south, while I said unkind things about Frederick and all his ancestors to the twenty-fifth generation, though after thinking about it more, I doubted this was his fault. He'd orchestrated a coup with the Sinaloa cartel that the governments of two countries would never have been able to manage, but at the last moment—everything had gone terribly wrong.

Another RPG came in from the north and blew one of the outbuildings into oblivion. Whoever was responsible for this was well armed. Cautiously, I slipped through an empty lot. Construction material littered the ground, and I squatted between a pile of lumber and a rubber-tired cart, while I surveyed the terrain ahead. Nothing out of the ordinary appeared, so I took a deep breath and sprinted for the jungle. When I reached the edge of the trees, I dived into the soft dirt while I watched for any sign of pursuit. The night was eerily quiet. The only sound was the far away sporadic traffic in the town. Nothing emerged from the smoking ruins of the building I'd so recently vacated, at least not yet. That undoubtedly would change, and I had no desire to be around to witness it. I rose, and carefully ghosted through the dense grove of what the locals called *Bálsamo*, angling toward the south and the Costa Rica border.

Before I'd gone fifty yards, I spotted the man off to my left, but only because he slapped at a mosquito. He lay with his rifle balanced across a fallen log, his whole attention focused on the recently blown-up building. A stalk would be risky, but this might be my only chance to acquire a weapon, and I was fairly certain that soon I'd have need of something other than a bamboo club. My casted arm clumsily slipped around his throat, which fortunately was his first warning of my presence. My knife automatically slid out of my belt, and I stuck the razor-sharp point at the top of his ribs. "Do not move, or you will die."

He froze, which is what most reasonable people do.

"Who are you?" I whispered.

He didn't answer, and I put enough pressure on the point of that Bowie blade to draw blood, which was about a quarter-inch of steel past comfortable. "Who do you work for?"

He groaned, "Beltrán-Leyva."

WITHOUT REDEMPTION

I should have guessed. The Beltrán Leyva cartel were another of the bloodthirsty scum that held a knife to throat of the Mexican people. I slid my own knife back into my belt and jammed his face into the log while I frisked him. Other than the AK-47, he had a very nice .45 caliber Beretta and a short-bladed toad sticker in a hip scabbard. I considered throwing the rifle into a nearby drainage ditch but decided to keep it along with the other weapons, though one handed, it was doubtful I could shoot anything but the pistol. I pointed him toward the smoking building. "Walk. If you stop, you are a dead man." He glanced around at me, the whites of his eyes large against the night sky. I pushed him away before he noticed my injured arm. He never hesitated. Once, he looked back, but didn't seem inclined to ignore my instructions. Let Chapo deal with him—if he'd survived. In the meantime, my only chance to live was to skin out of here.

My mind raced as I slipped through a patch of deadfall, trying to pick up a game trail headed south toward the river. What crappy luck! How had the Beltrán-Leyva cartel known that Chapo had an agreement that would allow the *Federales* to wipe out Los Zetas as well as some of their smaller allies? Those two cartels were on cozy terms, and both were powerful and dangerous. Arguably, they weren't in the same league as Chapo's Sinaloa cartel, but their operatives controlled vast swathes of the country. Chapo would be certain we had double-crossed him. Nothing I could say would convince him that this was not our doing. And Chapo's vengeance would be swift—and final.

If I wanted to live, it was now imperative for me to reach the U.S. border. But what about Clarissa and Conor at that ranch back in Costa Rica? Could I warn them? I fingered the cellphone on my belt, checked the bars to see if I had coverage. Should I call her? What could I tell her? That she should take the car and go . . . yeah, but where? And alone with Conor? We'd been under surveillance since that first day at the beach. How much time would it take for Chapo to block any exit? He knew exactly where we were, and he would have every escape route locked. The last thing Clarissa could do was go to an airport, or just simply drive away. No. I had to go back and get them. Frederick had given us an emergency evacuation plan. I'd insisted on it. All I needed to do was pack my family up for a three hour hike. After that, Stirling would whisk us back to Texas and home, where this near-death experience could be chalked up on the wall along with about fifty others. The difference was that those others hadn't put Clarissa and Conor at risk. Anger filtered through every recess of my body, and I jammed the cellphone back into its holster. It wouldn't work to call her. What could I say? How could I tell her my boss had not really been in control of things, and that now we were in the greatest danger of our lives?

As soon as I was certain there was nobody behind me, I set a straight course south toward the Nicaraguan border with Costa Rica. No matter what else happened, I had to get to Clarissa and Conor before morning. I'd call Frederick. He'd know what to do. He always had a plan when things went wrong. But a lead weight in the pit of my stomach kept shouting that this time, it wasn't just me, and home was fifteen hundred miles and three countries away.

WITHOUT REDEMPTION

Two hours of slogging through the jungle brought me down to a dirt track that a mile later narrowed to little more than a cow trail. There was some risk in following it, but I figured I had until morning before Chapo's vengeance would fall on my head. It would take him that long to muster more troops—if he was alive. I had a strong suspicion that he and at least some of the men in that room had survived the Beltrán-Leyva attack. They'd been lined up against the wall like dominos, but even if half of them had been killed, Chapo would have more forces nearby, and their number one priority would be to kill me.

I broke into a ground-eating dogtrot, trying not to joggle my now throbbing arm as I followed the narrow shoulder of the road. The border was only a few miles, and before the dark ribbon of the river that separated the two countries came into view, I left the road and quartered through a field dotted with towering, leafy Guanacaste before plunging back into the jungle on the other side. Moonlight glittered through the high canopy. Yellow, glittering cat eyes shone briefly in the darkness ahead of me, and I clawed for the Beretta I'd taken from the Beltrán-Leyva goon. Shooting whatever crouched behind those eyes would be a last option. This close to the border, gunshots would only bring more trouble, and I had enough of that without having to deal with a Nicaraguan army platoon. Ahead of me, the eyes blinked before moving toward me. I backed away and flicked off the safety. What a time to only have one useful arm. Now I could see the outline. It was definitely a cat, whether a puma or jaguar didn't really matter. I had no wish to kill him, but neither had I any intention of being kitty chow. I backed away which in hindsight was the wrong thing to do, but in the dark, it seemed the only option. Several times, I scraped around with my foot for something to throw at him but found nothing. Once, I aggressively stepped forward, but the cat went into a crouch. If I could have brained him with a big stick he might have gotten the message that there was easier prey, but in that murky jungle, I found nothing that would suffice. Once more he sunk to his haunches, ready to spring. Now, only ten feet separated us. I winced and pulled the trigger.

Excuses are for the dead, and I've never been prone to making them, but it was pitch-black in that thicket. Though I could shoot with either hand, my right was not my best. The sharp crack of that pistol never even slowed the cat. He had to take two jumps to reach me which didn't give me nearly enough time for a second shot. I braced against his charge and held up my left arm. His powerful jaws snapped shut on what should have been flesh and bone, but of course in my case was hospital plaster. It gave me the split second I needed to pull the trigger, even as his claws raked a couple tracks down my skinny ribs. This time the bullet embedded deep into his brain. He slumped to the ground. I staggered back from his carcass panting with relief while I tried to still my shaking hands. Some things I'd been trained for. Fighting hungry jaguars wasn't one of them.

I squatted in the damp mud and listened. Far away, I heard a shout in the night, followed by a staccato voice barking orders. I had no desire to hear more. I peered at the cat carcass in front of me. Even if I'd been inclined toward recording the event, this didn't seem the time for safari self-

WITHOUT REDEMPTION 109

ies. Swiftly, I tucked the Beretta into my belt and quartered off to the left, away from the voices. I had no wish to tangle with Nicaraguan soldiers. Though they were only doing their job, languishing in one of their flyblown jails, with the possibility they might sell my scalp to the highest bidder didn't strike me as productive. Chapo would undoubtedly be the winner in that scenario.

Fifteen minutes later, I'd left the voices behind. Just to make sure, I continued east for another mile before cutting back toward the river. Not for the first time, I pondered just how I would get my family out of this mess. Frederick had promised a quick solution in case of trouble. When he'd mentioned the possibility of danger, I should have bailed. That option had passed. Now, it was a long, long way to the U.S. border and home.

Chapter 14

Paolo squatted and fingered the leaf mold in front of his feet. Less than a quarter mile from where the stranger had overpowered the watching man in the jungle, the tracks abruptly turned and headed due south. He swore softly. He should have found out more from Chapo. If he could be sure who this man was, he would have a better idea of his destination. Once, as he followed the trail, he turned and glared at the silent figure behind him, wondering if he knew anything of value. He was only a hired gun. The chance of him knowing anything helpful was zero.

The man at his back had seemed distracted, almost disinterested in the proceedings as Paolo tracked the stranger over ground that seemingly held no clues. In the bottom of a low swale, they stopped for a few quick swallows of water. The bodyguard clipped his canteen back on his belt and shuffled from one foot to the other, clearly uncomfortable.

"I do not have the skills you have on a trail, but perhaps I can help."

"How's that?" Paolo snarled. "I need to know who this guy is in order to understand how he thinks. If I lose the track, it would be helpful to have some idea where he would go."

"He will cross the river into Costa Rica."

WITHOUT REDEMPTION   111

"How do *you* know?" Paolo asked, the darkness only partially masking his contempt.

The man never answered, his face tight with sudden anger.

Paolo tensed, sensing danger. A Chapo bodyguard was no ordinary killer, and if he was going to spend the rest of the night at Paolo's back, it would be wise to not have him angry. He choked off the frustration that threatened to erupt.

The bodyguard squatted, laid his assault rifle across his knees and pointed at the faint track in front of them. "Paolo, you are obviously very good at this, but perhaps you should presume that the rest of us excel at something as well. I know who this man is, and where we will find him."

"Why didn't you tell me before?"

The bodyguard's voice dripped with his own disdain and anger. "You were too wrapped up in yourself to ask." There was little light to see the man's face, not that Paolo needed any. The condescending tone told him he'd made a bad mistake. This man might or might not be his equal, but the only way to find out meant that one of them would die. "So, where will he go?"

The man's big-boned hands caressed the barrel of the M16 that lay across his knees.

Paolo stiffened. His hand slid sideways until his fingers were within easy reach of the knife scabbard that hung concealed under his left arm.

The bodyguard held up a hand. "Stop. We are in this together. If you fail, Chapo will treat neither of us kindly."

112   *David Griffith*

Paolo shrugged. "You are right. But if we are to succeed, I need whatever answers you might have. Please, tell me what you know."

"I was on duty when Chapo negotiated with the American intelligence firm. The stranger with the broken arm works for a company called Stirling—"

"I don't care who he works for." Instant silence ensued, and Paolo again sensed danger. He should not have interrupted.

The bodyguard propped the butt of his rifle in the dirt, his left hand clasping the stock, his right dangerously close to the trigger. His words were now even more clipped, his anger apparent in every syllable. "This company does contract work for the U.S. government. When they feel they need to meddle in our affairs, Stirling calls in their Mexico expert—the Indian."

"The Indian?"

The man's chuckle came from deep in his throat, and Paolo felt at a huge disadvantage not to be able to read his face.

"Yes. His name is Lonnie Bowers."

"Where is he from?"

"Nobody knows. Though he has often posed as a Mexican, he isn't. Some say he is not even American, that he is actually a Canadian Cree or perhaps Chipewyan. Not that it matters. What *is* important is that he is dangerous."

"I have heard much of him. He's overrated. Besides, he can't be that good. He bungled this hit on Chapo."

The man shrugged. "He may not have been sent to kill Chapo."

"Then what is he doing here?"

WITHOUT REDEMPTION

Marco shrugged. "The boss negotiated an agreement—immunity from U.S. prosecution in exchange for a list of high-level names and Los Zetas safe houses. I presume he came to consummate the deal."

"So, you don't think this Indian betrayed us?" Paolo asked. The ensuing silence gave him time to mull over what the bodyguard had told him. He waited for an answer.

The light from the rising moon cast teasing shadows across the bodyguard's chiseled face. Suddenly, he stood and picked up his rifle and held it loosely in the crook of his arm. "No. I don't. He had no reason to sell us out. The information Chapo offered was too valuable. But somebody else knew about that meeting, either Los Zetas, or perhaps the Beltrán-Leyva cartel, both scum from the same sewer."

Paolo showed no expression, but inwardly he scoffed. What nonsense. This Stirling group had decided to play a bigger hand. This was the deal of the century. They would get a list of all the Los Zetas commanders, where they lived, their safe houses—everything. But immunity for Chapo? The Americans would never agree to that. They'd decided to kill him and be done with it, except their timing had been off. When the blast had taken out the wall, the last thing he'd heard was Chapo attempting to renegotiate some item. He tried to remember. Chapo had given the stranger an envelope. It no longer mattered what it had contained. When he spoke, he carefully measured each word, his previous anger well in check. "Whether this Indian is guilty is not our concern. When we catch him, Chapo can decide his fate."

The bodyguard shifted his rifle and shrugged. "Then let us be going. He will go to his woman and child who wait for

114 *David Griffith*

him at a small guest ranch on the Costa Rica side, close to the border. Of the exact location, I am not certain. To find him is your job. Perhaps it would be good if you did not fail." His voice carried no threat. It was matter-of-fact, toneless, and deadly.

Paolo nodded. This man would be at his back through the rest of the night. Had Chapo sent him to get rid of the new man if he failed? As Paolo peered into the dark face, the certainty hit him with sledge hammer clarity. There would be no second chance. He rose to his feet, nodded, and picked up the trail. The tracks were easy to follow. A recent rain had dampened the forest floor, enough that he had no trouble following it south toward the border.

As he sorted through the telltale signs by the light of the flashlight, he tried to work out a picture of this man they called the Indian. Who was he? So far, his quarry had shown little incentive or skill in covering his tracks, but then why should he? It was dark. He had until daylight before any serious pursuit, so his first reaction would be to cover ground quickly, to get as far away as possible. Initially, he wouldn't be concerned with leaving signs of his passing.

An hour later, the tracks led to a deeply worn trail with a hard-pan bottom. It was as if the man in front of them had suddenly grown wings. He could find no more trace or track. Paolo shrugged. It didn't matter. The stranger obviously angled toward the small ferry crossing the locals used. They could pick up his tracks on the Costa Rica side. He turned. "Call the boss. Tell him the man we follow has crossed the river and headed south, possibly on the road to Los Chiles."

WITHOUT REDEMPTION 115

The bodyguard pulled his cellphone out of one of the myriad pockets in his battle vest and punched a speed-dial button. He spoke before he brought the phone to his face. "This may be a long night. My name is Marco."

Paolo nodded. With this dangerous *sicario* at his back, a truce was the best option. "Thank you. I should have asked—"

Marco's staccato bark into the phone interrupted Paolo's apologetic reply, and as his voice increased in volume, Paolo nervously edged off the trail, uncomfortable with the added noise. The stranger's tracks were very fresh, not more than a half-hour old. It didn't seem wise for Marco to be giving away their position. Fortunately, the conversation ended quickly, and they carried on toward the San Juan River and the border.

Nobody seemed inclined to offer them passage to the south shore at three in the morning, so they managed that on their own. Paolo untied the ferryman's boat and pushed off. Though the Indian must have swum the crocodile infested river, Paolo had no intention of doing the same. The ferryman would have to figure out his own way to get to the Costa Rica side to retrieve his rickety boat.

The southbound gravel road led from the water. Paolo quickly picked up a track where the Indian had come ashore. The ground still showed the dampness from his dripping clothes, which might be the only sign they'd find. Certainly, the hardened road top would yield nothing. The question was whether he would stay on the road, and if he did, where was he headed? Would he lead them to the little rancho where he'd apparently left his wife and child? Paolo tried to

116 *David Griffith*

dredge up any information he'd ever gathered about northern Costa Rica. That didn't take long because he hadn't any, and Marco knew little more. It was like tracking a man blindfolded. All he could do was follow the gravel road, and see where it led them.

Paolo moved the flashlight over the shoulder. Most men, out of habit, will travel close to the right-hand shoulder of a road. Rarely will they walk in the middle, even if there is no traffic. This appeared to be a seldom used route. Nevertheless, Paolo moved his flashlight back and forth, determined to miss nothing. Occasional scuff marks indicated the passing of someone recently, but there were never any clearly identifiable tracks on the hard gravel surface.

An hour later, and three miles from the river that marked the border between the two countries, Paolo was rewarded. The road made a long sweeping turn to the west, and in the middle of the corner, the distinctive tracks of the Indian's Raràmuri footwear skidded down the steep slope and struck off through some pasture land. They followed, but now it was slower, the trail harder to find.

From the time they'd left the river, Marco had remained silent. Now, Paolo turned and studied his features. He'd more than proved himself, and though he'd volunteered little more information, he seemed a man who was smart and watchful.

"Do you have any knowledge of this country . . . where this guest ranch would be?"

Marco's jaw muscles worked under his smooth skin. He stared at the track and then off to the south. "No, I do not. But—I wonder if he came alone to pick up this piece of paper. Or are there others waiting at this *ranchito*?"

WITHOUT REDEMPTION

Paolo studied the man's face while he digested what Marco had said. Though he'd long ago mulled that possibility, Marco's question was astute, and he mentally kicked himself. It hadn't been professional to lord it over this man. Every one of the twelve had been handpicked. Each would have special skills in addition to the ability to kill. Momentarily, he wondered about the man he'd sent back. His face burned with embarrassment—and a beginning trepidation. He'd spurned one of Chapo's chosen. Fear drained the blood from his face. The boss might view that as an unforgivable trespass. There could only be one atonement. The Indian had to be dead by morning.

Chapter 15

The sun had painted God's colors in the sky when I stumbled across the north pasture of the little ranch where we'd expected to have a memorable holiday. Quietly, I slipped between the calf barn and the round corral where they started the green colts. The small cabin where we stayed loomed ahead.

The early morning sun caressed the weathered boards with the first rays of warmth. I took the steps two at a time to the second floor and knocked on the sliding door. No answer. Panic rose in my chest. I knocked harder. Suddenly, the curtain jerked back, and I glimpsed Clarissa's sleepy face. The breath whooshed out of my lungs. She waited for *me*, the husband who was either always gone, or in a jackpot of some sort. She unlatched the door and slid it open. The only answer I gave to the question of where I'd been was to grab her and pull her close. I kissed her hair and every place I could kiss on her face before I let her go. When I stepped back, I still held her hands. "Get Conor. We have to leave—now!"

There were things that Clarissa and I still had to work out in our marriage. We'd both arrived at the altar with plenty of baggage, but somehow, more by God's grace than good management, we'd been able to mix it all into a glue that had held. That hadn't been a painless process, but we'd worked through most of the serious issues. This was one of those times we

WITHOUT REDEMPTION 119

didn't have to have an argument. Her questioning look said she wanted more information, but in the meantime she just turned to the task and started throwing clothes into suitcases.

"No."

She whirled at the seriousness in my voice.

"It all went very wrong. There are bad people coming, and they could be very close. We have to get out of here." I held up my hand at her stricken expression. "Don't worry. Frederick will bail us out."

She still hunched over the open bag but now she stared at me with that "Lonnie, you have really done it this time," look. Immediately she started tucking Conor's clothes into the corner of her suitcase.

"No! Hon, you don't understand. There is no luggage. We have to run."

She froze. "On foot?"

I clenched my jaw and nodded. "Gather up all the food we've got. We'll put that into my pack. While you're doing that, I'll fill the water bottles." I looked at my watch, worried, wondering if they'd arrive soon. "We may only have a few minutes before we need to be in the jungle."

Her eyes riveted to mine. "What have you done to us? This is your idea of a holiday?!" Her voice rose, the accusation of betrayal a blot on my character, and I understood. It was one thing for us to be in danger, but now our child was involved. Conor—her baby, and for this mess, I was responsible—in every way.

"Think of this as an adventure." I tried to chuckle, but it trailed into a weak laugh. Nothing about this was a joke, and

120 *David Griffith*

I turned to the little kitchen sink to fill the water bottles. Out of the corner of my eye, I watched her process the horror. She may have had more of a premonition of what was ahead than I did. I've heard it said that sometimes women do. Regardless, she squared her shoulders and started tucking necessary items for Conor into her backpack. We had little more than power bars and snacks. They went into my pack, along with all the milk and baby food we had on hand. As I packed, the anger built. Clarissa was right. How could I have exposed her and Conor to this danger? It may have been unfair to blame Frederick, but this shouldn't have happened. I'd been gullible, and stupid. I shouldn't have agreed to this—and now my family would pay.

I glanced out the window. Down on the highway, three white Chevy Suburbans turned onto the dirt track leading up to the ranch. Panic constricted my throat. I watched them wind up the hillside toward the buildings, with no doubt who they were. One of Chapo's men had tracked me through the jungle and down that gravel road, all in the dark? If that had been the case, that man was very skillful—and dangerous.

We had no more time. After I'd swung the food pack onto my back, I scooped Conor out of his bed with my right arm and signaled to Clarissa. We slipped down the stairs and into the low overcast of that rainforest morning. No breeze rippled the grass as we trotted the hundred feet to the murky jungle.

Once inside the cover of the trees, my heart dropped down around my knees. I knew nothing of this terrain. The few days we'd spent in the country, I'd studied the plants and

WITHOUT REDEMPTION 121

grasses, the trees and wildlife. All were of great interest. Likely, I could blame that fascination on the Indian side of me, or perhaps it was just that I'd spent so much time in the outdoors. As a kid, I'd disappear for weeks at a time in the British Columbia mountains and forests. Then, the wild places were a gentle salve of healing for the anger I'd carried at the system that stuffed me in a new home at regular intervals. But here, I knew nothing of the jungle, nor had I any knowledge of the dangerous cats and poisonous snakes that roamed these verdant wetlands.

Within a hundred yards, I picked up a southbound trail worn deep with the cloven-hoofed tracks of wild pigs. Those were occasionally blotted by wider prints of what I thought might be tapirs. Our guide had pointed out one of those crazy looking animals on the edge of the jungle. Larger than the wild pigs, they were thankfully, much less dangerous. Nevertheless, my casted left hand brushed the .45 Beretta tucked into the small of my back. We needed to put distance between us and the men at the rancho, and the safest way to do that was through the jungle. Any direction would do, just so we got far enough away. Later, I would contact Frederick in order to formulate a plan to get out of the country.

I glanced at Clarissa and marveled at her toughness. Scarcely twenty minutes ago, she'd been fast asleep. Now, with little effort, she matched my pace without a word of complaint. I grinned at her, and though I could see the fear in her eyes, she smiled right back. There wasn't time, but I stopped and squeezed her with my one good arm. "I love you, and you are the most wonderful woman in the world." I wanted to tell her more; how sorry I was, and how much I admired her indomitable spirit, but it was time to move on. Those words would have to wait.

We double-timed on up the mountain, trying to get far enough ahead we'd be able to stop for a rest. Conor, now awake was not at all interested in our plan. It was breakfast time, and he had little patience for anyone who thought they might put that on hold.

I'd never done what we called a surgical removal, a sanitized term for identifying and killing the enemy, though all of us were trained for that. My job had always been intelligence, which meant I didn't kill people. If I had to do that, it meant my cover was blown and I'd failed miserably. We had other guys who took care of those details, and when the need arose, they did it well. Would this time be different? Would there be a commando team to call in when we needed them? What if we couldn't stay ahead of Chapo's killers? I fingered the gun at my belt.

Clarissa and I had discussed the subject more than once. She didn't think it was right to kill another man. For any reason! In the heat of an argument, though I wouldn't admit it, I had great respect for what she thought. Consequently, I'd spent considerable time mulling over her logic. But in my line of employment, her pacifist mentality didn't seem to work, today more than ever. Now, more than ever, it didn't matter what either of us *thought*, and desperation clapped a titanium band of fear around my chest. I glanced at Clarissa, then pulled Conor closer to my chest. I loved these two people more than anyone in the world. To protect them, I would do whatever was necessary.

Chapter 16

A streaky red band smudged the eastern horizon with the first light of day when Paolo followed the tracks off the road and into a meadow. Here, in the verdant dew-tipped grass he could follow the tracks at a shuffling trot. The Indian had made little effort to hide his trail. He traveled as if tired, or was it just that he didn't expect pursuit? A slow smile creased Paolo's face. He suspected the latter. This man wouldn't suspect anyone could track him through the jungle and across a river in the dead of night. A slow smile split his lips. Chapo would forgive him for any trespasses he might have committed if he found and killed this double-crossing traitor. Paolo surveyed the area ahead, then broke into a trot. He needed to bring this to an end.

By the time the sun peeked over the highest of the eastern ridges, Paolo and Marco had traversed another of the high, cloud-topped ridges. The trail led steadily south and east, and an hour later they dropped into a wide valley, the steaming jungle now interspersed with fields kept lush and green by the daily rains. Twice, they stopped while Paolo quizzed Marco further on their quarry's destination.

The first heat of the day chased the last wisps of fog off the meadows when they slogged through one more of the dozens of trickling streams and climbed to a gravel road. The scuff marks were fresh where the Indian had crawled through

124 *David Griffith*

the barbed wire and scrambled up the sandy shoulder. To the south, brilliant emerald grass covered the rolling hillsides. Grazing dun-colored cattle spread away in a paddock to the south. Paolo constantly monitored the track, but apparently the Indian had no intention of leaving the road. His faint track ran straight down the shoulder, and a mile later a ranch headquarters straddled both sides of the pot-holed gravel track. Three white SUVs were parked in front of a single level lime-green building. Paolo didn't have to look twice to know they were same ones that had delivered Paolo and the other men to the meeting site last night. The boss had known where the Indian would run to. Paolo's long night tracking the man had only been insurance. Probably, Chapo's swift justice had already been administered.

When Marco and Paolo trudged through the door, Chapo glanced at them without comment. The spacious room, obviously a dining area held wooden restaurant tables. A stocky, middle-aged farmer in black rubber boots was backed up against the far wall, his face bloody and bruised. One of the twelve barked out a question, then jammed a gun butt into the farmer's expanding belly. The response was immediate.

"Yes, he was here. He stayed—with a woman and a baby." The farmer pointed out the offending cabin he'd been foolish enough to rent. Chapo dispatched Mavelio and two men to apprehend the occupants. He then turned in the chair and eyed Paolo curiously. "So . . . where is he?"

Paolo anxiously scanned the room. "He is here. His trail . . ." He spread his hands. "The tracks led to here."

WITHOUT REDEMPTION

Chapo stared intently. Paolo searched his face, trying desperately to read his thoughts, without success.

"Why did you send Jorge back?" Chapo's voice, soft as a baby's blanket, cut through the silence, the threat unmistakable.

"*El jefe*, I made a mistake, a simple misunderstanding. It will not happen again."

Chapo's gaze flitted around the room, his eyes momentarily resting on each man before they again leveled on his newest recruit. "I do not tolerate fools. When I say two men should go with you . . . I mean what I say." He rose and stepped forward, then placed a hand on Paolo's shoulder. The touch was supposed to be friendly, perhaps even fatherly, but Paolo flinched like a rattlesnake had dropped onto his body. Chapo smiled with his lips, but his nearly opaque eyes resembled the unblinking orbs of a hunting predator. "You are now one of my brothers. Never make that mistake again."

Paolo's head bobbed up and down. He'd been spared, but it was a lesson to be remembered. The dangers that threatened a common *sicario* were nothing compared to this. Another trespass of any kind would be fatal.

Suddenly, the outside door cannoned back against the wall. Mavelio strode into the room. "He is gone."

Chapo leaned forward, his voice expressionless. "Where?"

The man's jaw worked up and down as he contemplated the answer he would give. "Apparently, he left on foot—only minutes before we arrived."

126 *David Griffith*

Chapo stood, puzzlement threatening to wipe away the deadpan stare. "And the woman and child? Surely, they are not gone as well?"

The unfortunate Mavelio shuffled in front of him, crossed his arms, then clasped his hands behind his back. "They are not here."

Anger suffused Chapo's face. "What do you mean? Where did they go?"

Mavelio took a deep breath, like he didn't want to answer. "It appears they went into the jungle, *el jefe.*"

"Why would he do that?" Chapo's look of incredulity returned, and he chuckled. "He did that with a woman and a baby? Is he crazy?" He waved a hand in the air. "No, I think he is not that, but when he experiences the danger of the jungle he will be very afraid. He has made a stupid choice. This will be over by noon." He pointed to the dwelling their quarry had so recently vacated. "Go through that cabin. Something in there will tell us what this loco American intends to do." Suddenly, he whirled, his finger stabbing at the air. "Paolo, find their trail. Let's end this."

Paolo walked outside and stared up at the lush green mountain to the south. Soft, white clouds covered the peak, but angry, dark cumulous clouds had commenced their march from the east. The afternoon rains would be hard and heavy. Chapo was right. This man could never escape on foot with a woman and a baby. What a fool.

Paolo almost felt sorry for the man he'd tracked through the night. Now he would catch him easily. Then, he and his woman would die a painful, slow death. And the baby? He shrugged. It wasn't his fault the man brought his family in-

WITHOUT REDEMPTION 127

to this kind of trouble. He walked to the edge of the jungle nearest the cabin and studied the soft chocolate soil for fresh tracks, but his eyes kept returning to the volcano mountain to the south. This man would try to hide his trail which would be nearly impossible with a woman and a baby. Paolo studied the terrain. Where would the man go? He faced an environment for which he could hardly be prepared. The Indian seemed to know and be comfortable in the wild, but what could he know of jungles filled with every kind of poisonous snake and spider known to man. However, contrary to what Chapo thought, this man might not be afraid, which meant he might not react like other men.

When Paolo walked back into the room, Chapo paced like a caged hyena, anger etched over the day-old stubble on his cheeks. His voice, when he spoke, carried only anger and frustration. Paolo understood. Chapo wanted quick and accurate answers.

"So, Paolo, you did well tracking the man here. I am impressed. Where do *you* think he is heading . . . with a woman and a baby?"

Paolo's reply needed no thought. "There." He pointed toward the volcano mountain.

Chapo stopped pacing, and his lip curled. "This was the Beltrán-Leyva cartel, you know. It was that backbiting, vindictive scum, Arturo. He's the only one of them with the brains and resources to pull off the attack back there at the villa."

Paolo nodded, unsure whether an answer was required, or safe.

"I find it too much of a coincidence that they would attack at the crucial moment when the list of Los Zetas names appears. What is your opinion? Do you think the Indian is working for them?"

Paolo hesitated, considering his response. Was this a trap, a setup . . . payback for his earlier condescending attitude? "Perhaps there are others who would be better equipped to answer that question, but be assured, I *will* find him. Then he can be made to address the question himself—before the appropriate punishment."

Chapo's lips split in silent mirth. "Ah Paolo, well spoken. You are a cagey one." He glanced at his watch. "We are well armed, and shortly, we will be adequately provisioned from this man's kitchen." He waved dismissively at the bleeding *ranchero* in the corner of the room.

"How much head start do you think he has?"

Again, Paolo stared up at the forbidding mountain to the south. On a bald knob at the top of the ridge a flash of color stood out against the surrounding green of the jungle. As quickly as it appeared, it was gone, but what he'd seen was enough for him to know. The Indian had only a few minutes start.

He spoke confidently. "He has no more than a half hour start. We can easily catch him before noon."

Chapter 17

Before we trudged over the spiny ridge above us, I tried to count the men who trooped through our recently vacated *cabina*, while the others milled around in the yard. At least twelve, all with AK-47's or AR-15's. Not good odds, but better than they had been before the explosion. That must have killed three or more which hardly helped. The rest were elite soldiers. The only thing I could hope was to leave no trail for them to follow.

I pulled my phone out of the bottom of my pack, turned it on, and dialed Frederick's direct red-code line. Even from this distance I could see the man in dark camouflage who stood to one side, angrily pacing back and forth. Occasionally, he would look up at the mountain where I'd tucked in behind a big banana leaf. At the moment, most of my attention was focused on my GPS as I punched in the coordinates for our emergency pickup. However, I still kept an eye on the activity below.

"Don't let me down." My anger boiled to the surface, and I didn't give a rip whether that hurt Frederick's or anybody else's feelings. My family was in danger. I turned the phone off and took out the battery. It wasn't likely anybody down there had the equipment or available technology to monitor our position, but I would not take chances. The dark camouflage guy worried me the most. Through the night, I'd sensed somebody on my trail. Was he the one who had been skillful enough to follow me? I watched as he paced between the round corral and the cabin. Occasionally, he stared up at the spot where I'd taken cover. An uncomfortable premonition crept through me. He knew exactly where we were.

I would have given much to hear what those men were discussing down in that yard. Surely, they wouldn't try to follow us through the jungle? Probably they would just deploy to different points where they could cut off our escape if we tried to reach a road or airport? Once more, I studied the man in the jungle camo gear. He pointed up the mountain. It was as if his finger hit me in the chest. If they followed his advice, we were in trouble.

Like a Redbone coonhound, the tracker guy started casting around the house for signs. Even in the soft, pungent dirt where I watched, I could see he was exceptional. Within minutes he'd found our track. My heart sank toward my boots. How could I get my family away? This wet rain forest was foreign to me, and I had little knowledge of the plants or animals. I sent Clarissa down a faint eastbound trail with Conor while I hunkered down to watch the events below.

It didn't take long for me to be wrong in my assessment of what they would do. Chapo's men lined out behind the dark camouflaged tracker who followed our trail up the mountain like it was one long string of orange fluorescent tape. I'd seen enough. I sprinted ahead to where Clarissa hiked through the trees. When she saw me coming, she sunk down against an Encino oak and started to nurse Conor. I knelt beside her while I watched our back-trail. "We're in trouble. There are at least twelve men following us."

WITHOUT REDEMPTION 131

She cocked an eyebrow at me, then grimaced, trying not to disturb Conor's second breakfast. "Really? How profound?" Her wry grin took the sting out of her words. She reached over and touched my leg. "At least now we're together. I was worried when you never showed up last night."

"Hon, you have no idea how sorry I am, or how angry I am at Frederick, even though this isn't *all* his fault." I took a deep breath while I tried to come up with something to lessen her fear. Nothing came to mind, or at least nothing with a shred of truth in it. "This would be no big deal if you and Conor weren't here," I finished lamely.

She didn't answer that asinine comment which gave me a chance to explain. "There's a man behind us. He trailed me last night from across the river in Nicaragua."

"I thought you said there was a dozen of them."

"There is, but one of them is way more dangerous than the others."

"Well, maybe we can lose him. Let me finish feeding Conor. You'll figure something out." She looked up, her smile trusting and confident. "Hey, I was tired of all the ants in that cabin anyhow. We should have stayed at the beach." She reached for my hand. "Lon, I have faith in God—and you. Somehow, you'll get us out of here."

My throat got scratchy, and I had to swallow a few times, completely blown away by this crazy woman's faith in me. Or maybe her faith in God made up for my lack of abilities. There wasn't time to pursue that subject, so I walked back to listen for any sound of nearing pursuit. They were closing way faster than I would have thought was possible, led by that man in the dark camouflage. His tracking abilities were exceptional, and it didn't take much time watching him to know we were in big trouble. I trotted back to where Clarissa sat. "I need to get rid of their tracker. He's good—very good."

"How do you propose to do that?"

This was not the time to sugarcoat the truth. "Kill him."

She suddenly went still, then raised an eyebrow and shifted Conor to the other breast before she answered. "And you're okay with snuffing out a man's life, simply because he's following us?"

Angrily, I stared at her. "They are on our trail for one reason—to kill us, so if one or two of them have to die—I really don't care."

"Yes, you do," she said softly. "I know you."

She'd thrown the whole question of my employment, philosophy, and I might add, my religiosity squarely back in my lap. I'd prepared, trained for years, to be the best for a day such as this. But how did that equate with coolly pointing a rifle at another human being and squeezing the trigger to blow his brains out the back side of his skull. I glanced down at the little guy cradled in Clarissa's arms, then met the eyes of the woman I loved more than life. It didn't seem a hard choice. Our eyes met. "If I don't kill him—and they catch us?"

She didn't answer, and I dogtrotted back along the trail to again look and listen. They were too close. There wasn't any more time. Conor would just have to wait. After we got to our pickup point, he could eat to his heart's content.

Frederick never left anything to chance, and he always took great care to provide for unforeseen circumstances. Our emergency evacuation spot was eighteen miles away from the

WITHOUT REDEMPTION

rancho, at the base of a mountain and very close to a gravel road. Frederick's theory had been that in the unlikely event of trouble, we could drive there in a hurry, ditch the rental car, and an emergency rescue helicopter would sneak in and whisk us out of harm's way. Back in Texas, it had all sounded so easy—and unnecessary. If we could have jumped in the car and left, everything would have been fine. Through the jungle—well, that was a different story. Though we'd occasionally hiked that distance, eighteen miles with a baby was a marathon.

Even at that high elevation, we slogged through black muck and swamp for part of the day, most of the time with Clarissa and Conor in front of me while I slipped back to watch our back-trail. Even though we were both in superb condition, by early afternoon, Chapo's men had gained on us. I had to change tactics. The swampy, rain-forest terrain fortunately slowed them as well. Occasionally I'd taken the opportunity to lay a false trail, but it hadn't been enough.

Twilight near the equator is completely different than what we experience in the north, so when nightfall crept downward from the top of the mountain, it was only minutes before we were left inside a pitch-black void. We'd crossed a small creek for the fifth time, then slogged part way up a hill until we found an open spot on a little bluff. We had a sorry bit of shelter and very little water, but there didn't seem to be anything better ahead. The one blanket we had wasn't enough for the three of us, so most of the night I dozed with my back to a Gamba tree while I listened and watched for trouble. I hoped Chapo and his men were at least as exhausted as I was, and that they'd vote for a good night's sleep.

134 *David Griffith*

Wet and cold, I woke at dawn to a misty drizzle. I slipped away to scout our back-trail. I'd not gone a half-mile when I heard voices and smelled the smoke of their morning fire. A great fear clamped down on my chest. But no, Frederick wouldn't let us down—as long as I did my part. All I had to do was get Clarissa and Conor to that little clearing on the side of a jungle-clogged mountain far to the east. I sprinted back to Clarissa. "Let's go."

"But Conor's not done nursing yet."

"Doesn't matter. We have to get out of here. They're too close." She struggled to her feet and handed Conor to me. Of course he fussed at having his breakfast so rudely interrupted. I shouldered the food pack and coaxed a pacifier in his mouth. She grabbed the other one and we slithered up the wet trail, trying desperately to put distance between us and those who followed. The drizzling rain immediately soaked through my windbreaker. Clarissa's wasn't any drier. Our footwear didn't stand the water any better than our clothes. Within twenty minutes, we both squished up the trail. It wasn't like I could pick a better trail. In the jungle, everything dripped with water, and with Chapo's cartel goons so close, we had only one option—to run as fast and as far as we could.

Conor jostled in my arms with every slogging step. I remembered stories floating around about Indian babies not crying much. I don't reckon that's true. If it is, our little guy cottoned to his white side. He could howl with the best, but this time something in his tiny body recognized the danger, because he only whimpered a bit, then fell asleep on my shoulder. A father's pride tingled through my arms. Whatev-

WITHOUT REDEMPTION 135

er Conor felt, I wanted more than anything in the world to protect him, to shield him and his mom from the danger I'd brought to their lives.

The faint trail we followed climbed steadily along the side of the mountain, then leveled out and ran along a rough ridge, generally heading in an easterly direction. We shared it with no other human or animal, for which I was thankful. Enough trouble lay behind us; we needed no extra in our path.

Frequently, I glanced back at our trail and shook my head. To find us would be so easy. Unless we did something radically different, those behind us would be able to follow our muddy trail at a high trot. I scanned the terrain ahead. Every bit of it was new, and I wished mightily that I had some idea of what we would face. What if we dropped down the mountain and left the trail altogether? At a lower elevation, the ground might be dryer which would mean we'd leave less sign. That might at least delay the tracker. As I left the trail, I tried to find the sun. If I could see that, I wouldn't worry about getting lost. But the thick fog and low cloud obscured any sign of it. Clarissa was starting to drag, which meant I had to slow that tracker or we'd not last another five miles.

A quarter mile after we'd left the trail, the muddy track I followed abruptly swung northeast and down a long hill to a stretch of soggy ground bordering a creek. I stepped into the water, waded to the middle and pointed upstream. "Hon, take off your shoes." She slipped off her tennis shoes, albeit with a questioning look. "Give them to me." She did and I took my boots off and sort of jammed her shoes over my toes. I handed my boots to her. "Here, put these on and follow the

136   *David Griffith*

creek. Stay in the deepest water, if you can. Just go slow and easy so you don't fall. I'll catch up to you."

She nodded, then slipped my boots over her feet. I handed her Conor and she slogged up the narrow stream, but not before I glimpsed the building fear in her eyes.

I crossed the creek and stepped onto the bank on the other side, deliberately sliding through the mud so there wouldn't be a clear print. The tracker would have long ago sorted out which tracks were Clarissa's and which were mine.

Fifty feet north of the stream, I struck off into the jungle, continuing to step on any dry material or rock I could find. After another hundred feet, I slipped the moccasins on that I carried in my pack, and walked backwards to the stream. Hopefully, it would look like we had both walked out of the water. Once again I purposely slid through the mud, doing what I could to avoid making a clear track. With any luck, it would buy us twenty minutes—no more. That tracker would not be fooled longer than that. Within minutes, he would sort out the trail and know we hadn't left the creek. Then the only question for him would be whether we'd gone up or downstream. Even if we were careful, in this bubbling stream he would soon find a disturbed section of sand or a misplaced rock which would tell him the direction we'd taken.

Back at the creek, I splashed upstream through the fastest water to where Clarissa picked her way along the rocky bottom. "Here, give me Conor."

She handed him to me while she put her own shoes on. "How far do we have to go?"

WITHOUT REDEMPTION

"About thirteen miles. The problem is that this stream keeps veering north, which means it empties into the San Juan River. We need to leave it and head further east."

"Can we stay ahead of them long enough to get there?"

I didn't have an answer, but the danger was too great not to tell her the truth. "I'm not sure. I bought some time back there, but in another hour or so, they'll be right behind us again."

"How long will it take to reach the site?"

I answered with way more confidence than I felt. "We may make it tonight if we can find a good trail."

Though she wanted to believe me, we'd lived together long enough I recognized the doubt clouding her eyes. Nevertheless, she finished tying her wet shoes and stood, ready to carry on. I continued up the stream until the jungle opened up a bit, stepped out of the water onto a black volcanic boulder, then reached back and helped her out.

"Hon, place your feet directly where I step if you can." Carefully, I skipped from rock to boulder until we were able to jump into a dense clump of *braquieria* grass. From there, I jumped as far as I could, jarring Conor enough that he woke and started to cry. Clarissa did the same, and we followed the contour of a high ridge that angled away from the creek.

I hitched Conor higher on my shoulder, wishing I had two good arms.

"Here, give him to me for a few minutes." Clarissa dug a long scarf out of her backpack and made a sling. I eyed her skeptically, wondering what she had in mind. She cinched it tight enough that Conor could ride inside and nurse as she walked. I reckoned that was the most innovative thing either of us could have done, and I smiled at her with pride. When the going got tough, my wife was on the front line.

A shout from back at the creek drove us forward. A wave of despair surged through my chest. That tracker had already picked up our trail. Now, they would quickly close the distance.

For the rest of the day, I used every skill I'd learned. Time and again, Chapo's men would be almost within shouting distance, and I'd think up some dodge to slow them. But it was a long, exhausting slog, and when darkness covered the land, we crawled between the roots of a great Gamba tree, still too far from our destination. The whole day had been hard going. Too many times we'd had to double back on our trail and I didn't figure we were any closer than seven or eight miles from the landing zone. I dozed off and on, but most of the night I didn't dare sleep. Though I hoped the tracker wouldn't be able to unravel the last maze I'd left, I was by no means sure. As long as he followed, we were in great danger.

For a couple hours after the sun came up, Clarissa and I made good time. I heard no sound of pursuit, but that didn't mean they weren't there. I edged toward the higher ground, hoping the rain-drenched soil would be firmer and leave less sign of our passing, but my efforts were largely useless. Every square inch of that high jungle dripped with water. We left few clues to our passing, but to Chapo's tracker, trailing us would be child's play. I glanced nervously over my shoulder, convinced he was close.

"Give me Conor." I held out my good arm.

WITHOUT REDEMPTION

Clarissa looped the sling around my neck and slipped him inside. He was awake and fussy in the heat, and I hoped once we slogged forward, he would quiet down.

Ahead, a long bare ridge led downward toward the bottom lands. The grassy slope would probably increase the visibility of our tracks, but that appeared to be the quickest way off the mountain. If we could drop down a thousand feet, the rain might stop which meant the ground would harden enough we'd quit leaving these great slogging footprints in the mud.

We followed the ridge east to the bottom, then doubled back west along a dry hump. The last jungle patch of bamboo below seemed a reasonable subterfuge. I stepped onto a fallen tree, and though the slippery bark nearly upset us both, we managed to walk the hundred feet of its length before again taking an easterly heading. A simple ploy like that would never fool the tracker, but it would take him a few extra minutes to again pick up our trail. Twice, I heard voices far behind us. Once, a man laughed, a purposeful, taunting sound. I glanced at Clarissa. She tried not to show her fear, but the tightness around her mouth told me their terror tactics had worked. A building anger began to tighten my resolve.

An hour later, we broke into a small valley, and the drizzling rain stopped like somebody had turned off a tap. In front of us, the ground was dry, reflecting another completely different climatic zone in this country of diverse landscapes. My useless left arm hung at my side, the cast hot and itchy in the damp heat. Worried, I glanced at my wife. Her red face, streaked with mud, was slick with the perspiration that ran down her cheeks. Panic drove me forward. A gut-level instinct told me this wasn't going to work. I had only one chance left. We could stay ahead of the AK-47's and death—only if I killed the tracker.

Chapter 18

By nightfall of the second day, the men at Paolo's back were hot, sweaty, and angry. Unbelievably, they still had nothing to show for their work but more muddy tracks. As hard as Paolo had pushed, the Indian had stayed ahead of him. He seemed to sense when Chapo's men were close. In the last twelve hours, he'd become much harder to follow. Not big things, but every little dodge took precious seconds to unravel.

Paolo tried to picture the Indian's destination. If Marco had been right, the American company he worked for would try to evacuate him. Any of the mountain meadows surrounding them would work, or it might be an abandoned landing strip many miles away. He glared at the line of men strung out behind him. He needed somebody who knew the country, but none of them would be of any help. He took two swallows of water from the canteen at his hip, then did a slow circle to try to pick up the track that had again disappeared.

After dropping down from the volcano mountain, the Indian had led them into a low range of hills to the south. Now, though he followed no trail, the man showed uncommon bush sense. Often, he found the fastest way through the dense underbrush, all while leaving only minimal signs to follow. Sometimes, he would send the woman one way, then

142   *David Griffith*

head off through the jungle. After a wide circle, his tracks would again meld with hers. Each time he did it, Paolo had to unravel both sets to make sure they rejoined. Meanwhile, his quarry gained more ground. And there wasn't one of the men behind him, including Marco, who could track one of his mother's goats down a dirt road. He could send none of them to follow one of the trails when the Indian and his woman separated. All in all, it had been a frustrating day.

Paolo, far ahead of the pack of weary men sat on a broken stump and watched the supposed elite warriors straggle up the trail. The Indian had been on the run for over forty-eight hours. Often today, he must have carried the baby as well as whatever other supplies they had managed to throw together. He should be exhausted. However, he hadn't slowed his pace.

Dusk had turned to darkness when Chapo and the men gathered around Paolo. All wanted only to end this crazy slog through a foreign jungle. After considerable sniping at Paolo's lack of results, Chapo ordered them to make camp by a small creek. The temperature plummeted to unseasonal levels, and the never-ceasing drizzling rain drove the cold into their bones. Every one of them grumbled. Though battle-hardened veterans, and at home with any type of mortal combat, sleeping on wet, snake-infested ground remained outside of their job description.

At dawn, Paolo again picked up the track. The men behind him struggled through the mud, surly and hungry. Two hours later, the trail angled down toward the flat country, out of the jungle clad hills. In a small clearing, he caught a glimpse of the lush pastures at the bottom. For whatever reason, the Indian had taken that route. For the first time since the hunt had began, Paolo laughed. The man he followed had made a mistake. They would easily catch him in that vast expanse of grass. Before nightfall—he would be a dead man.

Minutes later, they broke into the open grasslands. Far ahead, Paolo saw the two figures he'd followed through the jungle, running. Immediately, Chapo ordered Marco to bring one of them down. He commenced firing, but it was a six-hundred-yard shot, and though they were all superior marksmen, the distance was too great for any accuracy with an AK-47. Then Paolo saw where the Indian was headed. An immense sugarcane field lay at the bottom of the valley. He swore under his breath. Once he reached that, they would never find him. "But," he snickered, "the cane can be a very dangerous place. To find their bodies would be good enough."

Chapter 19

I turned and squeezed Clarissa's hand. She'd not complained, though she was near exhaustion. What I'd decided to do carried a huge risk. A half mile away, a vast acreage of green waved in the hot wind coming off the nearby ocean. Sugarcane, fourteen feet tall with stalks that grew straight and close like fur on a raccoon. Nobody would find us in the cane—except maybe the critters. I shivered. Anybody who harvested can burned the underbrush before harvest. Coral snakes, the deadly bushmaster, and the aggressive and venomous fer-de-lance thrived in the mass of leaves and brush at the base of the cane stalks. I glanced over my shoulder, hoping we had enough time to reach the field ahead. There, at least the odds would be a little better. I gritted my teeth, wondering if I'd made a poor choice. It was too late for second guessing, so I grabbed Clarissa's hand and ran in a desperate race against death for that far away patch of green.

Halfway across the open field, the first shot signaled the men behind us had reached the edge of the jungle. I clawed at the .45 in my belt, then shoved it back. A pistol would be of no value at the distance they were shooting. The only bonus was that neither the AK-47 nor the AR-15 is real accurate over a quarter mile, though that was scant comfort. Conor, getting the jostling of his life bellowed like a gut-shot grizzly, but I never slowed down. Eighty yards from safety, I glanced

WITHOUT REDEMPTION

over my shoulder. Three of them were running hard, rapidly closing the distance between us. One of the men must have stopped to fire. Bullets skidded into the ground to our right, which provided plenty of reason not to stop and pick any flowers. Clarissa and I were side by side, her hand in mine. Once, I glanced at her face, hollowed by fatigue. Under the bone-weary exhaustion, anger pulled her lips back in a way I'd not seen before.

When we burst through the outer edge of cane, I let go of Clarissa's hand.

"Step directly in my tracks. Watch carefully. This won't be fun, but it might give us the time we need to escape." With that, we plunged deeper into the twilight forest of stalks. Once out of sight, I beat my way to the left, jostling the tall stems as little as possible. I had no illusions. We were not safe, but it would take much longer for the tracker to follow us here, and it was doubtful he would attempt to do that. If they were smart, they'd stake the perimeter and wait until we came out, rather than facing the poisonous snakes, never mind the wasps, giant spiders, and other undesirables that inhabited the somber labyrinth in front of us. All I could hope for was that we could quietly slip to the other side and escape after dark.

Minutes later, I smelled the first acrid whiff of smoke. My throat constricted with fear. I'd thought the cane was too green to burn this early in the year, and probably it was. However, the underbrush would burn quite nicely. I glanced back at Clarissa, licked my dirty finger and stuck it as high over my head as I could. The wind direction was hard to as-certain, but it seemed to be coming off the ocean to the east.

David Griffith

Immediately I struck off to the right, beating the ground with a broken stalk to try and drive the snakes away.

Before long, the smoke started to burn our eyes. I tried to move faster. Suddenly, at the probing of my stick, a fer-de-lance reared its ugly head. I beat at it with the stick and backed away, trying to kill it with the piece of cane. With lightning speed, it raced toward me. Clarissa was directly behind me. I had nowhere to escape. At the last moment, I raised my foot. It struck at my shoe, burying its curved fangs as I ground the writhing creature into the dirt.

Clarissa looked on in horror. "Are you alright?"

I took my hat off and wiped the sweat off my brow. "His fangs never reached my foot."

"What kind of snake was it?"

"A fer-de-lance. They often live in the cane. I know nothing about them, other than if they bite you . . . you die."

Clarissa shuddered, and for the hundredth time I wondered how an exotic holiday in what was supposed to be the safest country in Central America could have gone so wrong. I grabbed Charissa's hand and stumbled away from the flames. Now we would have to run from the burning cane, and probably straight into their guns. We couldn't escape, but I vowed that some of those men who waited for us to come gasping and coughing out of the cauldron of smoke would die before we did. I scanned what was visible ahead. By now, Chapo's men would be positioned on every side of the field, except on the southern boundary where they'd first fired the dry leaves. They'd know we couldn't run back that way, and they were right. The heavy undergrowth behind us burned fast and hot, the smoke from the green cane al-

WITHOUT REDEMPTION 147

ready suffocating, impossible to get through. We bent low to the ground and crashed through the nearly solid wall of stalks, away from the thickening cloud. How far to the edge of the field? From the mountain, the crop had looked to cover two or three hundred acres. Were we nearing the northern perimeter? I didn't know , and in the yellow, smoky light, there was no way to tell.

Suddenly, we broke into a long corridor, and what I both hoped for and feared lay before us. Irrigation ditches are common in the cane fields, and we'd just stumbled onto one. I didn't want to get down in the muddy water of that ditch. Conor would have plenty to say about that plan, but the smoke was too thick. We could run no longer. On the other side, guns waited.

The ditch wasn't at all appealing, but it would be a short reprieve. I scanned the water for snakes. The smoke would be pushing every crawling critter in the cane north, away from the flames. It didn't matter. We had no other choice, and I slid into the ditch. Clarissa crouched down beside me and gently lowered Conor's little body into the warm, gooey sludge. The water wasn't cold. He didn't squawk. Maybe he thought it was bath time. I reached into the bag for a diaper, and ripped it in pieces. We soaked them and held them over our faces while we hoped and prayed the snakes would detour around us. It took every ounce of willpower I had not to grab Clarissa's hand and run from the advancing fire.

The flames were now only a few yards from where we lay, the smoke thick enough we couldn't see more than a few feet in any direction. Our eyes streamed, and Clarissa held Conor down until only his face was above the muddy water.

148   *David Griffith*

He started to cry, because of course his eyes hurt. I watched my wife try to make the pain go away, knowing she couldn't any more than I could, and a great anger washed over me, because of what Chapo and his tracker had done to my wife and little boy. Every sinew in my body craved an opportunity to strike at these evil men in any way possible.

The heat became more intense, though as the flames closed in on the water-filled ditch, the smoke seemed to rise farther away from the scorched earth. We huddled together, knowing this might be the end of our lives. Several times we ducked under the sludge-filled water, and we took turns bathing Conor's face and head. I don't know how long we lay in that ditch, but eventually the heat dissipated. The worst was apparently over. Drained of any energy, I crawled out and peered at the smoldering, black ground to the west. Tall stalks of cane, free of underbrush, stood between us and the brilliant late afternoon sun which only drove the temperature higher as it broke through the drifting smoke.

Another ten minutes went by before I hitched Conor into the sling and we left the ditch, squishing through the blackened leaves in our soggy footwear. Before we'd gone a hundred yards we'd both been burned on our arms and shoulders by the still hot cane, but waiting longer wasn't an option, so we forged ahead. The shortest distance to the jungle and cover had been on the west side of the field. Chapo would hopefully presume we would try to stay in the heavy smoke that drifted to the north, and would have the majority of his men positioned there. Escape was too much to ask—of God or anyone else—but we needed some big breaks if we were to survive another run over open terrain. This time we

WITHOUT REDEMPTION 149

wouldn't have a head start, so to lose the tracker, we had to regain the jungle without being spotted.

With no leaves on the stalks, I saw the end of the cane field thirty feet before we reached it. I signaled for Clarissa to wait, handed her Conor, and slipped out to the edge. For five minutes I stood motionless, melding with the blackened foliage around me. A half-mile to the west, high hills separated us from the ocean. I'd hoped for more jungle. It wasn't, but if we were to survive, that's where we had to go. I clenched my jaw and jacked a shell into the chamber of the handgun. It wasn't much against an assault rifle—but it would have to do.

Chapter 20

I ghosted back to where I'd left Clarissa, picked up Conor, and led the way out to the edge of the cane. A brisk wind still pushed the billowing smoke to the north. Quickly, I surveyed the coverless terrain in front of us. It was like an act of God. Not one of Chapo's goons were in sight. I grabbed Clarissa's hand and jogged west toward the scattered jungle and hills. Every few steps I glanced over my shoulder. If we could reach the tree line without them spotting us, we had a sporting chance of making it to the landing pad. With any luck, it would take the tracker at least an hour to discover we were gone. To gather all the crew together and pick up our trail would take more time which would give us the head start we needed.

Fifty feet before the first tree, little Conor started to wail. He was wet, cold, and hungry, and besides, he had a dirty diaper and he was letting the world know that something had better happen soon to fix that long list of woes. I didn't blame him, but his crying must have carried a fair distance, because as we threaded our way into the trees, a man appeared from the northern edge of the cane. He looked like the tracker, but I couldn't be sure. Had he seen us? Maybe not, but I doubted if that mattered. He'd heard Conor. Whatever advantage I'd hoped for had been lost.

WITHOUT REDEMPTION 151

We quartered to the top of the hill and struck out northeast along the ridge. With every step, my mind darted through options. In a small clearing, I got a good view back to the cane field. My worst fear was realized. At the bottom of the hill, a shout drifted up to us. That could mean only one thing. They'd rapidly mustered the troops. We'd gained way less lead than I'd hoped for. We moved higher up the slope, and in another open clearing, I had a small window back toward the bottom. What I'd dreaded was now confirmed. The tracker followed our trail like a rabid bloodhound. I could no longer put off a decision.

The trail and surrounding area we now traveled over was nearly devoid of underbrush. For a short time, that gave us an easier way forward. At a sharp left-hand turn at the base of a ridge, Clarissa changed and fed Conor while I climbed farther up to gauge the proximity of our pursuers. After Conor had finished lunch, I slipped down and joined her.

"Stay on this ridge." I handed her the GPS with the rescue zone coordinates. "I'll catch up in thirty minutes."

"What are you going to do?" She looked at me, the fear of the last hours strong in her voice.

"I have to stop the tracker." I'd never been able to hide anything from her, and though I didn't say it, she knew what I meant.

"You will kill him?"

Grimly, I nodded.

Her eyes dropped to Conor. He hadn't quieted much, and his breathing was ragged. "Lon, are you sure that's the right thing to do?"

"It is if we want to live," I snapped.

152   *David Griffith*

She laid her head wearily against my shoulder. I hugged her with my good arm, sad that we had differences when neither of us might see the dawn.

When I stepped back, she turned her face to the trail ahead, but not before I saw a new hopeless exhaustion.

"We're in a world completely foreign to me, but I don't think I could justify killing a man—for any reason." A tear fell on the bundle in her arms and mixed with those on our little boy's fever-flushed face.

My jaw set, and I started to walk back down the trail. My decision was made. I didn't want to hear what she had to say.

"Lonnie?"

I turned and faced her, angry at the interruption.

"I will pray you do the right thing." With that, she turned and trudged forward, following the faint indentations in the earth that passed for a trail. I broke into a dogtrot, back toward the flat below us. I would do what was necessary.

My ancestors were people of the forest, but what I had planned was not something they would have used, at least not to my knowledge. This one I'd acquired in Stirling Associate's jungle warfare school, and I'd seen the perfect spot a couple hundred yards back on the trail. I worked quickly, every action twice as difficult with only one good arm.

First, I dragged the long trailing vines into place. Two of them I braided together, then shinnied up a big Guanacaste tree and tied my makeshift rope off. The crudely fashioned noose was placed directly on the far side of a rotting log. I was betting heavily the tracker would step over the log in the same way we had. A few yards into the jungle, a bamboo patch provided more of what I needed. The sturdiest stem

WITHOUT REDEMPTION

153

yielded a half-dozen six-inch pegs. I sharpened each one to a razor point, then gouged out holes in a nearby Encino oak until the flat ends of the pegs fitted perfectly into the holes. The points stuck out four inches, more than enough to accomplish what I needed. I only had time for a few. When I'd finished, the deadly spears bristled from the trunk. I bent a sturdy sapling toward the ground, tied the vine to it and ran it through a fork in the oak. Then I anchored the braided vine to the trip stick balanced between the two stakes I'd driven into the ground. It took all my strength to bend the sapling over into the trail. Carefully, I set the trip spring using a weathered stick for a trigger. I backed away to survey my work. Everything was well concealed. Even the tracker wouldn't be suspicious. Best of all, the sharpened pegs in the oak tree were at the perfect angle. He'd never see them until it was too late.

I turned and stared down our back-trail while I listened for any sound of their coming. They had to be close. I made a last check of the lethal trap I'd set while Clarissa's words tumbled through my brain. "I will pray you do the right thing . . . I will pray you do the right thing." This *was* the right thing. If I didn't kill that tracker, we would die. In the end, they would shoot us as easily as one would swat a pesky mosquito. So why didn't I leave? What great moral code said I shouldn't annihilate *him*—every one of them?

The question scrolled over and over through my brain, along with her repeated words. "I will pray you do the right thing." Her hazel-green eyes followed me, like somehow they were the eyes of God.

154 *David Griffith*

Once more, I examined the bamboo spears. They might get the tracker, but only because he would be intent on following our trail. He would never suspect anything like this, and before he realized he'd placed his foot in a trap, the hastily braided noose would tighten on his ankle, the tree would spring back and swing his upside down body into the oak tree and the sharpened pegs. They would drive deep into his torso. How fast he would die would depend on where they entered. If he was lucky, death would be instant—which would allow us to escape. None of the others would have his tracking skill. Yeah, the trap was good. It was our only hope.

So why wasn't I walking away? To stand here longer was dangerous. Our enemies could appear at any second. I clenched my jaw. My wife . . . my little son. That's why I needed to kill this man. I turned up the trail, walked a dozen steps and stopped. I couldn't do it. At least—not yet. For no reason I could explain, it didn't feel right. The hazel-green eyes had now definitely become God's, and a voice that didn't sound anything like my wife's gave me as definite a no as I'd ever had.

With that bonehead decision, I picked a cudgel off the ground and carefully skirted the noose. The wicked looking bamboo pegs shattered easily. Okay, so I wouldn't kill him, but I had no problem giving him a first-class headache—and maybe after this, he wouldn't be quite as cocky.

I trotted up the trail, then stopped and glanced back at the smashed remnants in the eucalyptus tree. It had been perfect, a trap I would only get to use once. I shrugged in disgust as I thought about the now wasted opportunity. At least

WITHOUT REDEMPTION

it would slow them down, and they would know—I could reach out and sting as well.

The trail rose slightly, and I jogged up to where it made a bend before angling along the ridge. I shinnied into a patch of tall grass and lay watching the trap below. Within minutes, the first man came into view, clearly the tracker, his head down, eyes fixed on the easily readable sign we'd left. He got to the log, and I couldn't have ordered it any better. He stepped over it, his gaze already casting further to the next visible sign of our passing. Suddenly, his leg was jerked high into the air. He screamed, as his torso described a swinging arc and splatted into the Encino oak where I'd pounded in the pegs. The men behind him froze while their gun barrels searched the surrounding area. The tracker's unconscious body, still suspended by one leg swung lazily in the wind, an offbeat sound to the coo of a mourning dove calling its valedictory sound of hope and farewell.

Chapter 21

Chapo warily stepped around the log. He inspected the crudely carved spring mechanism, then glared at his man who hung suspended by his left leg while his limp body swayed in the gentle ocean breeze. Finally, he circled over to the oak and examined the pegs I'd blunted before leaving. He walked back to the slowly gyrating, upended man, jerked a machete out of his belt and slashed at the vine that held him. The tracker slammed into the ground. After a few moments, he struggled to his hands and knees, groaning with pain.

Chapo's eyes followed the trail to where I lay concealed. It was as if he knew I was there. "Americano, what is wrong?" He laughed, a great guttural sound in the wind. "You should have killed him, but I think you are too weak. Now you will die."

I shivered. I had no fear for myself, but I did for those I loved. What if they *were* able to kill me? What would then happen to Clarissa and Conor? I'd stayed long enough. It was time to leave.

As soon as Chapo turned away, I pushed backward out of the grass to where I could crawl down the trail without being seen. What I'd done would help. Their star player would be of little use, at least for today. He'd be scraped, bruised, and hopefully groggy from hitting his head. Best of all, when he picked up our trail again, he'd be a lot more cautious.

WITHOUT REDEMPTION 157

That would slow them down. Every step would be taken with more care. His added caution might give us a fighting chance to get away, but deep inside, I still had an unholy wish that he was dead. When I'd blunted those pegs, I'd made the wrong choice. Clarissa's life. Conor's life. Both were at stake. I should have killed him.

Twenty minutes later, I caught up to Clarissa. I glanced at Conor and brushed his cheek with my fingers as I passed her. She didn't ask about the tracker, and I didn't volunteer what I'd done. I didn't want to talk about what now seemed a mixed-up, stupid decision, so I laid my head against the bark of a eucalyptus, closed my eyes for a minute and worried about how we'd get to that landing zone.

Clarissa's voice as she spoke to Conor broke through my reverie. "You're not doing too well with this, little guy. Don't worry, Daddy and Mommy are going to make it better, real soon." She continued talking softly to him, stroking his hair, but it didn't seem to help.

I stood and leaned over them, more worried than I wanted to admit. Conor's face was red, his cheeks and lips dry and chapped. "What's wrong with him?" I asked.

"He's hungry. I tried to get him to eat some of the baby formula, but he doesn't like it." She put the back of her hand against his forehead. "And his fever is worse."

I stared down the trail, desperation again washing over me, knowing that if I'd have killed the tracker, it would have bought us the time we needed.

I took Conor and the sling from Clarissa, which made him even fussier. If he kept crying, they wouldn't need the tracker. The sound would be more than enough to guide them.

Clarissa was a gem, tougher than I'd given her credit for. I trotted along the trail, trying to put more distance between us and the Sinaloa goons. We'd gone at least a mile before she stopped and leaned against a tree, clearly exhausted. "Lon, you have to slow down. I can't go anymore."

"Sorry, hon. We'll walk for a while. They're probably a long way behind us now," I said, though my voice carried little conviction. Our boots still cut into the soft red earth along the top of the ridge, and though our trail wasn't overtly obvious, our tracks would be plain enough to the tracker. I made an extra effort to keep to the harder patches of ground, but it was difficult in that spongy dirt.

By my reckoning, we were now no more than seven miles from the helicopter pickup point, but we'd never make it there before nightfall, which meant one more night in the jungle.

Conor finally quieted. The constant joggling seemed to have put him to sleep, and for that I was grateful. Even though his whole world was being turned upside down, he'd handled this well. I wanted to cover his fevered cheek with kisses. I didn't, because that might wake him, but I stared into his little sleeping face, proud and glad to be his dad. A great wave of protectiveness sluiced over me, which probably happens to every father at one point or another. However, most dads were never in the mess we were faced with, and again I wondered if I'd done right by not killing the man who would harm my son.

WITHOUT REDEMPTION   159

We topped a high hill. Far to the north, and across the river that divided Costa Rica from her northern neighbor, Lake Nicaragua spread out in front of us. An hour later, the trail we'd followed for the last several miles veered toward the lake, which was the wrong direction for us, so we quartered along the side of the hill, hoping to pick up another game trail to the east. The GPS said we were still three-and-a-half miles to the pick-up. With all our zig-zagging, that would take three hours . . . maybe four if it was tough slogging. I checked my watch, and the sun in the western quadrant of the sky. Not a chance. Even if the chopper would land after dark, we couldn't find our way to the landing zone through this terrain. Between snakes, cats, and the Sinaloa cartel, any travel at night was too dangerous. I was not willing to subject Clarissa and Conor to that.

One hour later, the sun decided we didn't need it anymore. With no apology, it slipped silently into the western sea, and left us in a quandary. We couldn't keep going. Occasional lights from scattered houses glimmered in the distance to the west, but I didn't want to go near any of them. Better to take our chances in the jungle with the snakes than find out too late we'd blundered into one of the human variety.

Conor started to cough, and now his little cheeks were even more flushed than they'd been earlier. Fear coursed through every artery in my body. Clarissa was exhausted, and Conor's condition was critical enough we needed to find some medical help.

I stared into the velvety night as we trudged forward, every step that much closer to rescue and the end of this nightmare. Crickets chirped in the blackness, and far off a howler monkey bellowed his stentorian challenge, warning intruders away from his family. I hoped he was more successful than I'd been. Tonight, he would curl up in the canopy high overhead with little to disturb his rest, and that would be after a delectable meal of bananas or some other fruit staple of the monkey tribe. What would *we* eat? Mighty little, though there might be some baby formula left for Conor. Clarissa and I would dine on two blueberry and oatmeal Powerbars. That was acceptable. What wouldn't be okay is if we missed connecting with that chopper.

Twenty minutes more of stumbling through the darkness, and I knew we weren't going any farther. I turned and faced Clarissa. She held her arms out. "Give me Conor. I'll try to nurse him, though I doubt I'm good for much in that department."

I eased Conor out of the sling and gently laid him in her arms. Then I squatted beside her. His breathing sounded raspy, and he was immediately angry at the lack of good grub, though it was hardly his mama's fault. She had to eat right if she was to pass on life-giving nutrition to him, and I hadn't made that possible. My shoulders slumped. What if we slipped down to one of the houses and asked for help? What would be the worst that could happen?

I walked up to a higher point on the trail, to contemplate the valley to the west. The hunger didn't bother me. Often while hunting, or just exploring, I'd gone two or three days without eating anything other than a few berries. That said, I'd not want Clarissa to have to do the same; for her sake, and Conor's. We had enough protein bars to last another day, and a couple cans of the emergency baby formula we'd brought

WITHOUT REDEMPTION 161

from the cabin. Could we risk a quick shopping trip to one of the towns below us? Not likely. I might get away with it, but Clarissa's pale face would stand out like Snow White at a coal miner's convention.

Chapter 22

Paolo struggled to regain consciousness. Tortured blackness seductively beckoned, but the agony in his body vaulted him unwillingly into the present. At least one rib was broken, because just breathing made him grit his teeth. Through pain-glazed eyes, he viewed Chapo's face. It obscured a good part of the blue sky above him, and somewhere in the fog of semi-consciousness Paolo heard him yell up the hill toward where the Indian must have gone. He was too groggy to make out the words, but they sounded threatening. If he hadn't hurt so bad and been retching the vile contents of last night's supper, he might have laughed with the realization that Chapo still did not understand. The man they followed would be contemptuous of threats. They would be lucky if the Indian didn't circle behind and kill every one of them.

Paolo wiped the vomit off the corners of his lips and struggled to his knees. They should cut their losses and run, far away from this throwback to a people who had survived untold hardship, ancient warriors who killed their enemies with only crude knives and flint-tipped arrows. Like elite warriors everywhere, this was a man to be reckoned with—and avoided. So far, he'd made fools of soldiers armed with the best and most modern combat weapons money could buy.

WITHOUT REDEMPTION 163

"And me," he thought. "I'm not doing too well against him either." Instantly, a white-hot anger replaced the swirling onslaught of speculation. He groaned, and pushed himself to a sitting position, then tried to stand. If someone hadn't caught him, he would have fallen. Two of Chapo's men steadied him until he regained some semblance of equilibrium. As his head cleared, the anger died—a spent, useless emotion. He tottered over and fingered the blunted pegs in the tree. This didn't make sense. He should have been dead. The Indian had beaten him, and yet . . . he had let him survive? Was he that confident and contemptuous of those who followed that he played with them—refused to kill them until he tired of the game? Or was he as Chapo thought; weak, unable to seize the moment, finish the job? He fingered the skillfully woven vine the Indian had used as a snare. No, there was more, something he didn't understand. Nevertheless, this stranger he followed had made a grievous mistake. He would not have a second chance. He would now kill this man who dared to laugh at him. He would do it alone, and before it happened, the Indian would watch his woman and *niño* die.

Paolo turned away from the tree, fighting through the pain. His eyes fell on the expensive sniper rifle in Chapo's hands. What if . . .? As the thought took shape, it became more appealing. Chapo was angry that he'd not been able to deliver the Indian, and unless he produced something very soon, his career as part of Chapo's security squad would end.

"Señor." Paolo's voice cut across the group as he spoke to Chapo. "What we are doing is not working. He is playing with us."

164   *David Griffith*

Chapo's eyebrows rose, his mouth tightening into a hard line. "I couldn't agree more. Your skill is obviously overrated."

"Let me borrow your sniper rifle. I can finish this now." He stared at the rising trail in front of them. "He will not be far away."

Chapo eyed him with a cold, quizzical stare, and Paolo wondered whether he was within a heartbeat of death.

"I think I have made a mistake—something I don't do often. I should not have chosen you as a replacement for José. However, I'm going to give you the rifle. When you return it, your other hand had better hold the head of this traitorous Indian. Do not fail me again."

Paolo nodded and reached for the expensive gun. He slung it over his shoulder and limped away. The Indian's left stride was shortened, as it had been all day, and because of the broken arm, the right foot indentation was shallower than the other. What calamity would this man create if he had two good arms?

Each stumbling step to the top of the ridge was a small triumph over the pain. At the top, he found what he'd expected. Like a great cat watching its prey, the Indian had lain in the tall grass and watched while his trap worked its havoc. Paolo went to one knee, his hand testing the disturbed foliage. The man had stayed too long. He couldn't be more than a few minutes ahead.

A stifled groan escaped Paolo's lacerated lips as he struggled back to his feet. The pain from the rib was intense. Regardless, nothing would undermine his final push to find and kill this unpredictable foreigner.

WITHOUT REDEMPTION 165

Often over the next hour, he had to stop and fight the nauseous pain. Within a quarter-mile he picked up a good set of tracks from the woman. They were deeper than some of the others she'd left, which meant she carried the baby. As he had before, the Indian pyramided one small dodge over another. When darkness melded the sky with the forest, Paolo had not caught up to them—and then the tracks disappeared altogether. Panic constricted his throat. How would he explain to Chapo that he needed more time? As he ran that conversation through his mind, he knew—it would not end well.

He squatted in a small depression and waited for the men to reach him, dreading the coming confrontation. By tomorrow, he had to catch the Indian. Perhaps if he'd been around longer, he'd have had time to establish credibility. He hadn't, so this was it. He would succeed or be killed on this, the toughest assignment he'd ever had. Fairness had nothing to do with it. He was a *sicario*, and the rules were harsh. If you failed, death was your destiny, and often he'd seen men die in a manner that was neither simple nor quick.

When Chapo and his string of bodyguards straggled up the hill, the boss's quizzical stare lacked any outward malice or blame. But the look in Chapo's eye told Paolo he had little time left to find their quarry. The growing resentment was mirrored on the men's faces. Paolo glared in self-defense at those who dared to grumble. Most now viewed him as an over-rated failure. As long as Chapo thought otherwise, he was safe. But Chapo's attitude had changed. The Sinaloa cartel wasn't known to carry useless personnel, and Paolo knew unless he produced immediate results, his life could be measured in hours.

Chapo strolled to the edge of the steep hillside. He peered at the lights that twinkled far down in the valley from the windows of scattered farmhouses. "We will camp here. At first light, we'll pick up the trail again."

The troops built several small fires, cooked their meager rations, then huddled in the few thin blankets they possessed. A driving wind blew off the ocean, picking up speed as it moved inland to buffet the shivering men who huddled on the damp earth. Tempers heated, and dawn was a long time coming.

Chapter 23

The lights below beckoned me with their welcoming fluorescence. The lack of a moon to shed any light on our trail made them appear close, but whether those lights were rays of welcome, or dancing devils, luring us toward disaster, I could not tell. I slipped through the trees and stood on the edge of the hill that sloped down to the valley. The only sound was the high pitched whine of the tiny bugs that raised great bloody welts which made our lives even more miserable. Conor's cough was worse, each breath harsh and gravelly. He had to have medicine, and Clarissa needed rest. Though we'd not come far in miles, the constant fear of knowing you're only one bad decision away from dying had sapped every bit of reserve she had. Could there be medicine and a safe and warm place for the night behind one of those beckoning windows in the valley below us?

The GPS indicated our rendezvous point lay directly on the other side of a low range of hills to the east. If we were on the trail at dawn, we should be there by ten o'clock at the absolute latest. I'd taken great pains to obscure our tracks when we'd left the ridge and slipped down into the valley. With any luck, in the morning we'd be out of the country before Chapo and his tracker even found our trail. Tomorrow night, we'd be sleeping at a Best Western, or maybe a Hilton. Hey, we could even be back in Texas.

168   *David Griffith*

I slapped at another mosquito and again scanned the lights below us. Did I dare go to one of them and seek shelter?

Conor started coughing again. Clarissa's eyes met mine with a growing concern she could no longer disguise. "He's getting worse. I don't think we can wait until we are rescued."

I studied our baby's face. His breathing was rapid and labored, but it was the bluish tinge around his mouth that worried me. Though I had little knowledge of childhood ills, his condition was enough to scare me into taking risks I might not have otherwise taken. I rubbed Clarissa's slumped shoulders with my one good hand. "We can't. It's too risky. Isn't there something we can do for him?"

"No, he needs medicine, or at least Tylenol. He needs a humidifier—and if he gets worse, oxygen. Only a hospital can provide that."

My face twisted with pain. This was my little boy. No matter the risk, we had to take the chance. I stared at the twinkling lights. They were only peasant farmers down there. Surely none of them would have anything to do with drug cartels. We could find a doctor, and maybe even a bed away from the snakes and other larger predators we'd have to contend with here. Somewhere in my weary reasoning, I knew I ought to come up with a better plan than just knocking on a door and hoping for the best. But no other idea came to mind so I just headed down the steep slope toward the nearest lights. The terrain was treacherous, and I turned and reached for Conor. The slope was treacherous enough for Clarissa without packing an extra bundle. After I'd adjusted the sling so we were both reasonably comfortable, I reached

WITHOUT REDEMPTION 169

down and fingered the cold steel of the gun that remained tucked in my belt.

Clarissa never wavered. When I slid down a gravel chute she was right behind me. At the bottom, we found a well-worn trail and followed it until it intersected with a narrow dirt road. What would happen when we knocked on somebody's door at this time of night? Not that it mattered, we had no other choice. Our fate rested in the hands of God. I hoped He was inclined to save us.

The terrain around us consisted mostly of the light jungle that covers much of northern Costa Rica. A mile from the bottom of the hill, we approached a hacked out space alongside the road with a house in the middle of the clearing. A mongrel dog showed his teeth and bayed at us. It was pitch dark, so his heritage may have been better than I'd judged. For a few steps, he and I played chicken. I won, at least enough to get to the house. The current residents didn't seem to think their yappy mutt was anything to worry about, because nobody came to the door, even when I rapped on it. After a more robust second attempt, it swung open a crack.

"Hola." I gave the beady eyes that peered at me a view of my dentist's best work while I attempted to appear as harmless as a butt-wriggling Border collie pup. From the scowl on his swarthy face, the man on the other side of the door wasn't impressed. He stared without speaking a word, so I just carried on introducing myself and Clarissa in Spanish.

Suspicion clouded his features. He shifted his heavy frame to better peer behind me into the dark yard.

I shrugged, and held out my open palms. "It is only us."

170   *David Griffith*

The scowl deepened. "No. We have nothing. We cannot help you." He started to close the door.

"We don't want anything, but my little boy—"

Suddenly, a woman appeared behind the man. The moment she spotted me, corrosive fear tightened the deep, middle-aged lines around her mouth and cheeks. She stopped, then backed toward the far wall of the room. "Go away. We have nothing."

"I would only like a little help. Then we will go."

"We cannot give you anything." She too peered fearfully into the darkness.

"Please, our baby . . . he is very sick."

The man shook his head and again started to shut the door. My hand held it open, my face pleading for understanding.

"Where is he—this baby?" The woman timidly shuffled forward and tried to peer past me.

Clarissa moved into the light spilling from the doorway. Conor's rasping breath needed no explanation, but I tried to give it anyway. "He has . . . he has—" I struggled to come up with the Spanish word for croup. Though I spoke the language well, medical terms often stumped me.

The door opened a few more inches. The woman elbowed past her husband, who stared suspiciously at Conor as if he was somehow faking the labored breathing. She pulled the dirty blanket away and peered into his flushed face. "Bring him into the light." She motioned Clarissa into the house. "I cannot see anything out here."

The man glared at me as his wife beckoned us inside. He clearly wasn't happy with the turn of events. Something

WITHOUT REDEMPTION

171

else lingered in those shifty eyes, but at the time, I was too concerned about Conor to dissect the meaning. We stood in the middle of the room, and they both stared at the ragged, muddy bundle in Clarissa's arms. The cotton blanket he was wrapped in had seen much abuse throughout the day. It was torn and covered in mud from the irrigation ditch where we'd hunkered down to get away from the fire. Pity flickered over the woman's rugged face as she inspected Conor. Her compassion turned to instant anger when the man started to protest. "Diego, let me deal with this. You know nothing of these things."

Sullenly, he closed the door behind us and watched while his wife gently picked Conor out of his mother's arms, and though Clarissa didn't look keen to turn loose of him, there wasn't any other option. If we were to get help, this woman was our only ticket. Even so, the blood pounded in my head, and I went into what a friend of mine called agent overdrive. My eyes widened enough to take in every facial expression and eye tic of both the man and woman. If either of them made a bad move, they would pay dearly. I didn't need a gun for that.

Diego sullenly eyed the whole procedure for another minute, then shrugged and slouched into a chair against the far wall. He was a big man, perhaps more efficient than he appeared.

The woman unwrapped Conor and stared at his little red body. "Diego, the baby needs a doctor. Call Esteban."

Diego stayed rooted to the chair he'd staked out as home base and stared at her like she'd lost her mind. I catalogued every move he made. My whole life had been built around instant assessments, of horses and men. His eyes gave me little confidence we'd made a good choice, but I pushed my misgivings aside as he dragged out a cellphone and dialed a number I hoped would summon the help Conor so desperately needed.

Chapter 24

Within the hour, a fist hammered at the thin metal door. The woman opened it to a sallow-cheeked old Costa Rican with black whiskers and a weathered brown bag. The single, bare light bulb allowed him to make his diagnosis, give instructions, and administer some liquid aspirin. It wasn't much, and hardly seemed worth the risk we'd taken, but after a while Conor's breathing quieted which gave us time to get acquainted with the Torres family. More important, I was able to study Diego. He still wanted nothing to do with us, and the more he talked, the less I trusted him. Though he didn't drop any names, he talked about a major Mexican drug lord in the area—looking for somebody. A sly smile flickered over his features. He seemed way too interested in who we were, and I carefully fielded each probing question. Stopping here had been the right choice for Conor and Clarissa, but I'd best keep an eye on this weasel? The minute we walked out the door, he would sell us out. The best thing to do would be to have him where I could watch him, at least until we were out of danger, so I offered him a job.

Diego made no bones about not wanting to serve as our guide to some vague point I refused to identify—unless the price was right. I hardly needed him to take us five or six miles, which is what it would be if we had to take a roundabout way to avoid Chapo's crew. Diego might get us there

174 *David Griffith*

faster, though I wasn't inclined to bet much on that prospect. Besides, a wad of bills in his pocket would hopefully nullify thoughts of other mischief. Though I'd shared only a bare outline of our situation, the crafty look was proof enough he suspected we were in grave danger, and running, probably from said Mexican drug lord. Greed in a man can be used, manipulated—as long as you're the highest bidder. I intended to be just that. Our safety depended on my ability to keep him well paid, and under close supervision. The minute either of those conditions changed—he would be dangerous. He named a price. When I offered him double what he'd asked— two hundred and fifty American bucks for the first day, and fifty more for any afterward, he couldn't nod his head fast enough. There wouldn't be any days after tomorrow, but I dangled the offer in front of him anyway.

I was under no illusions. For today, I would be the *jefe*—the boss. Tomorrow? With Diego, I hoped there would be no tomorrows. I tried to shrug my misgivings away as I counted out half of the money into his sweaty palm. He'd get the rest when we reached the landing zone, or at the end of the day, whichever came first. In the meantime, I hoped the promise of future riches would at least keep my family safe through the night. I would deal with tomorrow when it came.

After the doctor left, Diego pointed us to a spot in a corner of his modest country house to bed down. The floor was hard, but there were no poisonous snakes and only a few cockroaches. However, between the *cucarachas* and Conor's labored breathing, I lay awake and worried about the coming day. The bigger cockroaches, the kind that walked on two

WITHOUT REDEMPTION 175

legs and packed heat were the biggest inhibitor of sleep, but maybe by tomorrow night we would be safely out of the country. Clarissa's voice as she murmured to Conor was the last thing I heard, and though I shouldn't have listened, I couldn't help myself. Her barely audible words soothed our baby boy as she nursed him.

"Hey, little guy. We were scared today, weren't we? We had to run through the snakes and spiders in the sugar cane, and all Mama could do was pray. I guess that's what everybody does when they face trouble ? Suddenly, God is real enough to petition for help."

I was too sleepy to think through the theology of that statement. Her soft voice lulled me closer to sleep, and I hoped it had done the same for Conor.

"Then we laid in that muddy water. We had our eyes closed, didn't we baby boy—because of all the smoke, and a big black and yellow snake slithered right over Mama's arm. I'm glad you didn't see that."

Wow, I wanted to reach over and squeeze her hand. Instead, I shut my eyes tighter, trying not to intrude or eavesdrop, but it was too late for that.

"I'm so thankful for Maria calling a doctor, and that your breathing is starting to get better. It makes me believe even more that God is here, and that He cares. Hmm . . . but then the reverse of that is: what if He allowed something to happen to you? Would that mean He isn't here, or that He doesn't care? I'm afraid that's much too heavy a question for us tonight. Mama's so tired. I don't think I can slog through another day in the jungle."

For a while, the common sounds of the night permeated the room. I was nearly asleep when Clarissa's soft voice broke the silence. "Your daddy wanted to kill that man today, but he didn't. Always before, Mama would have said he did the right thing. Now, I'm not so sure. I look down at you, my sleeping baby, and all the answers I thought I had don't seem clear anymore."

I opened one eye and watched her as she tenderly kissed Conor's hot little face, then tucked him into a nest of blankets. Her eyes, like mine, wouldn't stay open any longer.

LONG BEFORE DAYLIGHT filtered into that tiny mud-brick room, I lay wide awake, cataloging each sound. What had awakened me? Had it been a noise outside the house?

Clarissa's breathing beside me was quiet and regular, a stark contrast to Conor's. Though better than last night, it remained a gurgling whistle, labored, and not at all what we'd hoped for. Today would be a mad dash for safety. To do that, he needed to be well, not struggling for every breath. Guilt lay heavy on me. This was *my* fault. I'd gone against my better judgement and agreed to Frederick's proposal. Now, I somehow had to extricate my family from this mess.

Other than a dueling pair of crowing roosters, no unusual sound broke the silence before dawn, but still I listened. Clarissa now tossed fitfully beside me, trying to find a comfortable position on that hard floor. As the first purple colored the eastern sky, I slipped on my clothes and stole out of the house. Before I left the yard, I stood quietly and studied the hills to the north and east where we had to go. The

WITHOUT REDEMPTION

mongrel dog trotted up, stiff-legged his way around me, then growled his resentment at my presence in his territory. After he and I talked for a bit, I gave him an ironclad guarantee I would only be a short-term guest who had no designs on his resident family or feed supply. That seemed to satisfy him.

As soon as my yard friend quit growling, I hiked toward the high plateau Clarissa and I had abandoned last night. The sun was just beginning to shed its first light into the jungle, so I moved carefully, not wanting to come face to face with any hostile creatures of the two-legged variety. At the top, I backtracked down the trail to the point of land where we'd seen the lights of Diego's house. A few hundred yards beyond, we'd crossed a low swale. In the bottom, a trickle of water burbled over the rocks. I reckoned that was where they would be camped. I counted their inert bodies, each with a gun near to hand. One of those bodies would be the tracker. I squatted in the tall ferns and watched one of the sleeping forms stir and sit up. It was time to go. I edged backward into more cover. With any luck, Diego would get us enough of a head start that, even with the tracker, they wouldn't be able to catch us. Quietly, I slipped off the ridge and made my way down to the farmhouse.

The mongrel woofed at my appearance, but quieted at the sound of my voice. He seemed to remember our agreement. I softly opened the door, but there was little need for quiet. Clarissa sat with a blanket over her shoulder nursing Conor while she talked softly to Maria. As near as I could tell from last night, Maria had about five words of English. Clarissa had about the same level of Spanish but they seemed to communicate well enough. Maria flitted around the tiny

178   *David Griffith*

kitchen fixing food. Diego paced back and forth through the room. When I entered, he turned abruptly.

"We leave in a half hour. Eat." He pointed a thumb toward the table where Maria had laid out tortillas, rice, and black beans. No eggs. No coffee. I clenched my jaw, mildly irked at the absence of coffee in a country overrun with the stuff. Eventually, I shrugged and tried to put the small inconvenience into perspective. As long as I kept my cool, it wouldn't be a lack of morning coffee that would kill us. Besides, this family had offered what they had. Gratefully, I accepted a plate, bolted it down, then stepped outside and called the emergency number.

Calvin Parkin, one of Frederick's office intelligence people handled the call. Everything was in place. The minute we reached the drop zone they would whisk us out of the country. When we got within fifteen minutes of the area, I would notify them. There would be a chopper on the ground when we arrived. I tried not to picture how nice it would be to be in Calvin's shoes, sitting in a warm, spotless office in Albuquerque, his second or third steaming cup of coffee by his hand as he effortlessly stick-handled one more agent out of trouble.

We left the little rancho in single file. Diego led, Clarissa in the middle, and Conor and I brought up the rear. Clarissa had re-fashioned the sling to make it fit better. I smoothed Conor's hair away from his face with the tips of my fingers, careful not to rub the rough cast against his tender skin. He wasn't as flushed as yesterday and his breathing had improved dramatically for which I breathed a grateful prayer. By this af-

WITHOUT REDEMPTION   179

ternoon we'd be out of here, winging toward the best medical help in the world—and safety.

We'd not made it to where Clarissa and I had dropped off the ridge last night when the distinctive snap of a high caliber bullet stopped me in my tracks. The following crack of the rifle tripped a coiled spring in my head, the one that demanded instant action. I shoved Conor into Clarissa's arms, grabbed her hand and sprinted for cover. A dozen rifles opened up. Twenty feet before the tree line the grass got sparse and we had to *really* run for it. I pushed her ahead and zig-zagged back and forth. The distance seemed like a thousand yards. Bullets pflunked into the rain-soaked dirt around me. They were shooting at me as I knew they would. A bullet took a chunk out of my leg and though it didn't immediately hurt, blood flooded down into my shoe like a West Texas oil well. The pain would come later, and I'd soon have to stop the flow, but the important thing was that I'd kept their attention long enough for Clarissa and Conor to escape. That was all that mattered.

When I reached the safety of the jungle, I grabbed Conor, shoved Clarissa down behind a boulder, then dove in after her. That didn't go well as I had Conor in front of me. I landed on my left side and grunted with pain when my broken arm skidded into the ground. Conor of course, started bellowing like a branded steer. I clapped my hand over his mouth, which only made him madder at me and his whole life situation in general. Clarissa tried to jolly him into silence, but that didn't work either. We crab-scuttled further into the rocks and I scanned the surrounding area trying to spot Diego. He was nowhere in sight. Maybe he'd been shot.

180 *David Griffith*

Cautiously I raised my head higher to scan the surrounding area. Nothing. He'd disappeared. A bullet clipped my ear and I dove for cover, though I kept an eye on the ridge. The guns opened up again as three of them scrambled down the slope. Occasionally, I caught a glimpse of two others circling around to cut off any retreat. I turned to Clarissa. "Get out of here—and find Diego. I'll catch up later."

She shook her head. "No, we have to stay together." She pulled my pant leg up and examined the wound. It wasn't a bad one—as long as the bleeding stopped, I'd survive. She bound it up with a piece of clean diaper. She even had tape in that bag, though why, I'll never know.

I reached over and touched her shoulder while I gazed into her eyes. "Hon, do what I say. If we stay here, we will die—Conor will die. They're working their way down the slope. Within minutes they'll have us surrounded."

"But Lon, I don't trust Diego—and neither do you."

"We don't have a choice. Give me a couple of hours and I'll be right behind you. The only way I can hold them off is if I move now. I can't do that if I have to take care of you and Conor. Trust me sweetheart, this is what we have to do. By this afternoon, you . . . we'll be in that chopper and out of this nightmare. Now go." I shoved the GPS into her hands and squeezed her arm.

Our eyes locked. She reached for my face, and I tangled the fingers of my good hand in her hair. Time stopped. The guns were silenced as my lips met hers. "I love you."

"I love you too, Lonnie Bowers, and if you get hurt again, *I'll* kill you—or something!" Then she tucked Conor close and ran for it while I laid as much lead over that hillside

WITHOUT REDEMPTION   181

as a nine millimeter can manage, which doesn't come close to AR-15's and AK-47's. I was badly outnumbered and out-gunned, and when I scrambled a few feet to my left, they let me know with an answering barrage that I was going nowhere. My family had escaped at the last possible moment.

Minutes later, I peeked around the side of the mossy rock I was bellied up to just to see if any of those killers were try-ing to creep in close and finish me off. What I had for brains escaped by two inches, but they sure ruined my expensive tourist hat, and the truth slowly dawned on me. This grassy niche behind a black chunk of volcanic lava would be my last stand. I'd not see another dawn.

Chapter 25

As the first sliver of light turned the shadows from black to gray, Paolo slipped out of the wind protected swale where they'd camped for the night. In the light of the rising sun, he rapidly worked out where the Indian had dropped off the ridge. For nearly a mile, he followed the track, but grew increasingly apprehensive. Other than the first few hundred yards, the trail from last night was easy to follow—too easy. Why? Most of the day, the Indian's trail had been difficult to find. Why had he now lost all caution? Was there something else bothering him, a matter of so much importance that he didn't have time to hide his tracks? Paolo dropped to one knee and scanned the terrain ahead. Scattered trees, tall grass . . . slowly he backed away, his eyes darting over each tree, every bush and clump of ground. Was this another trap? The careless tracks screamed ambush. Paolo studied every inch of soil before each step. Yesterday, the Indian could have so easily killed him if he'd left the sharpened pegs. Why hadn't he? The question bothered him. Suddenly, like a corrosive explosion of lava, the answer burned deep into the most vulnerable part of his being. The man was taunting him, choosing to prolong the game, convinced he had outwitted and would continue to defeat those who followed him. Paolo snarled and turned away from the trail, his rage breeding a momentary contempt for his adversary He made his way back to the

WITHOUT REDEMPTION   183

top of the ridge and slithered inside the roots of one of the giant rainforest trees, the sniper rifle resting across his knees. As the rising sun brightened in the east, he tried to understand his adversary. Why had he'd taken his woman and niño down toward the ocean and people. What did that mean? Chapo needed to know.

Paolo had started to rise to his feet when he spotted the figures below in the ghostly fog. The Indian and his woman followed another man up toward the trail they'd abandoned the night before. At the same time, Paolo sensed movement above and behind him. He swiveled and peered toward the night's campsite. Chapo had the men out, trooping toward the top of the ridge, ready for whatever might come. As they neared, Paolo slipped out from amongst the tent-like roots. By now, the Indian was directly below, carrying the kid, a good omen. The baby in his arms would make him less mobile.

Frantically, Paolo motioned for Chapo and his troops to take cover. Special Forces guys don't need to be told twice. No matter whose army they're in, they know how to disappear, quickly, and well. All of them now watched as the party below moved closer . . . and then, somebody shot. For a millisecond there was silence, before the rapid chatter of semi-automatic rifle fire drowned out whatever oath Chapo had for the fool who had given their position away. Later, nobody would own up to doing it, but Paolo was incredulous. The pair was barely within range. Why had some idiot fired? There was no excuse. It was like an act of God.

Paolo scoffed under his breath. Professionals? Veterans of a hundred operations? What a joke. Every one of them

184 *David Griffith*

should have known better, and yet somebody had panicked like a first-year rookie. He caressed the stock of the sniper rifle, almost hoping the Indian would outwit the fools at his back. He so wanted the man in front of him to die. But it must be slowly, humiliated and afraid, the fear eating through his vitals like a rogue cancer. Those behind him didn't deserve to be part of the final success. Paolo quickly moved away from the firing line of men and worked his way to the north, then down through a hidden draw toward where he knew the man would hole up. If the Indian had been hit by the bullets from the ridge, he must reach him before he died.

From now on, it would be only the two of them—he and the Indian. He would kill the Indian alone, without help from the others, but first? Yes, there was something that must come first.

I RELOADED THE PISTOL in my hand. It would be little help against a dozen assault rifles, but fiddling with it gave me time to think.

In front of me, a mostly bare hill led up into the jungle. At my back, the grassy slope slid into the valley below where we'd stayed with Diego and his wife, Maria. Neither direction had much for cover. They'd have the hill well covered, so that was not an option. I was thankful Clarissa had gone. I'd not want to watch her and our little boy die here in a hole in the ground, far from the country we'd come to call home. To my right, a steep brushy spine ran perpendicular to the ridge from where Chapo's men had fired. They were still up there,

WITHOUT REDEMPTION 185

and if I wanted to put up any kind of resistance, I had to find a better spot. I jammed the last of the shells into the nine shot magazine, then scanned the broken, rocky slope to my left. Skittering into those rocks was my only chance. Not that I'd get away. That option had closed when I sent Clarissa after Diego. Now, I needed to pick a place to make a last stand. I wouldn't survive—but if Providence was agreeable—I would hold them off for as long as could to give Clarissa and Conor time to get away, and yes, I would take some of them with me.

In the end, I would have to decide what to do with the last bullet. More than a few times in the past, I'd choked back the stark horror and rising vomit at the mutilated corpses left behind by the Sinaloa cartel. If Chapo captured me alive, he would make very sure it took many hours before death would release me from the excruciating pain they would inflict. Could I go through that? I glared at the barrel of the gun in my hand as questions cascaded one after another. Would I be able to use it—my final act on this earth a suicide to escape the coming torture? Was there a moral weakness in that action? I'd always thought suicide to be the ultimate selfishness. Now that the bleak decision loomed in front of me, the answers I'd blithely spouted had deserted me.

Sporadic fire from the top of the ridge kept my head down. I couldn't shoot back. I only had a few bullets left, and they were out of range for my hand gun. Those at the top were well concealed, while others worked farther around the spine to my right to cut off any escape. Once more, I glanced at the jumble of boulders to my left. Those rocks offered the most short-term security, but it was a dead-end. Once I broke

186   *David Griffith*

that way, there would be no return, and no way forward. In those rocks, I would either die or be captured.

I studied the lay out on both sides and below me. A dozen yards behind me, a dry wash led down to a shallow streambed. If I hugged the ground, I might reach it. Not that the odds were good. Any moment now, one of them would break over the spiny ridge. Then, it wouldn't matter. They'd easily be able to see down to where I'd squeezed behind the rock. I'd be the target in a first-class shooting gallery, an easy hundred yard shot. None of them would miss. The streambed would at least provide a small amount of cover, and from there—who knew.

With no other decent options, I jammed the pistol into my belt and scurried down the slope. Better to be shot trying to get away than die like a rat in a trap. This way, they'd have to kill me.

Seconds after I reached the rocky streambed, I saw the first movement up on the spine. It didn't take long for the bullets to start flying again, but I was now partially concealed and they were shooting down a steep hill, which is tough for even the best shooter. I suspected these guys were capable marksmen, but their killing was mostly done at point-blank range on city pavement.

I darted down into the coulee, rolled twice and scrambled to the end. A moss covered boulder provided some protection, but when I dived behind it, my broken arm wedged between one of the boulders and my knee. I groaned, weary with the constant pain, and for several moments just rocked back and forth on my knees with my eyes shut while I fought off the nausea. When I opened them, my arm seemed a small

WITHOUT REDEMPTION

187

issue. Three feet in front of me, the tracker squatted, a high-powered sniper rifle pointed at the middle of my chest. It was over, and now I'd even failed Clarissa. They'd not had nearly enough time to get away.

I waited for the bullet to smash into me. I had no wish to face the other alternative, and yet I knew that if he didn't shoot, the time they took to interrogate and torture me would give my wife the time she would need to reach the landing zone.

My eyes moved from the gun to the tracker's face. It was surreal to finally see him up close. Sure, he'd been in the room back at San Carlos, but I'd been focused on Chapo, and paid little mind to any of the others.

A sardonic grin slowly creased the tracker's narrow, hard features, then faded away. He never spoke as I stared at him, waiting for the bullet that would take away my life. His eyes were a shade too close together, unblinking and cold, like the eyes of a shark. For an eternity he crouched without any movement, though I could see his trigger finger twitching like the tail of a rattler. Suddenly, he stepped back and lowered the barrel of his gun, his evil grin now replaced with a sneer.

"Two can play your game, Indian. Go." He pointed to a narrow trail that led up the coulee. "Quickly. I have given you your life. We are even. I would not want any of the others to have the pleasure of killing you, but before the day is over, you will die." He raised the barrel of his gun and fired two quick shots into the air.

I stayed frozen on my knees. I wondered why he would let me escape. Maybe in the end, he wouldn't.

After firing the shots the tracker lowered the rifle. Hatred and disdain surged over his face. The hatred I understood. But the disdain? Suddenly, it came to me. He'd been foiled—by a man with a woman and a baby in tow. He would see the blunted pegs back at the trap as a slur on his ability. I'd shown contempt for him. No matter what other motivation he had, his pride now demanded that he show the same contempt for me. He had to let me go, not as a sign of mercy or gratefulness, but because I'd disrespected him.

I nodded my thanks, brushed by him and left at the fastest trot I could manage. When I reached a bend in the trail, I looked back. He was gone. By whatever twisted code he lived, he had granted me life. The next time we met—there would be no quarter given. One of us would die.

Chapter 26

After Paolo had granted the Indian his life, he circled around to where Chapo held the men. For fifteen minutes, recriminations and backbiting dominated the conversation. Like a rabid pack of wolves they snapped and snarled, waiting for the weakest to go down under their combined weight. Paolo stayed as far away as he could, refusing to answer their veiled insults. That he could have held the Indian's life in his hand—then let him live would be beyond any comprehension to the men behind him. He didn't care. They meant nothing, and they didn't need to know why he'd done it. He would give the Indian to Chapo in his own time, in his own way. In one of the rare moments when the griping was directed elsewhere, he slipped away.

In a glade carpeted with native sawgrass, Paolo picked up the Indian's trail again. The barely visible track meant the man had again employed his considerable skill. Paolo walked back and signaled for Chapo's troops to follow, but to stay clear of the tracks. If he lost the trail and had to backtrack to pick it up again, he didn't want to have to sort through the boot marks of these bumblers.

Ahead, the country opened into more grassland, but all that did was allow the Indian to move faster and leave less sign. By noon, Paolo knew he'd lost ground, and tempers behind him frayed like a dog-chewed sarape. He understood.

These men were tough, but they were city guys, more than weary of slogging through this jungle heat. As always, the collective finger pointed at him. Once more, their quarry had slipped through their fingers because of his perceived incompetence.

An hour later, Paolo picked up the deeper track of the big man they'd seen that morning with the Indian and his woman. His trail had come in from the west. He'd met the Indian. They'd squatted in the middle of the trail, obviously talking. Then their tracks separated. Why? The woman had to be somewhere ahead. Had this new man left to join her? It took more time to work out the trail sign. The Indian had then veered to the east, toward a range of low mountains. The man with the deep tracks had gone straight north toward the Nicaragua border. Would they rejoin? He had a hunch they wouldn't, at least not right away. It appeared the Indian had sent the big man ahead to find the woman, knowing his pursuers would be more intent on him. He was right. By now, Chapo thirsted for revenge at any price.

An hour later, Paolo squatted in the trail to rest while he scanned the low, wet ground. With only one set of tracks to follow, he'd made good time. After making sure of the tracks and the general direction the Indian had taken, he moved out at a fast walk, his eyes riveted to the scraps of information in front of him. An hour later, he felt the familiar tension in his joints that meant he was close. Leaping onto a fallen tree, he climbed high enough to scan the terrain ahead through the scope of the sniper rifle. The Indian had led them steadily higher through the lightly forested rolling hills. Now, the fresh scuff marks angled downward, heading through a long,

WITHOUT REDEMPTION 191

open ravine with steep sides. Off to his right, a razor-backed east-running ridge presented Paolo with the opportunity he needed. He waited for the men, then squatted in front of them as he revealed his plan. Their quarry was very close. All the men had to do was follow the Indian's trail for a mile. They would probably lose it, but he was reasonably sure the man ahead of him would stay in the ravine, so if the men just walked up the bottom of the arroyo, that would be good enough. If they managed that, what he had in mind might work.

Paolo watched as Chapo paced back and forth while he talked. When he nodded approval, Paolo didn't wait for him to change his mind. He zigzagged to the top of the ridge and jogged parallel to the Indian's track in the glade below, all the time making sure he stayed out of sight. His whole plan was a gamble, but the Indian likely wouldn't deviate from his chosen direction. This was a perfect chance to put an end to this spectacle, and regain his lost standing with the boss.

A half-hour later, he spotted the quarry. Head down, concentrating on each step, the Indian limped forward. Paolo chuckled as he studied the black haired man with the now familiar straw hat. He lifted the rifle and cradled the soft butt-plate into his shoulder. His eye automatically focused on the crosshairs of the expensive scope. Almost without effort, they centered between the man's shoulder blades. Paolo's index finger slipped with practiced precision through the trigger guard. Could he hit him from this distance? The range had to be three hundred yards. What if Chapo's gun wasn't sighted in at this distance? He wanted so badly to shoot, but no—it was too risky. He had to be closer. This

192   *David Griffith*

time, there could be no mistake. As Lorenzo had taught him, he ghosted through the trees like a hunting mountain lion, unseen, always behind the man's left shoulder.

Down the slope to his right, he watched as Chapo and his men narrowed the gap between them and the quarry. They were within five hundred yards and getting closer, though of course they didn't know that. He watched as the Indian climbed out of the swale. At the top of the ridge, he stopped to scan his back-trail. Paolo froze, glad he was well concealed on the edge of an immature patch of *Matapalo*. Again, he leveled the rifle, this time balancing it carefully in the fork of a small tree behind a blackened stump. He'd gained some ground. The distance had narrowed to probably two hundred and fifty yards. The little tree swayed with the weight of the rifle. He needed a steadier rest, but would he get a better shot? Not likely. His quarry stood stock-still, watching as Chapo's men appeared below him. The Indian's head, slightly above the crosshairs bobbed as if he were counting the men coming toward him. Suddenly, Paolo panicked. That's exactly what he was doing. As soon as he realized a man was missing, he would instantly be gone. His trigger finger caressed the trigger of Chapo's expensive sniper rifle. The death he wanted for the Indian would have been much slower and infinitely more painful. Nevertheless, this would have to do. The Indian would die.

Chapter 27

When I caught up to Clarissa she slumped into my arms. Too worn from exhaustion and the constant strain for mere tears, my wife had reached the end of whatever rope she carried. I held her and Conor close. I'd not expected to be able to do that again. Then, we trudged north toward the landing zone, relieved this nightmare was nearly over. By mid-morning, the GPS told me we were within spitting distance, so I made the call. Though we'd seen no sign of pursuit, giant bullfrogs hop-scotched in my belly. Something wasn't right.

When we approached the grassy clearing, I heard the first thump of the helicopter blades as the chopper edged around the side of the mountain. Within minutes, it swooped over the landing zone and hovered. Immediately, gunfire erupted from the jungle. The pilot banked away and poured on the power. I pulled out my cellphone and punched in the number. A voice crackled over the whump of the blades. "Lonnie?"

"Who else would it be?"

"We can't land. They're right behind you. Listen, I'm going to dump the two commandos we brought about eight miles to the north of you. They'll secure the site and talk you in."

194 *David Griffith*

I glanced at Clarissa long enough to see the fear and despair on her face.

"I'll give you the coordinates as soon as I get over top of the site. And don't worry. It looked like less than a dozen men behind you. The guys have adequate ordnance to handle that many. They're well-prepared."

Whoever occupied that chopper would have plenty of firepower, but I needed more than two commandos, and I needed them here—not eight miles away. They wouldn't be able to work their way back to us, and it wouldn't do us any good if they tried. This jungle was too big, too dense. Besides, Conor and Clarissa had contributed all they had. Another eight miles? They didn't have it in them.

Without asking, Clarissa knew what had happened. My face gave it away. I was angry, scared, and more discouraged than I'd ever been in my life. But if the guy in that chopper was right, we didn't have time to sorrow over our misfortune. I hitched Conor up in the sling, and we high-tailed over to the north side of the overgrown clearing we'd worked so hard to reach. At the edge, I handed him to Clarissa and told her to go on ahead. After she disappeared, I bellied into some tall grass. Within three minutes, the first goon appeared at the edge of the clearing. The pilot had been right. If the chopper had landed, they'd have shot all of us into oblivion. To make it to the next drop zone, we'd have to lose them, or at least slow them down. But now it would be more difficult. The tracker would be warier. Every step he took would be taken with care, knowing there might be a trap. The liana vine had worked. Though hastily done, he'd hit the pegs I'd buried with enough force that he would have died. I shook

WITHOUT REDEMPTION

my head. Why? Why at the last minute had I smashed the pegs so he'd escape the justice he so richly deserved? Though Clarissa had influenced my decision, I hadn't done it for her. Up until now, I'd been convinced it had been a voice right from God, but now, we were in deeper trouble and a lot closer to dying. Whatever faith I thought I'd possessed had flown with the crows. If I didn't solve this, we would die. It was that simple.

I slipped back into the jungle while the men on the other side still cautiously surveyed the grassy glade that should have been our last view of Costa Rica. Just before I caught up to Clarissa, the chopper pilot gave me the new coordinates. She trudged wearily forward, each step forced and deliberate.

"Lon," she laughed, low in her throat. "I'll be alright. I'm just getting tired, that's all."

"Hon, we're going to make it out of here." I reached for her hand and held it while we duck-walked down the middle of another swift-moving creek. When we reached the other side, I pointed out a faint trail that switch-backed up the ridge on the other side, kissed her, and gave her the GPS with the coordinates they'd just given me.

She looked down at it. "Wha . . .?"

"I'll catch up to you, but this is going to take a little longer. Just keep going at a steady pace. Don't worry. I will rejoin you in a couple hours." I squeezed her hand. "I love you." I handed her my phone. "Don't be afraid to call the chopper. They'll figure out a way to pick you up or get those guys to you." She nodded through the tears forming in her eyes. "I'll try. Maybe you should have . . . not killed him, but somehow

196   *David Griffith*

stopped them." She trudged forward, then turned. "God will provide an escape. I know He will."

Anger and frustration threatened to erupt. Quickly, I turned away from her trusting eyes, splashed back through the stream and up the other side to where the trail dropped off the ridge. When I looked to where she'd been standing, there was nothing but tall grass swaying in the wind. I wished I'd hugged her and not spoken so harshly. She was exhausted and scared, but still fighting, doing her best.

I studied our back-trail and shook my head in disgust. If Clarissa was going to make it, I had to slow them down again. No! Not slow them—stop them. Up until now, my strategy had only delayed the inevitable. How I wished for that sniper rifle the tracker had. But I didn't have it, and other than the .45 in my belt, I wasn't likely to get another gun of any kind.

A sudden breaking branch to my left stopped my heart. I hit the ground, rolling away from the bullet that was sure to follow. When I came to a stop, the pistol was ready, and how I'd managed that with only one good arm, was a mystery.

Over the end of the sights, Diego stared at me.

"It took you long enough," I growled. "I thought they'd killed you."

He relaxed, the air leaving his massive frame like a plastic punching bag with a hole in it. "Well, I'm not dead—at least not yet."

"Good. We need to stop these guys."

Diego shrugged. "That is not so easy, when you don't even have a rifle."

WITHOUT REDEMPTION

I pushed slowly to my feet. My arm hurt from the tumble and the new wound in my leg was bleeding again. I set my teeth and motioned for him to follow.

We backtracked down to the creek, and I showed him the direction I'd sent Clarissa. "Catch up to her and keep a steady pace north to the landing site. Do not try to cover your trail. Leave lots of sign. When I have finished, I will need to find your tracks. Never mind about them." I pointed back toward where Chapo's goons would soon show. "You will be safe. They will follow me."

Diego's face remained expressionless, but his hooded eyes flashed a moment of wary cunning. Would he double-cross us? Had Clarissa been right? Diego's story of leaving the trail to avoid pursuers was improbable. Did that mean he was somehow connected with the cartel that doggedly followed our trail? I studied his face. My mind shouted against letting him be anywhere near my wife and son, but I had no choice.

I glanced pointedly at the gun in my hand. Then my eyes moved upward until they locked onto his. "Do not let anything happen to them." My voice was barely above a whisper, but in the quiet of the forest he heard—and understood. With that, I turned and trotted back up the trail. The Sinaloa cartel had declared war. Now I would meet iron with iron, death with death, the only response they understood.

On a sharp corner in the trail, I went to work. A thick patch of bamboo provided the opportunity I needed. With my knife, I cut and sharpened one of the bigger wooden shoots, then lashed it to a long springy willow which I bent backwards across the trail. I let it spring forward. Perfect. The bent stake struck at lightning speed. The sharpened bamboo

198 *David Griffith*

dagger was fastened at chest height. The first man in the line would be severely injured, possibly killed. The tracker would probably see it before it could do any damage. That didn't matter. He would know I was setting traps, which meant he would move with extreme caution, which was exactly what I needed.

When I'd finished, I trotted two hundred yards up the trail and climbed into the fork of a Gamba tree, my heart pounding, more from anticipation than the run. Maybe the tracker would miss it. With any luck, he would die. I shifted, trying to find a more comfortable position. No longer did I care. No, I did care, but I cared more about Clarissa and Conor.

Suddenly, my eyes riveted on the trail. A face appeared at the top of the hill, then a body with a cluster of men behind him, each man tense and uneasy as they scanned the surrounding jungle. They expected trouble, which is what I'd wanted. I watched as the tracker moved back and forth, searching for sign, then dropped to one knee. The seconds ticked by as he studied my tracks. Slowly, his head came up, his eyes studying the terrain in front of him. They settled right on my hiding spot. Suddenly, he sniffed the air just like an old hound dog, rose to his feet and signaled the rest to follow. Silently, I slid to the ground and slipped into the tangle of ferns behind me. The sharpened dagger would hopefully do its work. Regardless of the outcome, it should slow their progress.

After I was out of sight, I trotted down through a draw and zigzagged past a big Madero, its leafy branches soaring a hundred feet in the air. A howler monkey suddenly bel-

WITHOUT REDEMPTION 199

lowed overhead. Instant high voltage current froze me in my tracks. After my heart started again, I slogged through the bottom of a muddy wash and switch-backed up the other side. I would have liked to watch the tracker reached the stake trap I'd set. Would he blunder into it? Had he died, or would it be one of the others? I stared at my back-trail as a new level of antagonism boiled through my chest driving whatever compassion I'd felt to the four winds.

I spent a few minutes creating a jumble of tracks around a little stream. If the tracker survived my trap, I didn't want him to think Clarissa and I weren't still together. Though it was difficult creating a set of tracks that looked like hers, I did my best. Her smaller tennis shoes had a distinctive herringbone tread. When I'd finished, I moved on, less than satisfied with my efforts. However, with any luck, the punji stake had finished him for good and what I'd done with the tracks wouldn't matter. I tiptoed into the little creek and followed it downstream for a few hundred yards before again angling up the hillside. I laid a trail north and east. Clarissa and Conor should be to the north of me now, well away from the men behind me. Nevertheless, I had to be careful not to get too far away from their trail or I would have a difficult time reaching the new drop zone. After another hour, I veered back toward where they should be, constantly scanning the ground. I could not afford to make a mistake. There would be no opportunity to backtrack if I missed them.

Once, as I slipped through a low swale, a silent shadow slunk away from me into the deeper jungle. I stopped, not daring to breathe. The dreaded black panther wasn't usually antagonistic, but one was wise to give them a wide berth.

After the panther retreated, I limped onward, still angling northeast toward the San Juan River. Always, I scanned the leaf mold in front of me for any sign of disturbance while keeping a careful eye on my back-trail. If my trap had not disabled or killed the tracker, my immediate future would be difficult. I scrambled to the top of a hill and squatted in a leafy thicket with my back against the smooth, gray bark of a giant Ceiba. It was time I found out what had happened back there. I needed to know, because if he still followed me, I had to come up with a different plan.

What if I couldn't shake them? A dozen escape possibilities paraded through my mind, none of them good and most of them impossible with Clarissa and a six-month-old baby. I discarded each one while my eyes riveted to the trail below me for the first sign of the approaching men. One appeared, followed by another. Soon they all stood in the open, apparently arguing over their next strategy. I started to count them, anxiously trying to pinpoint the tracker. I ticked them off my list as each man appeared. Nine. I waited. One was missing. Instantly, I realized the tracker was not in the bunch below me. Had I missed him? I counted again while I scanned the surrounding jungle. No, they were one man short. Instantly, I panicked.

I never heard the shot, but then one never does until after the bullet splatters fragments of metal and bone through your body.

Chapter 28

When that bullet drove me backward, I rolled frantically to the right, then crawled away, searching for cover in the thick laurel behind me. Panic shot adrenalin to every corner of my body. More than anything else, I needed an escape, a place to hole up and assess the damage. Desperation forced me into a staggering trot. A red stain spread over my right shoulder. Blood dripped down my sleeve and off the ends of my fingers. Now, neither arm worked, and my mistake loomed large in front of me.

Through a moment of carelessness, I'd let the tracker get to me. No more shots followed the first one, so I skittered down to a decent hiding spot in a leafy bowl and scanned the hillside to the left from where I presumed the shot had come. Finally I spotted him, far up on the knob, but only because he lifted a hand toward his face. I doubted he'd slapped at a mosquito. More likely, it was a salute to the dead.

I'd seen enough. A determination to survive forced me to stumble further over the backside of that hill. Carefully, I threaded my way into the midst of a jumbled pile of lava rock until I found a hiding place. It was time to assess the new damage—and stop the flow of blood. I leaned back against one of the boulders, panting heavily, trying to breathe through the knife-like pain slicing through my upper body. My shirt, when I pulled it away was now soaked with blood, and when I surveyed the damage, I found the whole right side of my chest had been hamburgered into a grisly mess. Like it or not, I needed to take a minute to clean it up and do whatever else was necessary to keep infection at bay. And, I really needed to figure out how to buy Clarissa more time. I had little doubt—I was done for. Several times, I raised my head to search the surrounding jungle. My carelessness had cost me my life. Worse, I'd endangered Clarissa and Conor, because now I would no longer be able to keep the tracker busy enough for them to escape.

I leaned my head back against a rock. Until I'd noticed the missing man, I'd been sure I was safe. Foolishly, I'd dismissed that higher knoll to my right. It had been at least two hundred yards away, but that would not have been a difficult shot for the tracker.

Suddenly, the birds around me went silent. That meant danger, and I dived down behind the rock.

MAYBE THE INDIAN HAD heard him move, but Paolo didn't think so. The man, like a wild jaguar, sensed when there was danger. The moment he'd pulled the trigger, his prey had disappeared into the rocks. Paolo snapped off one more round, but only had a quick glimpse of what he thought might be the Indian ghosting through the trees. His bullet had been wasted, uselessly spent where the man had been a millisecond before it arrived. Once more, this Stone Age adversary had eluded him, and now Paolo had a sickening feeling that this morning, his pride had forced him into

WITHOUT REDEMPTION 203

a grave error. He should have killed the Indian when he had the chance.

Paolo slipped from tree to tree, constantly scanning the jungle ahead, a carbon copy of what he'd done a thousand times with Lorenzo. What was he doing wrong? He should have easily killed the man long before now—and then he saw the bloody trail. The Indian was hit, bleeding badly, scrambling to get away. Excited by his discovery, Paolo scanned the scuff marks in the rotting leaf mold. More blood spots. The man couldn't go far this way. He jacked a shell into the chamber, confident that he would soon come on his body. Nevertheless, he kept a close eye on the trail ahead. This was not an ordinary man.

Once, he glanced over his shoulder. Chapo and his men were close. They'd heard the shots and would wait for a report and further instructions, but he couldn't waste time. The Indian would be *his* kill. This, he would do alone. Those behind him could figure out the trail on their own. He trotted forward, alert to any possible ambush, confident the grueling chase was nearly over. In one sense, he felt disappointment. He felt a curious bond with this man, one that was hard to explain. How had he come by the skills that had kept him alive, when he should have been dead five times over?

The blood-spotted trail held his attention as he slipped forward. His pace quickened. No one could lose that much blood and survive, never mind be a threat. Still, he would take no chances. This man would be dangerous until he cut off his head.

Like a wounded animal, his quarry had moved uphill, as if some primordial instinct had taken over, like he was trying

David Griffith

to get upwind to pinpoint his pursuer. Paolo shook his head. That was crazy. Wasn't it?

The tracks led through a patch of tall grass and into some dense bushes. Paolo stopped. The hair stood up on the back of his neck. With his back to a tree, he scanned each foot of the trail. Inch by inch, his eyes dissected every bush and waving clump of grass. Something was out of place. He could feel it.

The Indian was so well hidden, Paolo had failed to see his outline. The first out-of-place item that registered was the dusky, blued barrel of the pistol surrounded by green background, a near match for the hair that fell over the man's forehead. Underneath that black lock of hair, hard, unblinking eyes stared at him, different than this morning. They were almost sad, and they held Paolo's like a vise. The voice, when he spoke was low, and his Spanish words carried a distinctive lilting drawl.

"Let us be done with this. I am not who you seek, nor do I wish to harm you. But if you want to live, go home and take those who follow me with you." The stranger said more, words that hardly registered.

Paolo tried to speak. He had a need to say something before he died. He didn't want to be afraid, but he was—more than he'd ever been in his life. Somewhere in the conversation, Paolo realized he was walking back the way he had come. Chapo's sniper rifle lay on the ground behind him—but he was alive. Once, he turned, wanting desperately to see the man's face again, to ask the question that burned his tortured soul. For the second time, the Indian hadn't killed him? Why? And the eyes . . . they hadn't taunted him.

The Indian truly did not *want* to kill. What made him different? He possessed the jungle skills of the ancients, more than anyone Paolo had ever encountered, and yet for some reason, when the opportunity came, this strange man had not pulled the trigger. Was it some moral compass that guided him, some insane creed that wouldn't allow him to kill his enemies? The man was badly wounded. He must understand he could never escape. Paolo shook his head and rubbed at his eyes with the back of his hand. What karma did the man have that was so powerful he would risk his wife and *niño*? Because if the Indian died, they would die as well.

WHEN I SPOTTED THE tracker on my trail, I eased my broken arm around to the small of my back and tugged the nine millimeter out of my belt. Blood still oozed from my chest, and my right arm was numb. I holed up in a clump of brush and held the gun clumsily in front of me, the barrel resting on a branch as I watched the tracker follow my trail. He peered to the left and right. His life, like mine. was attuned to danger. He sensed something. Nevertheless, he kept coming, his eyes searching the foliage in front of him. I was well hidden and completely still, but he was no fool. His eyes widened at the sudden recognition of the dark barrel of that pistol in my hand. It was as steady as I could hold it, aimed right at his second shirt button. Little did he know, because of my debilitating wounds, that pistol as the twigs surrounding it.

For what seemed like a month, our eyes locked. He figured he was going to die. I did nothing to dissuade him of the notion. I was tired, hurt, and though I wouldn't have admitted it, scared—for me, for my wife, for my little son. Without the use of either of my arms, the fight was over, and because I'd lost so much blood, escape could never happen.

When the tracker spoke, his voice was low, holding a new fear, and the sound of it barely reached me. *"Eres un hombre fuerte."*

"I am strong enough to defeat those who follow. You will *not* be able to kill me. Drop the gun." My voice was flat, devoid of any emotion.

Slowly, he lowered the expensive sniper rifle he held in his hand to the ground.

"If you do exactly as I say, I may not kill you. Then again, I might. I am really tired of your people following me. I was not responsible for what happened back at that meeting in San Carlos. Do you understand?" Though I doubted he believed or cared what I said, I wanted to at least sow a seed of doubt—and take that high-powered rifle. As long as he had that, my chances of survival were slim to none. With it, I could kill him anytime I chose—and he would know it.

"Walk back the way you came."

He turned and started down the trail. A hundred feet away, he glanced over his shoulder, and even at that distance I read the disbelief in his eyes that he was alive. The nine millimeter in my hand zeroed into the middle of his back, my index finger curled around the trigger. But with two useless arms, cocking that gun had been impossible.

Chapter 28

When the assassin walked out of sight, I scrambled out of my inadequate hideout, fumbled the sniper rifle strap over my shoulder and stumbled into a running walk through the jungle. Things had changed for the better. I was now fully armed—that is if I could force my arms to work well enough to shoot this thirty caliber nail driver. Whatever moral code had stayed my hand was no longer existent. If they got me, then Clarissa and Conor would be easy prey. Besides, anybody in their right mind wouldn't think twice about skewering every one of those miserable coyotes.

I tried to hunch the rifle into a more comfortable position on my shoulder. Now, I avoided any trail, and though rocky ground was scarce, I did my best to cover my tracks. Another spasm of pain from my newly injured arm elicited a groan, and I sank to the ground. The time had come to slip my shirt off and inspect the wound. If I was going to die, I needed to prepare in whatever way was necessary. A rotting log by another of the constant streams of trickling water provided an adequate seat, and I sat and stared down at the bloody mess around my right shoulder. My shirt peeled away with a minimum of discomfort. It hadn't been long enough for the blood to really dry and stick, so it came away easy enough.

Every piece of wood in that wet jungle steamed in the afternoon heat, probably an ideal environment for every kind of infection and sepsis known to man. I steeled myself to focus on what could only be a bloody mess of cartilage and bone toward my right shoulder. The tail of my shirt served as a washrag, and I dipped it in the stream and started to bathe the congealed blood away to better see the actual damages. As I stared at the raw meat, I tried to recreate the actual shot, the angles, and the possible damage. A deep crease in the skin between my chest and arm still seeped blood which ran down under my belt. The hole in my shoulder sprouted the edges of a twig. I grimaced, afraid to disturb it but knowing there was little choice. Again, I tried to remember where the shooter had stood, up slope and off to my right. The angle made no sense, and suddenly I understood what had happened. The end of the sliver of wood stuck out a quarter of an inch, hard to get my nearly useless fingers around. Finally, I got a grip on the pieces of wood in my chest, grimaced with pain, and pulled the remains of the staub out of the deep groove it had carved in the muscle. The bullet had probably clipped the edge of the tree trunk beside me, then ricocheted off and sliced along my bicep and chest. Other than causing a lot of pain, there should be no life-threatening damage. It had clipped a vein which spewed blood everywhere, enough to have convinced me I was mortally wounded. I would survive, albeit with considerable stiffness and discomfort.

After I'd soaked off most of the blood and cleaned some bark and other debris from the furrow in my chest, I struggled into my shirt, and hoisted the sniper rifle sling over my shoulder. The sun, now lower in the western quadrant, had

WITHOUT REDEMPTION

settled at the top of the trees. There might be two hours of daylight left, never enough to make it to Clarissa or the landing pad before dark.

I trudged through the dense undergrowth, leaving more signs than I had all day. To the tracker that would read like a two-inch newspaper banner. But the fact that I had the sniper rifle would loom large in his mind, and though he would follow me easily, he would be cautious. The leather strap of the rifle felt warm and gave me a sense of security I'd not had until now. I pictured myself lying well-concealed in a clump of bamboo or sugarcane, the high-powered optics exactly two and one-half inches in front of my right eye, the crosshairs of the scope centered on the tracker's chest as he walked into the sights. It wouldn't matter where I hit him. I didn't even especially want him dead, only that he was incapacitated enough to quit following us.

The bullet hole in my leg hurt more than it had all day, and my chest wound had now started to throb and spasm. I tried to work my arms and fingers, but it did little good. The ground had turned soft and sludgy, slowing my progress. Hopefully it hindered those behind me as well. Constantly, I scanned the ground in front of me for snakes or other lethal critters. One foot in front of the other became my motto—my life. I wanted nothing more than to find a path forward, a way to win this suicidal game.

It was then I spotted the tracks. I stood over them willing them to be older, different, but they were no more than a few hours old. Clarissa shouldn't have been this far to the east, which meant she wasn't at the helicopter site. Diego's heavy tread was clear, but now there another set had joined them which sent a new set of muscle spasms across my chest.

Farther on, the tracks mingled under a spreading Guanacaste tree. A tired grin creased my stubbled face. Conor had slowed their progress. Good for him. Four feet away from the base of the tree, fresh dirt covered a small square of ground. I scraped the soil away until the tiny edge of a dirty diaper peeked out of the soft earth. Clarissa always took great pride in leaving a camp undisturbed, with no sign of our human presence. She had deliberately left that for me, knowing I would find it.

I limped around the edges of the area where they'd rested. Toe scuff marks. A half-smoked cigarette butt lay carelessly thrown where the new man had paced back and forth. Clearly he wanted to be moving. My squalling kid slowed their progress. How long would they put up with that? My jaw clenched, anger battling with a mushroom cloud of fear. Painfully, I sank to the ground to trace Clarissa's track with the tips of my fingers. I shouldn't have trusted Diego. I'd stifled the uneasiness because I needed him. For that, I'd been a fool.

Quickly, I smoothed over the tracks, then backtracked a hundred yards. Hopefully, the tracker would be intent enough on my trail, he would miss the ones I'd rubbed out. When I carried on, I made sure I left lots of signs, enough it would appear I'd walked ahead a few feet, then changed my mind in order to veer farther east. After I'd laid a good trail into a small creek, I doubled back to follow Clarissa's track. With danger both ahead and behind me, it had become even more important to catch up to her.

WITHOUT REDEMPTION 211

The last rays of the evening sun had enough heat to warm my back and dry a small portion of the ever-present dampness from my clothes as I hurried forward. Who really was Diego? Was he allied with one of the cartels, or was he just a freelancer looking for a quick buck who thought he would be generously rewarded for turning over Clarissa and Conor to Chapo. If so, then he understood little of their savage barbarity. If he was very lucky his reward would be a quick and mostly painless death, and that would only happen because they were busy with me. El Chapo never left loose ends, nor was it likely he would be ready to advertise his presence in this country, at least not yet. And who was the man who had joined Diego? To that, I had no answer.

The gathering darkness now made travel difficult. Since I'd taken the rifle, I'd not seen or heard anything behind me, but the loss of blood and my stiff arm were a constant reminder of my worsening situation. When I could no longer find my way, I stopped to rest while I contemplated a plan. Though I'd been able to move at a reasonably good limp, I doubted I'd gained any ground. Diego had swung to the northwest, toward Los Chiles on the Nicaraguan border. Would they use one of the rural boat or ferry operators to take Clarissa into Nicaragua and the safety of the vast jungle to the north? Once there, he could disappear and take his time in making the most lucrative trade, if he hadn't already. The other man's presence meant that was a distinct possibility.

Diego and the new man had a woman with a baby, and I might add, at times a cantankerous one. Whether it was the Indian or the Irish in him, that little guy knew what he wanted, and if he got shorted on grub, trouble would follow, which made me worry. What would they do if Conor wouldn't stop crying? I stumbled over a log and grimaced as I skidded to the ground on my knees. Painfully, I slumped forward until the pain subsided and I could again struggle to my feet.

An hour later, a faint, acrid odor touched my nostrils. Instantly I crouched lower in the tall grass. My eyes searched the surrounding Matapalo, and the intertwined roots of the soaring Encino. Carefully, I eased the still useless handgun out of my belt. Then I spotted the source of the smell and exhaled my held breath in a wave of relief. Three feet in front of me, a still smoldering cigarette butt lay in the grass. This was the right direction. Clarissa and Conor were ahead of me.

A bearing by the stars isn't as good as a GPS but you don't need batteries, so I set a course the same way my ancestors would have done, and became one with the night. What I was doing carried tremendous risk. If Diego changed direction, I would not be able to go back and again pick up their trail. But I could never sit and wait for daylight. Other than the occasional firefly, the stars above provided the only relief from the blackness of the night. Somehow, I would find my family.

Chapter 29

I ground the still live butt into the dirt, hitched the heavy rifle higher on my shoulder and ducked from one tree to the next. How far away was the big river that separated Costa Rica from Nicaragua? That still appeared to be their destination. A quick glance overhead confirmed what I already knew. A large bank of cloud would soon obliterate what little moonlight I had. Going forward would be increasingly more difficult.

Twenty minutes later, I dropped down to the edge of a small meadow and followed it north. At the far edge, a tangled mass of vines and bushes concealed anything that might resemble a way to the river. To strike off through the jungle would be pointless and dangerous in this inky blackness. Besides, though I knew a ferry landing lay somewhere ahead, I had no idea which way it might be.

The night chorus of the jungle surged around me. Far-off, the deep bellow of the ever-present howler monkeys competed with the closer squeals of wild pigs fighting over territory, mates, or whatever else pigs argue about. Some kind of carrion bird swooped in and landed on a branch over my head. No doubt, he reckoned the odds were at least even that I would be his next meal in this paradise of death. I tried to remember the last map I'd so casually studied at the ranch. The road running north to Los Chiles should lie to

214 *David Griffith*

the west. Would they go that way with Clarissa and Conor? Diego would have no desire to spend another mosquito-infested night in the jungle, and he probably would know exactly where to hole up safely—on either side of the river.

A rising sense of panic and fear threatened to choke any rational decision I might make. Would Diego and his new partner take his captives upriver to San Carlos, or did they have other options deep in the jungle? My best chance of success was to get to the river before they did. Knowing I hadn't the strength to jog and pack the heavy sniper rifle as well, I slipped it off my shoulder. I ran my fingers down the thick barrel, hating to let go of the security it had offered. Nevertheless, I dropped it into a dark tangle of leaves on the edge of the trail. Whatever happened, I would have to do without it.

Scattered cloud now obscured a good portion of the sky above me. I'd tried to make my way by the stars but they were all strange to me, and there were few recognizable constellations. The ground generally sloped to the northwest, so I struck out in that direction, hoping that would be the easiest route to the river crossing. Once, the distant mutter of a car confirmed the presence of a road somewhere to the west. Several times in the moonless gloom, I stumbled over a hidden root or vine which shot spasms of pain through most of my body. Nevertheless, I carried on. Clarissa and Conor depended on me. I would not let them down.

Before I'd gone another mile, the jungle gave way to a long open valley. The ground ahead was sparsely treed, which greatly helped my progress.

WITHOUT REDEMPTION

Farther down the hill, I broke into a trot, the knee-high grass swishing against my pant legs. I kept a wary eye out for hostile critters, hoping the snakes and jaguars were off on other business. It wasn't to be. Before I'd stumbled through a hundred feet of that lush forage, one of the country's most feared reptiles reared up in front of me. The only snake that large was a Boa Constrictor, and even in the dim moonlight I could see he stretched to nearly twelve feet. Instantly, I had the Beretta in my hand. Though I'd been unable to cock it earlier, that snake caused involuntary muscles fueled with adrenalin to work overtime, and I no longer worried whether I'd be able to handle it when I caught up to Diego and his partner.

The big snake's head and body weaved back and forth. When he crawled forward, I backed away. I'd heard it said at the ranch that Boas aren't real aggressive unless they're threatened or hungry. That was small comfort, even though I had no intention of threatening this one. I had no hankering to blow his head off, simply because the shot would make noise, and I could ill-afford to draw any attention. I had enough trouble without drawing more.

I backed up further, but it didn't do any good. The snake's head weaved back and forth as he crawled toward me. Probably he smelled my blood-crusted shirt, which put him in the mood for a bedtime snack. I tried to be as uncooperative as a human can be, and for a moment he seemed to get the hint that I'd not be an easy meal. Then his head went down and he came straight for me. My constitution and natural temperament have never been inclined toward snake wrestling. I put a bullet in his head, or thought I did. Wherever the bul-

216   *David Griffith*

let had gone, he made a hard right and crawled away through the tall grass while I cringed at the shattering noise I'd wanted desperately to avoid.

Worry over the noise I'd made would accomplish nothing, so I again broke into a tortured, limping trot, focused on reaching the river crossing before Diego. If my worst fears were realized, and he took them into Nicaragua, anything could happen. It was possible they would just disappear. Fear caught at my throat, and though my doubts were a lot bigger than my faith in a God who cares, I pounded out a prayer as I limp-trotted down the trail. If there was ever a time I needed help, it was now. Between the loss of blood, stress, and lack of sleep, I had little reserve left. Weariness threatened to pull me down, but each time I thought about slowing, anger surged through me. I would make it, because my wife and son depended on me. Winning was now more important than at any other time in my life.

Within minutes, the ribbon of water that divided the two countries came into view. In the distance, the thick band of jungle clustered along each shoreline. Now that I didn't have the weight of the rifle, I picked up a gear. Trotting was out of the question, but I limped faster, angling toward what I hoped would be the ferry crossing. A cluster of lights twinkled far on the other side of the river, which by my reckoning had to be San Carlos.

With little warning, I broke through the thin band of trees stretching down to the river bank. Instantly I froze. Two men sat on the far side of a campfire, both staring into the flame that burned fitfully in front of them. I squatted in the underbrush and peered through the trees. One of them ap-

WITHOUT REDEMPTION 217

peared to be young, barely more than a kid, but I well knew in the cartel culture, kids cut their teeth on gun barrels. A few were seasoned *sicarios*—killers before they reached their teenage years. The other man was stooped, with long gray hair touching his shoulders. The kid sat on the ground, but the old one perched on a broken stump, his chin resting on the butt of a crook-ended walking stick. Poverty appeared to have hovered over them like a flock of hungry turkey buzzards. I moved cautiously forward, then silently stepped into the light of their fire. Both heads instantly swiveled my way, their faces startled by my unannounced presence. Instant fear touched the youngster's face, but the old man's eyes moved up and down my frame with no expression. His weary gaze rested on the gun in my hand. Being cautious by both nature and training, I held it more to ward off trouble than to start any.

My words broke through the silence. "I come to your camp with no ill will." The only sound other than my voice was the occasional crackle of the little fire in front of them.

The kid's furtive eyes riveted to the pistol barrel. "We don't have any money." He dug at the damp earth with the short stick he held in his hand.

"It's not your money I seek." I moved closer and stood across from them, careful not to look into the flames, the gun held easily at my side while I watched and listened for any other sound. They might be harmless, but I would take no chance, and if trouble came, I would not want my night vision to be hampered by the light of the fire.

218 *David Griffith*

"Where are you going?" My eyes moved back and forth, but mostly I watched the young one. If trouble started, it would come from him.

The old man answered, his gaze still wearily fixed on the burning coals. "Home to San Miguelito."

"You are Nicas?" I asked, using the local slang term for Nicaraguans.

Both heads moved up and down in unison.

"What brings you to this side of the river?"

The old man pushed a stick into the fire. "My son worked here. He was killed. I came to get my grandson." He gestured toward the boy beside him.

I nodded. His words had the ring of truth but I still kept a wary eye on the young one. The initial fear on his face had now turned to a sneering bravado. His hands fidgeted restlessly. One started to creep behind a rock beside where he sat. I raised the gun slightly and moved the barrel until it zeroed in on his belly. His eyes flickered to my casted arm. I couldn't hide that, but I stayed far enough from the fire he couldn't get a good look at my blood-soaked shirt. It would not do for him to see more signs of weakness, and in the dark, he'd not see that the pistol wasn't cocked.

The old man struggled to his feet and leaned heavily on the cane. "My son got involved with drug people." He stared across the fire, then his shoulders sagged. "But he wasn't bad. They shouldn't have killed him."

"Quiet, Grandfather. This man is a stranger."

The old fellow dropped his eyes to the ground and shuffled from one foot to the other. Now satisfied that these two weren't an immediate danger, I stepped backward, away from

WITHOUT REDEMPTION 219

the fire. In my condition, I should have been more careful. My foot dropped into a hole and I went down hard, hampered by the gun and my injured arms. All in all, it saved my life. The staccato bark of an AK-47 and the sharper snap of an AR-15 made the place I'd so recently vacated by my clumsiness a death zone. Hastily, I crawled into the underbrush. A hundred feet into the trees, a thicket of bamboo promised a decent level of protection. Whoever was out there would be wary of coming after me in the night. And they wouldn't have to. I was going after them.

Occasionally, a shot rang out. Several bullets scuffed the dirt, way too close to what remained of my beat-up carcass. I scuttled farther to the south of the fire. The last thing I'd seen before I tumbled over backward had been the furtive scowl on the old man's face. He'd known about those guns, and as much as I wanted to slip away, I needed to know which enemy hid in the grass on the other side of that fire.

Chapter 30

Why? Every step, that word pounded into Paolo's brain. How could he have walked into another of this bushman's hidden traps, and why had the Indian not killed him? Was he still playing some weird psychological game? Even though Chapo's men were close, he could have easily fired a couple of bullets and escaped. Paolo stopped and leaned against a eucalyptus. Great gusts of oxygen filled his lungs. He still lived, and no experience or background in his violent life could explain why.

Far back, the first of the men rounded a bend in the trail. What would he tell Chapo? How could he explain that he'd shot at the Indian with one of the best sniper rifles in the world and not killed him? That he'd walked into an ambush and the man had taken his rifle—no, Chapo's rifle? To the boss, he would look to be the most incompetent of fools. Slowly, the realization hit him. Unless he killed, or better, captured the Indian, whatever career he'd had with the Sinaloa cartel was over, which might be the least of his worries. Very likely, Chapo would order him shot on sight. Any conversation with Chapo must start with the Indian's bloody head in his hand.

The decision made, Paolo hunched out of sight, then scrambled into a dry creek bed. From there, it was easy to quarter up the hill on the other side and head north. His

WITHOUT REDEMPTION

221

job had suddenly become much more complicated. Now, it was crucial that he know where both Chapo *and* the Indian were positioned. It wouldn't take long for Chapo to realize his tracker had ditched his responsibilities. From now on, it wasn't only the Indian that would be hunted. He would be as well. Paolo scowled. He still had the pistol, but the Glock gave little comfort. He trailed a man who not only had a handgun, but was now in possession of a very accurate rifle. Behind him, nine angry men, each with semi-automatic AK-47's would shoot him on sight.

Paolo squatted at the top of the hill and watched Chapo's men as they arrived at the copse where the Indian had ambushed him and taken the rifle. The men milled around the small clearing, confused as to which way he'd gone. They waited for him to appear, for some signal as to where to go next. Well, they wouldn't get it. He took one last look at what might have been, then slipped into the trees.

What should he do? Strike south for Panama, or even Colombia? No, that was too far. The Nicaraguan border lay only a few miles to the north. If Chapo's men somehow caught up to him and he needed to do a quick escape, he could slip across the river and hide in the jungle. That seemed a dismal prospect. What then? Where would he go? What would he do?

At the top of the ridge, he shrugged and cast his fate with the Indian, or at least the direction he had been traveling. Everything he'd worked for had disintegrated like burned paper. Now his life was not worth a week-old tortilla, and the fault lay squarely on the man he followed. Paolo swore bitterly. For that, he would pay. Behind him, Chapo's men lusted for blood, and though none of them were skillful enough to follow this man through the jungle, they would not quit. Sure, they would leave—go back to Mexico, but Paolo knew; Chapo would marshal every one of his considerable forces to find him. Here in the jungle it would be child's play for him to lose Chapo's chosen. Long term—the odds were dismal. If Chapo wanted you dead—well, you were going to die. To survive, he had to have a peace offering. He had to have the Indian's head.

A hundred yards up the trail, a thought smashed into him like a striking fist. Why had he been so stupid? He didn't have to catch this man. The woman . . . he should have followed her in the first place. It wouldn't even be necessary to grab her, at least not right away. All he needed to do was watch, and be close. Sooner or later, the Indian would come to her. Let *him* stumble through the jungle. But was it too late for that? She had split off miles back, probably with the man who made the deep tracks. But the big man wouldn't have the skill of the Indian. They would be easy to catch, and then . . . a dawning plan brought a slow smile to his face. It was time he set a few traps of his own.

How he wished he still had the sniper rifle. To have it in the crook of his arm would have been comforting, but then maybe not having it was an advantage. He needed to make up for lost time, and the rifle had been heavy. Somewhere ahead, there might be other ways to acquire whatever firepower he would need.

After a wide circle around Chapo's men, followed by a long slog back to the scuffed tracks where Paolo had found the hidden cigarette butt, he found the trail he wanted.

WITHOUT REDEMPTION

Night had fallen. The woman was obviously exhausted. Her stride had shortened, and frequently she stopped, possibly more for the *niño* than for her. He squatted and touched the track with two fingers, testing the viscosity. Beside hers, the track of the big man had sunk deep in the mud, but now, another man had joined them. Paolo's hand momentarily rested in the heel print, feeling the crumbled earth, like the pulse of a live animal. Before dawn, he would catch them. What would he do to them—to her? He fingered the knife in his belt. Whoever the two men were, they would die. The woman? She must be used with finesse, played like a good poker hand to draw the Indian.

Two hours later, the trail dropped toward the bottom lands, then abruptly turned north to the remote ferry crossing a few miles east of Los Chiles. As Paolo neared the water, everything suddenly became more puzzling. The tracks of six or seven other men mingled with the two he followed. Who were they? None of those behind him could have reached the ferry crossing ahead of him. He sifted through each track. Though some of the boot soles were close, none fit the sharply ridged prints he'd observed around the areas where Chapo's men had camped. Within sight of the river crossing, the trail disappeared. Lorenzo's words hammered a near-forgotten message into his ears. "Never presume. If the story doesn't fit the tracks, then find out why." And nothing fit here. This sudden disappearance made no sense.

Paolo backtracked to study the new tracks. Who were the men who had taken the woman—and what was their destination? Within a few hundred yards he knew they were headed for the ferry which would take them north into

David Griffith

Nicaragua. He trotted toward the crossing, more worried than ever. Chapo's men might be close. And who knew where the Indian was at? Not for the first time, Paolo considered abandoning the quest, but by the time he'd arrived at the river, anger had annihilated every thought other than killing his quarry as quickly as possible. It was then he saw the flicker of firelight through the trees. He crept closer, wondering whether it might be the Indian's camp? He quartered down the knoll, staying well concealed in the trees, but still close enough to study those around the fire. Four occupants shared a meal. His eyes riveted on the big man with the grey plaid shirt. He'd caught a glimpse of that shirt when Chapo's men had opened fire on them. Plaid shirt sat beside an old man with a long wispy beard. They seemed to be in deep conversation. The two on the other side of the fire quietly ate; one a boy, the other probably the man who had been with the big one. Two assault rifles leaned against a stump. Paolo scowled. This morning, when he'd seen the big man running behind the Indian and his woman, he'd not had a rifle. Where had he found one? Surely not the old man at the fire, unless they were more than harmless *campesinos*. Were they another cartel—either Beltrán-Leyva or Los Zetas?

With no warning, a gunshot high on the hill to the east reverberated over the valley. Paolo whirled and scanned the jungle, but nothing materialized in the dusky gloom. Below him, the big man snatched up one of the guns and signaled for the other man to follow. He watched as they moved back a hundred feet from the fire, their heads barely visible in the tall grass.

WITHOUT REDEMPTION 225

Paolo remained hidden while he continued studying the situation. The old man and the boy talked softly, their voices too low to reach beyond the glow of the fire. Then, as if a tree had suddenly uprooted and moved, a man stood in the firelight. Paolo stared at him. The Indian held a pistol, almost carelessly, as he talked to the two at the fire. His voice floated on the night air, wispy and indistinct. Suddenly, gunfire erupted. The Indian went down as if he'd been shot—or had he? Paolo would not make the same mistake again. Once more, this strange man had disappeared. Dead? Maybe, but he doubted it.

Paolo unsheathed his knife and slithered down to the grassy clearing. He stopped while still high enough to keep an eye on the other side of the fire. The two shooters had both sunk into the grass between his position and the fire. The Indian? Who knew. Within minutes, Paolo could make out his form, moving silently forward in the grass far to the right. A chuckle built low in his throat. This time, the Indian would find out he was second best. Paolo pinpointed both of the shooters ahead of him in the tall grass. Both would die. Then he would deal with the Indian.

He was nearly in striking range of the first man when the Indian yelled. The man in front of him foolishly sprayed lead in the general direction of the voice, exactly what the Indian had wanted. The shooter had foolishly given away his position. Paolo used the night noises to cover his approach. His left hand covered the man's mouth. Simultaneously, his knife plunged deep into the right side of the soft throat. The body immediately went slack.

David Griffith

Paolo silently slung the man's assault rifle over his back. Now, for the other one. He must get to him first. He wanted the Indian to find both of the men dead, to feel that first creeping dread, and know that somewhere in the tall *Estrella* grass, death awaited him as it had these others.

Paolo slipped in behind the second man, the big one with the plaid shirt. Killing him was almost too easy. But in that last second before he sliced through the pliable throat tissue, he realized there was no resistance. The man had been unconscious. Instantly he froze, and fear gripped every muscle in his body. There could be only one reason. The Indian had already been here.

Frantically, his head swiveled back and forth. How had it been possible for the Indian to be that close, and where was he now? He wiped the blade of his knife on a patch of dry grass and slithered away from the dead man as quickly as he could. His confidence fled. This Indian from the far north was even better than his old teacher, Lorenzo. Quietly, he slipped through the grass and far into the jungle. He would no longer play this game. The Indian would win, despite his injuries.

A quarter-mile upriver, the ferry man seemed reluctant to offer information, but after Paolo jammed the knife blade under his chin, he rightfully understood the gravity of the circumstances. Yes, an hour ago a woman had crossed with a small baby—and six men. He stuttered out a description of a couple of the men and suddenly, answers started to click into place. This was no longer only about Chapo, or the Indian. Those who had crossed with the woman belonged to the same cartel as those who had blown the east wall out of that

WITHOUT REDEMPTION 227

building and killed three of Chapo's men. Paolo's scalp contracted, prickling as if he was being watched through a gun sight. Too many players had a stake in this crazy game. Following the woman had just become a lot more dangerous.

He leaned over the ferry rail and fixated on the water that led to the foreign soil ahead. His lips peeled back in a snarl. Dangerous or not, he would find the woman, because if he had her, there would be no more slogging through the jungle. The Indian would come to him.

Chapter 31

Time has little meaning when death threatens, so after I'd inadvertently stuck my foot in that hole, then fallen over backward, I had little comprehension of how long it took me to crawl through the grass to the other side of that clearing. Every time I raised my head, I was grateful that the lights of the nearby village were at my back. The two shooters who lay hidden in front of me would be hampered by that light. I tried to pinpoint each position. The muzzle blast of that AR-15 had been to the left of where the old man sat, but I wasn't sure of the location of the other rifle which made me doubly cautious. I peered through a tangled patch of underbrush. The clearing was now deserted; the only trace of human presence the intermittent flicker from the coals of the dying fire.

Cautiously, I inched forward. A stirring breeze ruffled the tall grass but I could discern no human movement. Wherever the shooters lay, they had no intention of showing themselves. I crawled farther to the left. If they wanted to play "Injun in the bushes," I wasn't exactly a novice. Each time I moved, I reached ahead with the palm of my hand to identify every twig or stick that might betray my presence, something my hunter ancestors learned to do reasonably well in order to eat. This was not a time to disgrace them.

WITHOUT REDEMPTION

The night is never still in the jungle. Though the gunfire had silenced a far-off bellowing howler monkey, a whole herd of frogs now competed with a trio of chirping geckos somewhere in the small strip of trees that screened the river. The night noises felt ominous, like whatever was out there had grown wearily used to gunfire and the evils of man. Farther upriver, sporadic traffic in the town sounded a discordant note, incompatible with the deep earth smell of the jungle floor. I slipped my hat off and again raised my head to peer through the tall grass. An icicle of fear stabbed toward my belly.

Directly in front of me, a size twelve sandal obscured my vision. My eyes followed the heavy leg toward the man's back and shoulders. A fatigue cap covered some curly hair, and his face was tucked into the butt of the offending AR-15. I'd found one of them. Where the other hid was anybody's guess, but he had to be close. I slipped the knife out of my belt and focused on his carotid artery. It had to be fast. With another man out there, it would not do to let this one make any sound. I rose on my haunches, the knife in my left hand.

Though not common knowledge, it is difficult to cut an enemy's throat soundlessly. For what I had to do, there could be no more noise than a whisper in the grass. I had no wish to be shot by the other man, nor did I want him to escape.

I leaped forward, my knees extended, aiming for the point between his shoulder blades. The landing was textbook perfect. The air whooshed out of him like a punctured killer whale. I stabbed down at the base of his neck. The problem was—I couldn't do it, I suppose for the same reason I'd let the tracker go. It was that crazy Christian God thing. You don't kill—just because you can. My teeth ground together in frustration. In my profession that didn't work. These were bad guys. They, or some of their buddies had Clarissa and Conor, and they were here for one reason—to kill me. Besides, this cartel goon likely deserved to die ten times over. Nevertheless, when my one hundred and eighty pounds hit the middle of his back, I let him have the butt end of that knife on the point behind his ear. He crumpled like a soggy beach towel. I left him where he lay and started for the next one. Careful to make no sound, I inched to the right. There had been a sliver of moon earlier, but now it was obscured by cloud which made finding the other man more difficult. If I wasn't careful, I'd be right on top of the guy before I even sensed his presence. As I crept toward where I thought he would be, I tried to hurry. My last-minute decision not to kill the first man had been . . . well, there was no sense going there. If I'd killed him, I could have just out-waited this one. Eventually, he would move, and I'd have him. But if the man I'd thunked with my knife woke up, he'd groan and thrash around, causing untold grief for me. I inched forward, scanning every tuft of grass. So far, nothing stirred. Had he slipped away? Suddenly, I froze.

Something had moved right at the edge of my peripheral vision. I couldn't pinpoint it, but something was out there. I wanted desperately to ease my head above the waving grass to get a better look, but I didn't dare. If I'd seen him, he may have seen me. He was to my far left, farther from the fire than I'd thought. The position I was in meant I would be silhouetted against the fire. He'd have to move very little to have me in the sights of that AR-15.

WITHOUT REDEMPTION 231

I crawled forward another six feet. Who were the two shooters, and what did they have to do with the old man and the boy? And most of all, where were Clarissa and Conor? Fear for them must have made me a bit crazy. There's no other way I can explain what I did next. My hand rested on a chunk of tree limb. It looked to be about two feet long. I closed my fist over it and threw it in the general direction where I'd glimpsed movement, then yelled into the darkness. "Your friend is dead, and now I'm coming for you." Immediately, I shifted over behind a tree and it was a good thing because he opened up on full automatic, which an AR-15 isn't supposed to do. It obviously had been modified to spray a lot of lead in a hurry. He hadn't needed to do that. A professional would have stayed quiet, and not given away his position, which would have made me very cautious. Whoever lay there was scared—with a nearly empty rifle, though I'd not bank on that.

I left the cover of the tree, making no more sound than a prowling big-horned owl. The man had been at least fifty feet away when he shot, and I'd seen no movement after that rifle burst. I worked around and came in behind him. At the last, I worried because after the wild shooting, he'd made no sound. Had he somehow crawled away and escaped? Finally, ahead of me I saw the outline of his boots sticking out of a patch of tall grass. One slow inch at a time, I slipped closer. He made no move, seemingly oblivious to my presence. I half stood, and when I did I felt the blood again run down the inside of my arm. It scared me. The wooziness made me unsteady. One step closer . . . same move . . . knees extended. Make sure he had no wind to yell out a warning. At the last moment, the moon peeked out from behind a cloud. My forward momentum stopped, and I slid down beside him, patting the ground, searching for the rifle. The AR-15 had vanished. His head lolled sideways at an odd angle, the mouth slack. Dark fluid stained his cheek and chin, his arms splayed out in front of him. I reached for his neck. The still body and jagged wound in his throat told me everything I needed to know. Diego was dead.

Chapter 32

My chest constricted with sudden fear. Whoever had killed Diego now had his rifle. Were the sights trained on me? I slipped a dozen yards away from his body and lay unmoving in the tall grass. Was it the tracker who had stabbed his life away? And where had Diego left my family? Unanswered questions bombarded me, each exploding like a hand grenade in my chest, and I didn't like any of the possible answers. I well knew how little respect the cartel had for life. Mostly they killed for a reason, but sometimes, like rabid wolves they spread blood and mayhem solely for the perverted joy of killing. I searched the surrounding area, then, partially concealed by a tree trunk, I stood and scanned each section of grass and brush between me and the smoky bed of coals where the old man and the boy had sat.

It's not in me to be superstitious, and to my knowledge, none of my ancestors ever claimed to have the gift of second sight, but I had a sixth-sense feel of lurking danger. Could it have been the old man or the boy who killed Diego? That hardly seemed possible.

Now, not killing the first man seemed like a stroke of divine guidance. One way or another, he was going to talk. I inched back to where I'd left his unconscious body. He lay without moving. I frowned and stuck the back of my hand over his carotid artery. He should have stirred by now. No

David Griffith

pulse, and my hand came away covered in blood. Unable to roll him over with either arm, I tucked a knee under his torso and turned him face up. His head lolled back against the ground and a sudden chill ran up my spine. The deep slit across his throat was mute evidence of how he'd died. But how . . . when I'd been so close? Nobody could have done that—except the tracker. I peered into the dead man's face, more disturbed than I'd want to admit. By the light of the moon, nothing in his face was recognizable. He wasn't one of Chapo's men, at least not one of those who had been in the room at San Carlos. Besides, if he was Sinaloa cartel, why would the tracker kill him? And what about the old man and the boy? Were they really only a couple of peasants, like so many others, caught in the crossfire of the drug wars that spanned a good portion of the continent? That seemed believable, but believing in coincidences wasn't my strong suit. Nothing here added up, and though it was unlikely I'd ever find who Diego had *really* been, I had little doubt who had killed him.

I eased away from the body while twinges of fear ate into my belly. Now more than ever, every move I made had to be precisely calculated, because the man who was out there was as good, maybe better, than I'd ever been—and he had two arms. With painstaking care, I again scanned the whole area. It took me over an hour to work my way back to the other side of the still smoky campfire. When I felt it was safe, I stood in the shadows and listened to the night sounds, straining to hear any offbeat sound, to discern anything out of the normal. Far off, a bird of prey screeched its familiar hunting cry. In the clearing, no sound broke the silence, which too

WITHOUT REDEMPTION

often meant death and danger. Even the frogs and the geckos hid in their holes. I leaned into the rough bark of a towering *Kapok* tree, attempting to become one with the jungle. Like a dysfunctional flock of barn swallows, every option flitted through my mind. This terrain was foreign to me, but the animals here had the same survival instinct as the wild ones in the mountains of Montana or the deep bush country of British Columbia. The hunted avoided the hunters, the small ones gave way to the large, and in season, every male and female made the mating sounds and moves that led to the wonder of procreation. My back slid down the tree and I squatted in the damp, clingy leaf mold. I would have liked to talk to that old man again. I had a strong hunch he'd been well acquainted with Diego and his partner. There was a good chance he would know much about where I could find Clarissa and Conor.

The river crossing lay less than a mile away. The last tracks of the men who had Clarissa and Conor had pointed that direction, so I struggled to my feet and trudged toward the same ferry crossing I'd used before.

The hour was late when I arrived. There should be few customers this time of the night. Newvertheless, I waited and watched from the tree line, not at all inclined to stumble into any more unhealthy circumstances. This day had provided more than enough battles.

A flat barge made its way slowly through the current, unloaded two people on the other side and immediately returned. I strolled out to the ferry landing, looking like any other weary traveler at the end of the day.

"Hola, amigo. How much is the fare?"

236   *David Griffith*

"*Treinta córdobas.*"

Thirty Nicaraguan *córdobas* seemed like a lot, but I handed him fifty *colones*, Costa Rican money. Here on the border, it didn't matter what currency you had. Either would work.

He took the bills. I walked onto the barge, and he started for the far shore. As he worked the boat out into the current, I leaned out over the rail. "Nice night. Had much traffic?"

He shrugged. "A bit."

Out of the corner of my eye, I saw he was a big man, in surprisingly good condition considering his sedentary occupation. Light from the small bow lamp struck the side of his expressionless features, his eyes intent on the chocolate current ahead of us. I decided to take a chance. "Did you have a woman passenger tonight, one with a small baby?"

His eyes flickered over my face. He stared at the water as if assessing whether he should divulge any information. Finally, he nodded. "Yes, one crossed earlier—six men with her. It would have been my best trip today."

"How long ago?"

He shrugged. "An hour." He glanced at his watch. "Maybe a couple."

"You said six men? Are you sure?"

He scowled. "Of course I'm sure. They never paid. I will remember every one of them. Drug cartels!" He spat the word out and instantly glanced sideways, wondering if he'd said too much. "Where are you from? You are not Costa Rican. Neither are you a Nica?"

I shrugged, trying to put him at ease. "Consider me a friend from far away. That woman. She had long, sandy colored hair?"

WITHOUT REDEMPTION 237

"*Si. Muy hermosa.* Very beautiful. Why do you look for her?"

"She is my wife."

"And the little one is yours?"

I nodded.

His eyes once more left the river ahead and riveted onto mine. "How did this happen?"

"We had trouble and had to run to escape. I trusted a man to take care of my wife and son while I led the evil ones away. It was not a good choice."

"You are a man of the jungle?"

"No. In my country there is no jungle, but there are great forests where I have spent much time. To survive in the wild places in this country is more difficult, but some things are the same."

He maneuvered into the landing and secured the boat, apparently in no great hurry to return to the other side. "What are you going to do?"

"I will follow them, no matter where they go. The woman and little boy are very dear to me."

"Of course. But you are one against six, or maybe a hundred. One man cannot—"

"I will do whatever is required. It is not in me to quit."

"Where do you think they've taken your wife?"

I shrugged. I'd made one mistake with Diego, and though this man seemed of a different stripe, I'd take no chances.

The ferryman nodded and stuck his hands deep in his pockets as he studied my face. "It is no business of mine, but

238 *David Griffith*

I do not like to see the Mexican drug cartels bring their destruction to our country. We have enough evil of our own."

"Yes, they care little who they hurt, whether their own people or others."

"That I well know." He leaned one elbow against the starboard railing and stared out over the water. "If by chance you go to San Carlos tonight . . . ?" His voice trailed into silence.

I waited, not wanting to pressure him. He was as wary of me as I was of him, and rightly so. It wasn't a country or a time to trust strangers.

Suddenly, as if he'd made his decision, he spoke. "Go to my cousin at El Lago Cantina. He won't betray you, and . . . he will know where they have taken her. Six men and a woman will not enter San Carlos without his knowledge. His name is Manuel. Tell him Raymundo sent you."

As I stepped off the boat, I nodded and thanked him, truly grateful for the help he'd given me. I started to walk away, but his voice stopped me.

"*Señor*, one more thing. A man crossed after the woman, one with very dark skin, of medium height. He asked about the woman as well."

"Did he have green eyes?"

"Yes, they are the first thing one notices, the cold eyes of a killer, and—"

"He had a rifle; a *cuerno de chivo?*"

The man nodded. "Yes, he was a man of the cartels. Every mother's son of them is armed with an AK-47."

Before the ferryman cast away, I handed him another fifty *colones*. "You have been much help. This is only a small token of my appreciation. Perhaps someday I can return the

WITHOUT REDEMPTION   239

favor you have done me." With that, I turned and followed the tracker toward San Carlos. He was ahead of me, but perhaps this Manuel had information he lacked. Clarissa could not be far, and if I had to move a mountain, I would get there.

Within the hour, I stumbled past the first dilapidated houses on the outskirts of San Carlos. Pain now washed over me in an unbroken wave, and weariness drug me down worse than any time I could remember. On the lake side of the town, I spotted the El Lago Cantina. The pistol lay flat against my back, and I pulled out the tail of my shirt to cover it. A gun in plain sight would only invite trouble, and I already had plenty. I had no need to borrow more.

A shorter version of the ferryman slouched behind a rustic plank bar. His eyes followed me when I walked through the door and slid onto a rickety stool.

He walked to the end of the bar where I sat. ""What would you like?"

"You are Manuel?"

His eyes narrowed. "I might be."

"Raymundo sent me. He says you would know if some men with a woman and a baby arrived in town tonight."

His eyes instantly slid away. "In these difficult times it is foolish to see too much."

I waited.

He set a glass down under the counter. "Do you want a drink?"

"No. I have much to do. If they are here, I must find them." I leaned an elbow on the bar. "Raymundo brought them across the river. They stiffed him."

He growled a curse and scanned the room. "Wait."

240 *David Griffith*

Three men sat at a corner table, dust-covered tradesmen whiling away a social hour before returning to their homes. Manuel signaled me over to the far corner of the bar, a good distance from any listening ears. He lowered his voice. "These men will be at Rudolpho's. They will take her there as well."

I leaned forward, my face close to his. "Rudolpho's?"

"It is a house on the biggest island in the harbor." He wiped at the moisture on another glass and nervously checked the door to the street. "Go down to the marina . . . maybe a mile."

"So who is Rudolpho?"

"You are not from around here? Everyone in Nicaragua knows Rudolpho."

I shrugged, while I studied the dozen bottles arrayed on the ledge behind the bar, hoping he would provide more information. I felt his eyes studying me, but I resisted the urge to meet his gaze.

Finally he spoke. "Rudolpho owns a liquor franchise for the whole country. He is very rich—and corrupt." His voice dropped into a bitter growl as he turned away.

"How can one get to this island?"

He uncapped three brown bottles and placed them on his tray. As he stepped around the end of the bar to deliver the drinks, he glanced at me. "I have said enough. I have to survive here long after you are gone. But go to the marina and ask for Javier." He shrugged. "He might help you."

It was my turn to nod, my heart full of gratitude. Like his brother Raymundo, he'd taken a big risk. "*Adiós*, Manuel. *Muchas gracias*. I will not forget what you have done."

WITHOUT REDEMPTION 241

His eyes darted in my direction before he hoisted the tray and turned toward the table in the far corner. "*De nada*. Be very careful. You will need God and all the angels if you expect to come back alive."

I had no doubt of that. To try to rescue my wife and son from what would undoubtedly be a heavily guarded island fortress would be impossible. Even if I could get to them, how would we escape?

A garbage-strewn boulevard led me to the lake, and from there I followed the shoreline until a small marina appeared in front of me. Three or four paint-peeled sailboats bobbed up and down, the steady breeze nudging them into rebellion against the lines tethering them to the short wooden pier. On the other side, a fishing boat with a hundred-horse outboard shared space with a thirty-foot yacht. It was long past dark, so no boat owners tinkered with sails or rigging. The place felt foreign, a world completely alien to my cowboy life.

I walked past the yacht. Silver fittings gleamed in the reflection of the sporadic overhead lights. At the end of the dock, the fish boat showed more activity. A wary brown face studied me as I approached. The eyes carried no welcome which didn't matter a hoot to me. I wasn't here to win a popularity contest. "*Hola, amigo*. Could you tell me where I can find Javier?"

"I am Javier. What do you want?" he asked sullenly.

"You."

"Why?"

"Manuel sent me."

242 David Griffith

"So? Manny sends lots of people. What is it you want? Fishing, or a sailing tour of the islands? Either one, I can take you tomorrow morning at nine."

"No. I want to go to the big island—now, tonight."

He peered at me in the murky darkness, his one word answer clipped and final. "No."

"Why? I will pay whatever you want—within reason."

His dark eyes narrowed. "No. Get somebody else. Tourists do not go out there, especially at night."

"Yes, I am aware of that, but it is important that you drop me there."

He stared suspiciously. "No! It is too dangerous. If I did that, I would be dead before morning."

"Not if I slipped over the side, and nobody knew I'd been on *your* boat."

Again he shook his head while he replaced the cowling over the engine.

I reached into my jeans and drug out a thick roll of American hundred dollar bills, licked my thumb for the proper effect and started peeling them off. The mahogany face in front of me contorted between greed and fear while he chewed over my proposition. His mind was obviously working overtime, while he tried to assess risk versus reward.

Contrary to Frederick's usual parsimony, this trip he had insisted I carry a wad of cash. He certainly hadn't given me any instructions for spending it, and the rolled up stash had been nothing but a pain, until now. When I'd counted out five hundred dollar bills, I ripped them off the pile and extended them toward him. He didn't even hesitate. His lips flattened and he shook his head. I put five more with them.

WITHOUT REDEMPTION 243

He eyed them, but his head still wagged back and forth. Still a no. This was no time to quit. I peeled off another three, stuck the rest back in my jeans and waved the crisp green bills within his reach. He stared out over the water, his face immobile, unreadable. Suddenly, he reached for them, but I pulled my hand back, cut the pile in half and gave him part. "The other half when I go overboard. And—we have to be no more than a hundred yards from shore. No more. You do not have to wait for me. I will find my own way off the island."

How I would find Clarissa and Conor and get us all back to the mainland was not something I wanted to think about. There was bound to be at least one boat there. An escape plan would have to come later. My right arm throbbed in unison with the ache in my rapidly stiffening left. I flexed my fingers, trying to regain some mobility. Each movement sent shooting pains down into my hand until I finally gave up.

Javier stuffed the bills inside his jacket. I moved to step onto the boat, but he held up his hand and motioned me to an older panga down the beach with an eighty horse Mercury that appeared to have been minted in the last century. "We will go far out past the island, then come back and approach it from the lake side. Perhaps they will think we are coming back to the harbor after a long day of fishing."

I nodded agreement and settled onto the middle bench, close to the starboard oarlock. Javier untied the painter and shoved the boat into the deep water. Though a shred of daylight still cast its last light over the bay, the moon had risen, bright and silvery on the western horizon. Deeper into the estuary, two cormorants grunted at each other, the curious sound reminiscent of a couple of pigs searching for leftover

David Griffith

scraps. Out in the bay, a dozen seagulls fought over the rotting carcass of a bull shark that was too large for any of them to carry away.

Despite the decrepit appearance of the motor, the electric starter produced an instant deep-throated purr. We idled away from the mainland, and he pointed the nose into a narrow channel between another swampy estuary on our right, and a long kidney-shaped island up ahead on the left. When we reached open water, he steered way out into the lake, then turned and ducked behind one of the smaller reefs. The brilliant, full moon illuminated every detail of the sheltered cays protecting the harbor. Javier edged in next to one of them. High in a leafy tree, three monkeys sat like solemn judges. As we approached, they skittered down to the lower branches, obviously associating boats with tourists and food, even at this late hour. My less than enthusiastic guide skirted the monkey isle, ignoring their screeching protest at the lack of free food. Ahead, a larger, nearly round island slid into view. I reckoned its area at somewhere north of five acres. A concrete and rock parapet topped by razor-wire encircled the shoreline that was visible, and when I questioned the boatman he said it girdled the whole island. A walkway had been constructed between the beach and the wall, probably designed to make it easier for guards to patrol the perimeter. It was obviously a well-guarded facility.

As we approached the island, I studied the wall, split by two openings that I could see. Metal gates with spear-pointed tops and more razor-wire filled those gaps. Each gate sported a menacing camera that had undoubtedly catalogued our supposedly innocent approach.

WITHOUT REDEMPTION 245

Once, Javier glanced back at me, apprehension clouding his dark eyes, and though the noise of the engine didn't change pitch, the nose of the boat slid a few degrees farther from the island.

I shucked my jungle-soaked shoes and tied them together. Carefully, I stuck my head between the laces and readied myself for whatever might come. It would be a long swim, especially in my condition.

When we were immediately adjacent to the last point on the island, I sat on the gunwale, dug in my pocket and handed Javier the rest of his money, then fell backward over the side. He never slackened the steady, half-throttle pace. I dog paddled with the current, trying to get as much mileage as I could out of the prop wash from the boat. It didn't last long. Within seconds, Javier and the boat had disappeared. I struck out for the shore, committed to I knew not what.

Chapter 33

Paolo stepped off the ferry onto the Nicaragua shore. Behind him, the ferry man stuttered a protest, his hand extended for payment. "*Señor*, I need to feed my family. You must pay."

Paolo growled a curse and pointed the Glock at the man's forehead. "Passage is free, you scum. You now deal with new masters. For protection from the Sinaloa cartel—*you* have to pay."

The ferry man stumbled backward, lost his balance and fell across a coil of rope as the boat drifted back into the swirling current.

The trail was muddled, the road too packed and hard for Paolo to sort through the jumbled array of tracks, especially at night. San Carlos lay ahead. The odds were good that those he sought were still there.

He hurried toward the town, desperate to find the woman, before the Indian or Chapo found her. However, his questions at every bar and cantina were shrugged off. No one knew anything of a foreign woman and baby.

On the far side of the plaza, a beggar held out a scrawny hand for some change. Paolo held twenty *córdobas* in his hand while he plied him with the same questions he'd asked all night. The beggar eyed the bills. Suddenly, he pointed down the street to the lake. "A woman with a baby and some

WITHOUT REDEMPTION 247

men passed here several hours ago. They are out there, on the island."

Paolo followed his crooked, dirty finger toward the island where he pointed, a short way out in the lake. "What is out there?"

"That is the castle of death."

"What do you mean?" Paolo slapped him, and the beggar sprawled onto the pavement.

"When they go there, they don't come back," he whined.

"What did the woman look like?"

"*Muy hermosa*, she—"

Paolo booted him in the ribs. "I don't care if she is beautiful. What did she look like?" he growled.

The beggar rolled on the ground and groaned.

Paolo wished he wouldn't have kicked him so hard. Now the man's ribs were broken. Precious minutes would be wasted before the wretch could contribute any more information of value. He turned and trotted down the street toward the sorrel-colored water of Lake Nicaragua. Was it Beltrán-Leyva who had taken her? If it was them, was it a simple kidnapping for quick cash, or something more sinister?

When he reached the lake, several boats rolled lazily against the wooden pier. A chunky, short Nica, stripped to the waist was bent over the transom pouring fuel into the tank from a five gallon jerry can. The scratched lettering on the dilapidated Mercury advertised it as an eighty horsepower model. Something about the battered craft sent up a red flag. Though he knew little of boats, this one seemed, at least mechanically, head and shoulders above the rest. The other fishing boats that rested on the sandy beach appeared hard-

248   *David Griffith*

ly able to float. Each sported geriatric power units from a by-gone era. This panga was a cut above the others, which meant only one thing. He made sure the pistol was loose and ready in his waistband.

"*Hola compadre.*"

Without glancing up, the boat man nodded a greeting.

Frustrated and angry from another long day of failure, Paolo jerked the pistol out of his belt and pointed it at the sagging back in front of him. "I need a boat. Yours will do nicely."

Without looking up, the man spoke. "I'm done for the day. Come back tomorrow."

For an instant, Paolo's anger turned white hot and dangerous. He centered the sights on the top of the bent head, but a millisecond before he pulled the trigger, reason prevailed. To kill this insolent fisherman meant nothing, but a gunshot might cause unintended consequences. He glanced out in the bay to the nearby island where the beggar had indicated the woman might have been taken. The job ahead of him had enough danger. He would be wise not to advertise his presence.

The cowling for the outboard rested on the dock at Paolo's feet. The man continued to pour fuel into the outboard tank, seemingly oblivious of his visitor's continued presence. Paolo stepped forward and kicked the cowling. He couldn't have planned it better. The metal jacket hit the man square in the butt. His arms flailed, but despite his efforts to maintain his balance, the boatman did a spread-eagle dive into the murky water. When he surfaced, the first thing he saw was the unforgiving black hole on the killing end of Paolo's

WITHOUT REDEMPTION 249

Glock. The squat Nica swam to the edge of the boat and grabbed the motor.

"Get out." Paolo's eyes were hard and dangerous. There had been too many failures.

Slowly, the man placed a foot on the transom plane, then hoisted himself into the boat. The whole time, his eyes never left the barrel of that unwavering gun.

"Sit." Paolo waved the gun barrel at the rear seat in the boat.

The boatman sat, facing his adversary.

Paolo kneeled, and reached a hand over to the outboard. As he suspected, it was still warm. "You have been fishing?"

"One always fishes. That is how I feed my family."

No gear of any kind supported the boatman's story. "You're a liar." Paolo raised the gun slightly, and pointed it between the man's eyes. "I should kill you. You are not a fisherman, so who are you? Be careful how you answer. I have no time for fables."

The man shrugged. "I do what I have to do to feed my family." His focus riveted on the barrel of the gun in Paolo's hand.

"You are in the trade?"

The boatman's eyes shifted away. "Sometimes."

"Who do you work for?"

He inclined his head toward the island. "Sometimes them, but at times others. One does what is necessary to survive."

"Did you take anyone out to the island tonight?"

"Yes."

"Who?"

250   *David Griffith*

"Only one man." He raised an eyebrow. "He will not return. They will kill him."

"Who was the man?"

"I do not know. He seemed very capable, and dangerous."

"He had a cast on his arm?"

"*Sí.*"

Paolo inclined his chin toward the island. "Who are they?"

"It is never wise to speak of those who are in the trade."

"Who?" Paolo's voice crackled with a white-hot anger.

The boatman inched backward on the seat. "If you insist. Some think they are Los Zetas. I am not sure. They may be Beltrán-Leyva. I have never asked." His eyes shifted away, but only for a moment.

Paolo knew the man lied, but who controlled the island had little importance. All that mattered was that the woman had drawn the Indian. Now to spring the trap. Quickly, he glanced over his shoulder. Chapo would have every *sicario* searching for him. He would be unable to avoid them much longer, and the only salve that would quench the fires of Chapo's burning anger was out there in the harbor. He needed to bring back the head of the Indian. And the woman? He would present her to Chapo as well.

Chapter 34

When I surfaced, the fading sound of the outboard engine left an unaccustomed loneliness in me. My nearly useless arms, and the overpowering worry about Clarissa and Conor left me feeling inept and powerless. Even if I got to the island and found them, how would we escape? I still had the nine millimeter tucked into my belt, but what good would that be against these tiger-tough goons armed with the best weapons drug money could buy? It wouldn't be unusual for them to be equipped with rocket propelled grenades, fifty caliber sniper rifles, and various other ordnance that usually only national armies carried.

I struck out for the island doing a bad imitation of a dog paddle. Before my feet struck the rocky sand of the beach, I was sure I would drown, which possibly would have been the best solution if Clarissa and Conor would have been safe at home. I stumbled onto the beach and surveyed the low beach wall. It looked to be scalable. Behind that, the eight-foot concrete and rock barrier topped by razor wire was a different story. Even if I'd had the use of my arms, it would have been difficult to cross.

I staggered up to the wall. There didn't seem to be any guards, at least none I could spot. My arms wouldn't work well enough to pull myself up onto the concrete walkway that encircled the entire island, so I turned to my left and scuttled

252 *David Griffith*

along the rocky beach while I tried to locate a better place to scale the wall. After a hundred yards, I'd still found no way to scramble up the vertical slope. However, there were plenty of rocks. I started to pile enough to get up and over the wall.

Suddenly, I froze. Voices ahead of me pushed away any thoughts other than escape. I lay flat against a massive rock, hoping the darkness would be enough to camouflage my dripping body. Were these sentries? As they drew closer, the words became more distinguishable. A man and a woman. Rapid, voluble Spanish—clearly an argument. I scrunched under the wall, hardly daring to breathe. I fumbled for the familiar grip of the nine millimeter at my back, but within seconds, reason prevailed. A gun would only give away my position. I listened carefully as they approached.

The man's hard, bass words echoed down to me. "Sandra, you are completely wrong on this one. My way is the best. Don't eliminate them—at least not yet."

A rough, tobaccoey female voice answered. "There is no reasonable argument for keeping them alive, even if they are Americans. They are only a burden, with little redeemable value."

"The key word is 'American.'" It was the male. "Nobody hates them more than I do, but eliminating this woman will only create more scrutiny and trouble. You have to weigh the benefits against the repercussions. As I understand it, she is the wife of some low-level intelligence agent?"

The woman answered. "Apparently. When I talked to Diego, he indicated she was in the country with her husband, the intelligence agent at the meeting with Chapo."

"And now Chapo's trying to kill him?"

WITHOUT REDEMPTION   253

The footsteps moved closer. I melded further into the wall hardly daring to breathe.

The man snickered before continuing. "Yes, we at least accomplished that. But you need to keep the woman alive. That American agent's meeting with the Sinaloa cartel can only mean trouble for us. The woman may have information we can use. And the man? We need him alive as well, which means your people have to get to him before Chapo."

The woman's voice rose. "I have no argument with what you're saying, but we wouldn't be in this situation if you hadn't bungled the attack. Everyone in that room should have been dead—the agent, Chapo, everybody."

The man's angry retort was indistinguishable.

Sandra spoke again. "Anyhow Ali, on this one, I doubt we have to worry about the Americans. Our source indicated he was not working for a government agency."

The footsteps stopped right over my head. If either of them looked down, I was dead. Seconds later, the clear evening air carried the sound of the woman's voice as they walked on. "It is little different than when you were in Afghanistan. This agent is simply a hired contractor. If they disappear, there will be few repercussions, and. . ."

I strained to hear more, but their voices faded away. Sandra had called him Ali? That wasn't a Mexican name. Afghanistan? Who was Ali? If he'd been involved over there, and was now on chummy terms with a Mexican drug cartel, it meant Frederick's warnings to other intelligence agencies had come home to roost. Al Qaeda had brought a new level of danger to the western world.

254 *David Griffith*

The last I heard were from the woman he'd called Sandra. Her words carried back to me on the still night air. "Besides, there's that squalling kid."

Ali's last broken sentence brought no comfort. "Sandra, . . . learn from . . . experiences. In Iran, . . . played this game much longer . . .."

Who was Sandra? Certainly not Mexican or Nicaraguan. It was a name nearly as foreign as "Ali." Some long-forgotten fact pushed through from the back of my brain. Somebody with that name had been discussed at a high-level meeting. I wanted to get a glimpse of her face, but they had already walked out of sight. Besides, it would have been too dark to see her anyhow.

After their voices faded, I followed the wall until I found a good handhold on a couple of protruding rocks. With great effort and not a small amount of pain I pulled myself up and onto the walkway, then limped in the opposite direction Sandra and Ali had taken. Frederick would be very interested in those two. However, he could somebody else to deal with them. My family had first priority.

As I trudged along the wall, I suddenly remembered where I'd seen the woman's name. The sultry Sandra had been accused of several trysts with drug cartel lieutenants, but she had been born a Beltrán, which meant she was now a sworn enemy of the Sinaloa cartel. Obviously, tribal blood ties held precedence over sex. Money trumped love every time in the drug world. However, all that was of little interest. Clarissa and Conor were here. Which cartel held them was secondary.

WITHOUT REDEMPTION 255

Every step, I searched for a way over the wall and into the compound. Nothing appeared encouraging. The eight foot rock barrier was topped with broken glass and war-wire, that razor-sharp coiled product that deterred even the most foolhardy of thieves. With my nearly useless arms, there was no way to scale it. If I did make it to the top, the wire would cut me to ribbons, and I couldn't afford to lose any more blood, at least not tonight.

Within a hundred yards, light spilled across my path from the windows of a substantial building. It didn't seem wise to try to slip through that, so I turned back and followed the concrete to where I'd come ashore. That was the farthest point from the house, and it seemed there was at least a small area the surveillance cameras didn't cover. My best chance of scaling the wall without being seen was here. But I couldn't even start to climb to the top. My shoulders slumped. A great weariness hit me in the chest with the force of a sledge hammer. I hurt all over, I couldn't remember when I'd slept last, and worst of all, I knew I would fail. I'd not get Clarissa and Conor out of the trouble I'd brought on them.

Suddenly, it was like a gentle hand came down on my shoulder and I heard a voice say, "Lonnie, I'm here. Just look up." Now I've never been one to believe in supernatural gimmicks of any kind—Indian or white. I turned to see who had spoken. Nobody stood behind me, so I had to conclude that maybe it wasn't just clap-trap. It might be God. That thought really spooked me. With all the big problems in the world, why would he mess with me? Then I heard it again, and though the voice wasn't as audible as the first time, neither

256 *David Griffith*

was it an exhaustion-induced hallucination, or something I'd just thought up.

Between television evangelists and the internet, who hasn't had more than an enough of preachers spouting about Jesus and Christianity? Most of the cowboy folks I socialized with had been exposed to about fifty truck loads too much of that stuff. I had too—until God backed me into a corner. He and I had done some face-to-face business on a lonely gravel road in New Mexico. For me—that changed everything. Still, talking to God on a regular basis seemed a bit presumptuous. Train loads of people needed help worse than I did. That said, no matter how much I wanted to, I *couldn't* help myself, never mind Clarissa and Conor. So—I looked up. The limbs of a massive oak tree obscured the night sky. I squinted at one of the larger branches. It ran over the wall, about ten feet off the ground. Was God trying to tell me to climb a tree, crawl across, and then fall ten feet to the ground with no arms, and little better than one leg? If that was the best He could do to help me, then he really did have bigger issues on His mind.

Because I had no better answers, I climbed the tree. Getting up there wouldn't have been hard if I'd had two arms that worked, because the tree had a big fork hardly three feet off the ground. But to get to the branch that hung out over the wall was considerably more difficult. When I reached it, I scooted forward, though with little help from my upper body. Half-way out, I peered through the leaves under my hands. My weight had bowed the branch to within a few inches of the wire on top of the wall. Was it electrified? Involuntarily, I sucked in my belly and squeezed the branch as best

WITHOUT REDEMPTION 257

I could. Would there be sentries inside the wall? I searched the grounds, looking for dark shadows where one of them might be hiding. A dozen lighted windows from the distant villa cast shadows in the grass and shrubs. Music drifted from one of them, the sad Spanish song a *narcocorrido* of drugs, extortion, and death. I waited, not moving a muscle while my eyes searched each bush, every crevice where a man might lie in wait. I saw nothing. Slowly, I inched forward. Suddenly, a match flickered. I froze. Cupped hands brought it close to a man's narrow, high cheekbones. The match went out. All that was now visible was the occasional flare of the red tip as he sucked the smoky tar deep into his lungs. That answered my question. The sentry had been concealed in some bushes to my left, completely invisible. Were there more?

After twenty minutes, my shoulders and arms could stand no more. I had to move. Obviously, the idea I thought had come from God had been pure imagination on my part. I wasn't going to get over the wall, at least not here. Not with that sentry sitting within thirty feet of me.

I started to push myself backward, which didn't work well because neither of my arms had strength enough to move more than a crippled fly. The cigarette suddenly gained altitude, which meant the sentry had stood. I dropped my head against the limb and froze, trying desperately to meld with the dark branch. Abruptly, the man turned and strolled toward the sprawling *hacienda*. When he'd disappeared, I crawled farther out on the limb. This might be the only chance, and though I felt in no shape to drop out of the tree onto the ground, I knew there was no other option. The branch narrowed as I shinnied forward, the wire now within

David Griffith

an inch of the limb. Whoever occupied the compound had an excellent chance of viewing fricasseed Lonnie. I glanced at the wire. It was going to touch. I had to jump. Electrocution had never been on my top-three list of ways to die, so I vaulted forward, not that one can do that very well when you're lying mostly flat on a tree branch. Really, what I did was push myself another foot on the branch before I tucked my legs and let go. The ground rushed up to meet me long before I'd braced myself, and I went down with my right arm buckled under me. My face ground into the dirt. Waves of searing pain shot through my upper body, and I lay in the cool grass, unable to even lift my head. Sadness sluiced through the pain. Could I carry on? Now that I was inside the compound, would I be able to find Clarissa and Conor? I spit most of the dirt out of my mouth and struggled to a sitting position. In between groaning with pain, I did my best to catalogue the night sounds around me. Not that it mattered. I would have been easy prey for man or beast.

The massive building sprawled a hundred yards in front of me. I had no plan, I didn't know the layout, nor did I have any idea how to get inside. Hurt more than I'd ever been in my life, weary beyond anything I could remember, I had little resilience left. Maybe that was why I slipped in the first door that was open. I had to start somewhere, and there didn't seem to be any other option.

Chapter 35

Voices rose and fell in front of me. Quietly, I slipped along the wide hallway looking for a place to hide until I could get some idea of what lay ahead. Banging pots and pans indicated the first doorway to the left probably led to a kitchen. A hallway broom closet had been built into the wall just before that entry. The only problem was that it had batwing doors. I slipped inside and tucked my feet behind a vacuum cleaner, hoping no passerby would glance toward the floor where my legs would be plainly visible. At the other end of the hallway, the sound of approaching voices panicked me. I held my breath while they passed. What was next? I needed to get past the kitchen doorway ahead? That area would be littered with cooks, helpers, and whoever else had anything to do with evening drinks and a meal. I slumped against several broom handles while I tried to picture how the building had appeared from the water. Wide, sprawling. Definitely, two levels. Where would Clarissa be? How could I find her when I had no idea of the floor plan, and with the enemy everywhere?

The chatter in the nearby kitchen allowed me to get a handle on the number of people in the room. I slipped out of the closet and tiptoed back to where I had come in. Nearly made it before a face popped around the outside door. He hurried, obviously late for whatever responsibilities he had.

260   *David Griffith*

If I'd have been healthy I would have just reached out and clotheslined him. Then I would have stuck the barrel of that revolver up his nose and suggested he talk—clearly, and fast. Now, I wasn't strong enough to make that option work. Besides, the cast on my arm tended to give people the impression that respect had less importance, so tougher measures were required.

The pock-marked face belonged to a middle-aged male. He hurried toward me with his head down, intent on reaching the kitchen. Maybe he thought I was just one more cartel goon. More likely, he thought I smelled bad and he hadn't a clue who I was—nor did he care. Before he even realized what was happening, I'd slipped my least bad arm around his neck and jammed his face into the wall. My voice held all the pent up anger I'd kept buried inside since Frederick had conned me into taking this crazy dangerous trip, and for effect, I fumbled my knife out with my casted arm and stuck the razor-sharp edge against his throat. That blade had never sliced anything bloodier than kindling wood for a northern campfire, but he didn't know that.

"Where is the woman, the one they brought in tonight?" I increased the pressure on the razor edge.

"*Señor*, I do not know of any woman." His breath rasped loud against the cold steel.

"A woman arrived here tonight with six men. Where is she?" A few miniscule red drops of blood appeared around the blade.

He stiffened. "There is a room in the cellar. Perhaps she is there."

WITHOUT REDEMPTION

I made a quick decision, one I hoped I wouldn't regret. I sheathed the knife and shoved him up against the wall. "I give you back your life. Do you understand?"

His head bobbed up and down in a syncopated beat.

"But it is at a price. Do not speak to anyone of my presence. If you do, I will come back and kill you." That was an empty threat, and if he had been anything other than a lowly cook's helper, he would have raised the alarm the minute I turned him loose. I'd bet heavily that he worked here for one reason—to feed his family. I doubted he would risk his job because of some precarious allegiance to Beltrán-Leyva—or whatever other cartel held this island fortress. He would not want trouble, and the best way to avoid that was to say nothing. Hopefully, he wouldn't have to explain the scratch on his throat.

After he'd disappeared through the door that led into the kitchen, I trotted to the end of the hallway and stepped outside—just in case. A gate with an inside latch would have led me out to the walkway around the entire perimeter of the island, but I took a hard right and faded into a small grove of trees and bushes that screened what appeared to be a water treatment facility. I stayed concealed for a good ten minutes, but no goons boiled out through the door, which meant I'd probably been right. My guy had stayed silent.

A quick survey of the exterior of the building showed no other entry, which meant that to access this cellar room I had to go back in the same way, even though kitchen help and serving staff were as thick as fleas on a mongrel dog. I'd have more of a chance of success if I searched a different area of the villa first. If Clarissa was indeed in the cellar . . . hold it!

262 *David Griffith*

A five acre island? Nobody would build anything here with a cellar. It would fill with seawater faster than you could pour the concrete. Likely, the man had lied which raised two problems. I still had no idea where they held Clarissa, and two, if the man had been brazen enough to lie with a knife at his throat, he'd probably already raised the alarm.

The hopelessness of my . . . no *our* situation stampeded me into a stumbling trot back the way I had come. My mind ricocheted through a multitude of bad options. So far, I'd discovered no way to get off the island. When I'd slipped into the sea, I'd entertained a vague idea of rescuing my family and taking one of the boats that must be tied somewhere. But as soon as they discovered my presence, those boats would be guarded like they were the crown jewels of Nicaragua. And if the cook's helper raised the alarm, every goon here would be looking for me. On this fifty cent island, killing me would be about as easy as shooting a tethered goat.

I reached the place where I'd dropped from the branch. Other than the few bushes around the water treatment plant where I'd taken cover, there was no place to hide. Frantically, I scanned the grounds. It would take a half-dozen men all of twenty minutes to search the whole island. I'd find more places to hide inside the building than out here, so when an open doorway at the back of the building showed, I went through at a high trot. My half-baked plan lasted about a third of a second. Directly ahead, two men walked toward me. Both carried AK-47's, the weapon of every tin-pot army on the face of the earth, the chosen gun of the drug cartels.

Despite the wide hallway, they moved in single file. One of them had just opened the door, and when I came through,

WITHOUT REDEMPTION 263

it startled him. He stepped back, for an instant at a loss as to my identity. That moment was all I needed. My foot caught the most vulnerable spot in his solar plexus. The air left his body like a pin-punctured birthday balloon. I followed up the kick with a casted elbow to his face. He ceased to be a worry. The man behind him already had his gun in position. He kicked off the safety, but I hit him with all of my adrenalin-charged one hundred and eighty pounds. He staggered backward. Despite my ringing his bell, he came back fast. The barrel of his gun made a vicious arc toward my head. I'd anticipated that and ducked away. In football lingo, he'd made a 'hail Mary' pass. It failed. When the gun barrel whistled by my head, the weight of the gun took his body in a half-circle with it. I hit him in the kidneys with everything I had, which wasn't much, then clipped the point of his jaw with my casted elbow. He went down to join his partner, which meant I had a decision to make. I couldn't shoot them. The noise would have roused the whole establishment, but to leave them unattended didn't work either. Neither was hurt bad. They would be at least partially mobile within minutes.

I shook my head in disgust. There was no good option. I gathered their rifles, closed the door to the outside walkway, and left them groaning on the floor. Sixteen odd pounds of rifle did nothing for my injured arms or my forward progress, but I was loath to leave either of them. If I found Clarissa, those rifles just might be my ticket out of here.

Every door in the long hallway beckoned me like one of those mindless TV game shows my foster parents had watched in my youth. What's behind door number three?

Only this wasn't television. It was life and death, and the pain in my body told me death was the more likely outcome.

Chapter 36

The first door to my right turned out to be a laundry room. On the left side of the hallway, another room contained a bed, dresser, and little else. Farther down the hall, a set of stairs wound downward to a landing. Still holding the rifles, I took them two at a time. No sound of pursuit followed me. At the bottom, the stairs made a sharp left and ended at what appeared to be a storage area. However, the small cubicle contained nothing but the dank smell of mold and seawater, which verified my hypothesis that cellars don't work on an island.

Packing those rifles up the stairs from that dank room took more than I thought I had in me. Somehow I made it to the top, then skidded the two groaning bodies in the hallway to the bottom of the stairs and dumped them into the cellar room. The door didn't have a lock on it, but I jammed a block of wood against it. That wouldn't keep them there for long, but they might stay contained long enough for me to find Clarissa and get out of here.

Before stepping back into the hallway, I listened for any further activity. From the doorway where I'd entered the building, sporadic voices filtered in from outside. They were coming closer, so I needed to hurry. I took a chance and hopped for the last opening on the right side of the corridor. Stairs led upward, and though my steps on the marble floor

266   *David Griffith*

were way too loud, I skipped to the top as fast as I could. At a landing, the stairs made a sharp left, then led up to a large open room. To my right, a short hallway led to a heavy wooden door. A pencil line of light at the bottom should have hammered some caution into my thick head, but I was beyond any reasonable responses. I laid one of the rifles on the floor, tiptoed forward and threw the door open, the AK-47 balanced across my casted right arm.

A small kitchen took up the lion's share of the room in front of me. A table with wood-backed chairs at both ends hugged the left wall. A woman sat at the far end. With her eyes half-closed, she spooned baby formula into the mouth of a little boy on her lap. She was the most beautiful woman in the world, and that kid . . . well, he wasn't bad either.

I dropped to my knees, then lowered the rifle to the floor. I wanted to rush over and take her in my arms, but none of my limbs would cooperate. Finally, I struggled forward. Neither of us spoke. It wasn't a time to talk. Now, the only thing that seemed important was to hold and cherish whatever moments we might have left together, because the odds of leaving this island alive were pretty much non-existent.

I knelt in front of Clarissa and gathered both her and our little boy in my arms, if you can call a plaster cast on one side and a bloody appendage on the other "arms." Neither of them seemed to object.

"I didn't think you'd find us." Her voice carried all the exhaustion of a soul-bending weariness. What was left of my heart squeezed into a hard knot.

WITHOUT REDEMPTION 267

"I love you, and I will always find you. Are you all right? How long have you been here?" The worried questions spilled off my tongue.

"Two, maybe three hours. They put us up here so I could quiet Conor. One of the servants brought us some baby food."

I pushed to my feet and stroked her hair. "We'll find a way out of here." My voice sounded more confident than I felt.

She reached up and caressed my face while her gray-green eyes searched mine. "How did you get rid of the tracker?"

"I didn't. He's still out there following us." Anger surged right to my fingertips. "If I had killed him—" I choked off the sentence. That decision, right or wrong, had been made in the past. I couldn't go back there and re-do it. We might only have hours, or even minutes, left to live. I didn't want to waste them with recriminations. My hands cupped the face of the woman I loved. "We have each other. That is enough," I whispered. My fingers twined through her hair, and I pulled her close.

Conor had fallen asleep. No wonder. Finally, those who were supposed to be his caretakers had made it possible for him to have a full tummy. I reached for Clarissa's hand. "Let's go. We need to leave."

Clarissa struggled to her feet. It was then that I heard the distinct sound of boots on the marble staircase.

"Wait." I pushed her back into the chair and reached for the AK-47 on the floor. I checked the magazine. It hadn't been fired. Forty-eight rounds. Would that be enough?

268   *David Griffith*

Painfully, I jacked the first round into the chamber. When they came around the corner, I'd do whatever was necessary.

My finger twitched inside the trigger guard as professional instincts took over, lethal responses Frederick's people had hammered into all of us until they became as natural as breathing. I leaned over the parapet, using it for support, simply because I couldn't hold the rifle steady any other way. The clump-clump came closer. I leaned the other rifle against the wall so I'd have it close, then took a deep breath. The landing in the middle of the staircase was twelve feet away from the end of that gun barrel. I had no need to aim. I dropped to one knee to cover my torso behind the parapet. Whatever happened, I would sell myself dearly. Before they got to my family, many would die.

I glanced quickly back at Clarissa. Conor appeared to be still asleep. She rocked him gently against her breast, but in that split second, her eyes met mine. They weren't accusing, or even questioning. She trusted me to protect them—to make the right decision.

Three men reached the landing below me before the first one looked up. His jaw dropped when he saw me and he stopped like he'd hit a brick wall. The second man nearly ran into him, started to say something, then looked up as well. It was like dominos. The third repeated the performance. Every one of them knew they were silhouetted in the light—and dead. Two of them carried the same AK-47 I had. The other one had some knock-off AR-15, but all had the guts to start shooting.

WITHOUT REDEMPTION 269

"Lay the guns down—gently." Nearly in concert, they set them on the floor of the landing. No doubt, each of them had at least one other weapon as well.

"Come to the top of the stairs."

They trooped up, and I took a better look at them. They appeared to be veteran troops, old enough not to have to prove anything, which was a bonus. I wouldn't have to worry about anybody wanting to be a hero. All had seen enough death to know exactly what the odds were.

"Line up over there, face to the wall." I pointed to the north wall.

Each of them complied.

"No. On second thought, face me, and crowd together. It goes against my grain to waste ammunition."

The youngest one blanched as I waved the stubby muzzle at his belly.

"Now, take your shirts off and throw them in a pile."

Two of them had short sleeve button down shirts. The youngest had a t-shirt. They complied, and threw them toward the center of the room.

"Okay. Let's see what you're hiding. Turn and face the wall."

The oldest one, a hard-bitten, pock-faced bodybuilder type hesitated. I raised the rifle. He shrugged and turned to the wall. The .38 tucked into his waistband at the small of his back was now in plain sight. I stepped forward and jerked it out. Other than a couple of knives, the other two appeared to be clean.

"Drop your pants."

The man hesitated.

David Griffith

I jammed the barrel against the back of his neck which facilitated his immediate cooperation. "All of you—get 'em off."

Two pairs of jeans and a set of gray sweatpants hit the floor. None of them said a word, which reiterated what I already knew. They were professionals. If I made a mistake, it would be my last.

Their bare legs started to pimple with goose bumps in the cool night air. The guy in the middle had another short, wicked little blade strapped to his left leg. We got rid of that while I ignored the odd wolf-like snarl of hate, disdain, and at least a small amount of fear.

"Kick the pants backward."

Each complied, and I slid them further toward the other side of the room. They had no more weapons. Everything seemed under control. Then the soft closing of the outside door in the hallway below washed out whatever misplaced hope I'd had of getting away. The steps on the marble floor below echoed calamity and disaster even before he reached the stairs.

Those three rifles still lay on the stair landing, so I gathered and stacked them on the floor in the little kitchen. The .38 I laid on the table in front of Clarissa. She rocked Conor and stared at the gun like it was a coiled rattlesnake.

"What do you need me to do?"

I gestured toward the pistol. "It's loaded. There's no safety, just pull the trigger."

"I'm not using a gun—so you might as well take it." She looked away.

WITHOUT REDEMPTION 271

I left the .38 on the table. This was no time to argue. I fervently hoped she would never have to make the choice of whether to use it or not. But what if . . . what if we couldn't escape? What if this was it?

I glanced at the three near naked *sicarios* against the wall. They'd heard the steps as well. Would one of them yell a warning?

"The first to make a sound will die." My voice, barely above a whisper carried enough warning they all seemed to get the message.

Just before the footsteps reached the landing, I walked slowly to the top of the stairs and glanced down the narrow hallway to the room where Clarissa still sat at the small kitchen table. Our eyes met. The caustic moment between us was over. Her face showed only trust and acceptance for whatever I had to do. For that I was grateful. If things went badly, I'd not want our last words to be harsh.

I lifted the rifle, and my index finger once more moved inside the curved steel of the trigger guard. A slight figure, in what apparently was the standard servant's garb, appeared on the landing. No gun. No knife. His gaze immediately focused on my still form at the top of the stairs. He hesitated, then seemingly oblivious to the rifle in my hands, he dropped his eyes and kept coming. I stepped back, my trigger finger relaxing. This man wasn't a cartel goon, but what should I do now? I'd already had one run-in with a servant—who I presumed had gone to his bosses with the news of my arrival. But what if he hadn't? Were there undercurrents of distrust I knew nothing about?

272 *David Griffith*

A dozen different options raced through my exhausted mind as the man reached the top of the stairs. He ignored me like I was a picture on the wall, crossed the room and unlocked the door at the far end. Had he thought I was part of the establishment, guarding the woman? No, that was impossible, not with three goons lined up against the wall wearing only their skivvies.

He stepped through the door, paused, then proceeded to close it, but before he did, our eyes met. His held for an instant longer than normal. That look might have meant nothing—or everything. One thing I was sure of—he had no intention of taking a stake in this deadly game.

Chapter 37

"Get the motor started. We go to the island. If you lied, the fish will pick the meat off your miserable bones." Paolo clicked the safety off and pointed the pistol, wanting desperately to kill this insolent fish monger.

Without a word, the boatman dug under one of the seats and pulled out a ragged, red shirt. He shrugged into it, buckled the cowling back into place and pressed the electric start button. The big Mercury coughed once, then rumbled to life. Paolo untied the painter, stepped over the bow and sat facing toward the rear. Fifteen minutes later, the fiberglass bottom scratched through the gravel at the farthest point from the soaring Royal Palms that shaded the walls of the sprawling hacienda.

"Where did you drop *him*?"

The boatman pointed over his shoulder with his thumb. "In the lake. Back there."

"He *swam* to the island—with a broken arm?"

"I didn't wait to see if he made it." The boatman's eyes darted back and forth. "They will kill us if they find us here."

Paolo scoffed. "I think not." A fleeting surge of exultation flooded through him that the Indian might be at the bottom of the lake. Then again, probably he wasn't. It would take more than Lake Nicaragua to kill that crazy man, no matter how bad he was hurt. Besides, he needed to take physical

274   *David Griffith*

proof of the man's death to Chapo. The only thing that would save him would be a bloody, severed head.

Paolo jumped over the bow and onto the gravelly sand. He pulled the boat farther out of the water and crooked a finger at the boatman. "You're coming with me."

The man's shoulders slumped, but he obediently stepped over the side and waded ashore.

Paolo tied the painter to the protruding root of a Gamba tree while keeping an eye on the concrete path and wall that encircled the island. Whether this was Beltrán-Leyva or Los Zetas territory didn't matter. Both were bitter enemies of the Sinaloa cartel. A run-in with either of them could be just as lethal as with the Indian. Momentarily, he considered leaving the boatman, either tying him to a tree with the painter—or perhaps killing him. In the end, he did neither. If he tied the man, he might escape and leave him stranded, and to shoot him would create noise he could ill-afford.

They scrambled up the bank and onto a walkway. The wall was forbidding, but Paolo had no intention of attempting to scale it, not with that razor wire on top. He led to the right. "Have you been on the island before?"

"Once or twice. My sister is a housekeeper here."

"There is a servant's entrance?"

No answer until Paolo prodded him with the barrel of the pistol. The man shrugged in resignation. "That small gate leads to it." He pointed directly ahead. Paolo made the man walk on his left side. With the gun in his right hand, it would provide more than enough time to kill him if he attempted anything foolish.

WITHOUT REDEMPTION

275

Ten paces later, a wrought iron gate gave a view of the grounds and the back half of the building. It wasn't locked, and Paolo reached through the bars and unlatched it. In front of them, a wooden door sported a hand-carved image of the sun god. He motioned for the boatman to open it. If it was a trap, he would catch the first bullet. The chatter of workers drifted through the hallway. He shoved the boatman ahead of him and tiptoed inside. Immediately to his left, a set of stairs led upward. The voices now were louder, and the banging of pots and pans suggested a kitchen. Second story first. He motioned the boatman toward the stairway.

Paolo's whole life had been lived with danger, and he had a well-honed warning system. A *sicario* either developed that skill—or died. And right now, a screeching parrot inside his chest shouted danger. He should have listened. When he turned the corner at the landing, he looked up to the top and into the same jet-black, steely eyes he'd seen in the clearing back on the other side of the river. Paolo's gaze dropped. The short barrel of an AK-47 zeroed in on his torso, more than enough to match the pistol in his hand. The Indian's index finger was balanced on the trigger. In a moment, death might speak, but Paolo doubted it. If the Indian hadn't killed him in the jungle, he certainly wouldn't kill here where a shot would bring every cartel *sicario* on the island. Nevertheless, he lowered his arm and let the pistol drop to the floor.

Without speaking, the Indian beckoned the two of them to the top. Paolo's sharp eyes flickered over the three near naked prisoners lined up against the wall, which meant the Indian's presence was still unknown. The corner of his mouth

276 *David Griffith*

tipped upward. He had only one man to deal with. When the opportunity came, he would be ready.

As Paolo and the boatman reached the last stair, the Indian stepped back a half-dozen paces. Like a lone wolf, he was canny, always aware of danger, and Paolo cursed his failure to kill him in the wild. Even hampered with a woman and child, this strange man had been too skillful. The realization stoked an uncontrollable jealousy, a desire to kill and be done with this enemy forever.

The Indian motioned him further into the room. Paolo complied, his eyes again darting to the three men against the east wall. One of them sported a Beltrán-Leyva tattoo, though with their hands crossed in front of their privates, and their faces jammed into the plaster, none of them looked like killers. Quickly, he scanned the room, then peered down the short hallway to his right. The woman sat on the far side of a small table, gently rocking her sleeping baby. Haunting gray-green eyes stared out from a gentle face, the expression resigned, tender, like a . . . a Madonna—but a Madonna of war. In front of her, taunting him with their closeness were four assault rifles, all leaned in a tempting row against the table.

High voltage anger spewed from an overflowing reservoir deep in Paolo's chest, down into his arms, until the knuckles of his clenched fists turned white. He'd had enough. This stranger had humiliated him for the last time. Everything Paolo had worked for years to accomplish had been taken away. How he would love it if the Indian could watch helplessly while he blew away his woman and kid. His jaw set.

WITHOUT REDEMPTION

277

In a pretense of interest in the semi-nude figures against the left wall, he sidled to the other side of the boatman. By a stroke of luck, the Indian limped forward. The barrel of the rifle dropped a few inches, and Paolo knew that would never have happened if the man hadn't been distracted by intense pain. It was the best opportunity he would get.

With the speed of a striking jaguar, he shoved the boatman into the Indian. The timing was perfect, his move totally unexpected, and both went down in a heap. The rifle skittered across the room, but the Indian was already clawing at the revolver jammed under his belt at the small of his back. Paolo scrambled around the boatman and kicked the gun out of the man's fumbling hand. He scooped it up, ignored the Indian and ran into the room where the woman held the baby. She continued rocking the little one, but her gentle eyes locked with his.

Seconds passed, and he felt himself drawn, as if the woman had some special power of enchantment, some great strength. He stepped behind her and placed the cold barrel against her temple.

Her voice rocked him back, the sound of it like an electric shock. "I will go with you. Just don't kill him."

He shook his head and tore his eyes away. Now, the haggard face of his enemy appeared in the doorway, the rifle leveled and ready. "Drop the gun—now."

The Indian never hesitated. The AK clattered to the tile.

Paolo winced, hoping it wouldn't misfire and send a bullet ricocheting around the room. "Back off."

The Indian shuffled backward three steps. Paolo jerked the woman upright and walked her forward. This was the best chance he'd have, and as much as he wanted to kill this man, that was not an option, not if he expected to escape. The best thing would be to take the woman. He could worry about her Indian later. At least he had one of them, not what he'd hoped for, but better than nothing. The tables had finally turned.

The boatman stood as far away as he could get, not wanting any part of other men's quarrels.

"Come." Paolo inclined the gun barrel toward the squat Nica who immediately scuttled to the top of the stairs. "You—back up to the wall." The Indian slowly backed toward the wall across the room from the three *sicarios*. Carefully Paolo reached for the rifle the Indian had dropped, hefted it to make sure the magazine was at least half-full and shoved the barrel into the woman's back. Though he couldn't know the exact number of rounds in the magazine, it would be enough.

Paolo stopped at the landing and picked up the Glock. "I want five minutes. If any of you move before then, you will die. But first, I will kill the woman. Here." He gestured toward the Indian as he clicked the safety on, then walked up two steps and slid it across the floor. The gun stopped about three feet from where the Indian stood against the wall. "You are still in charge. Keep order—and make very sure nobody appears at the bottom of these stairs for five full minutes. It would be unfortunate if such a beautiful woman should die because of your stupidity."

The Indian's gaze never wavered. There was neither fear nor hatred in his eyes. In fact, a slight smile played across his narrow, strong face and Paolo wondered how he could

WITHOUT REDEMPTION

be that confident? Didn't he care? Did the woman mean nothing to him? Wasn't this his child? He backed down to the landing, signaled the boatman to go ahead, then quickly prodded the woman toward the ground floor. The short-barreled rifle in his hands covered his retreat. Perfect! Now if they could just get out of this place without alerting any of these Beltrán-Leyva scum.

He shoved the barrel of the rifle harder into the woman's back and pushed her to hurry. They hit the long hallway and ran for the door where the boatman and he had entered the building. Twice, he glanced over his shoulder while he fumbled with the action on the gun. He pushed the release, and the magazine dropped into his hand. It was within a few rounds of being full. He rammed it back into the rifle and jacked one of the 7.62 shells into the chamber. A live round hit the floor. The Indian hadn't been bluffing. The gun had been loaded and ready.

Paolo made the boatman and the woman run ahead. He trotted behind them, ready to discourage any foolish enough to follow. A niggling thought dogged his step. Could he have quietly cut the Indian's throat? He still desperately wanted to not only win, but to present both the Indian and his woman to Chapo alive. Besides, to get that close to that bushman would have been foolhardy.

When he closed the gate he glanced over his shoulder at the door with the carved sun god motif. It was as if the man had some supernatural power. He was more skillful than any man he'd ever battled, but his behavior defied all logic. Shots would have raised all kinds of alarms, but Paolo was sure the

Indian had again hesitated to pull the trigger for some other reason. Why? As before, the answer evaded him.

Chapter 38

Whatever plan I'd had to escape with my family now lay in ruins. I reached for the revolver the tracker had skidded onto the floor in front of me. What now? To get out of here alive would take more than one lousy pistol. I needed a whole arsenal of guns? I took a deep breath, muttered a quick prayer to the God who seemed to have abandoned me. I limped to the top of the stairs, then addressed the three shivering monkeys along the north wall.

"I am leaving. That was my wife and son. The man who took them is Sinaloa. I am leaving now to find him."

They all turned and glared at me.

"I have no quarrel with you today, but do not get in my way." I punctuated each sentence with the business end of that pistol as I met each of their sullen eyes. If they wanted more of a stake in the game, then they would suffer the consequences.

I pulled the banana clips out of the AK-47's, grabbed one and tucked the .357 in my belt. When I hobbled down the stairs, they were scrambling for clothes. None appeared to be in a hurry to follow me, but they wouldn't stay put for long. I'd humiliated them, and they'd not forgive that.

As I hurried to the outside walkway that ran the circumference of the property, I considered my options. It was now dark. By the time I got to where the boatman must have

David Griffith

beached his panga, they'd be long gone. There would be other boats. I'd just have to find one.

The concrete sidewalk made a curving right, then ran toward the front corner of the house. Voices and laughter floated on the evening breeze, which seemed to indicate a party still in progress. I hugged the wall and shuffled forward until I could see around the corner.

A vast deck area broke off in a series of steps to the edge of the water. Beyond that, a concrete wharf ran out into the lake. Two fiberglass ruanbouts shared space with a gleaming white yacht. That one could stay. I needed one of the smaller boats. They'd be faster, and more maneuverable. But how was I going to get to them?

Four men and three women lounged on the marble patio. I stepped back and leaned against the wall. From the riotous laughter and loud voices, they appeared to be at least one cocktail past tipsy. Would they have automatic rifles? Probably not, but they were men who lived in a dangerous world where death was seldom more than a footstep away. Every man would have a handgun tucked somewhere, and the minute I showed my face, the shooting would start . . . unless—no, it would never work. I looked up at the star-strewn sky. The moon hung suspended over the jungle to the west. An errant palm leaf seemed to slice into its surface like a sprig of parsley.

Quickly, I retraced my steps to the servant's entrance. The main electrical panel had been mounted immediately inside the hallway door, kitty-corner to the broom closet. My hand froze just as my thumb touched the main breaker. Voices came from the stairway at the far end of the hall. Of

WITHOUT REDEMPTION

283

course. The three Beltrán-Leyva goons were barreling down the stairs. Quietly, I closed the panel and scuttled into my broom closet hidey-hole.

They trooped past while I did my best to meld my body with the back wall. The sound of their feet on the marble and concrete was easy to follow. Within minutes, they would raise the alarm and the place would be crawling with cartel goons. I should have made a run for one of the boats.

When they hit the sidewalk, instead of turning right toward the patio, they trotted toward the far end of the island where the tracker had taken Clarissa. Obviously, they figured I'd gone that direction as well. They'd be too late to find anything where they had gone, but it might give me a better chance to escape. Later, they would have to tell their tale of being disarmed and humiliated. It would be a hard story to tell. I doubted they'd want to divulge the more intimate details. If I wouldn't have been so tired and scared, I would have chuckled.

I waited another minute before I stepped into the hallway and over to the electrical panel and flicked the main breaker. Instantly, the whole building went dark. I headed for the wharf at a shuffling trot. When I reached the corner, I never even slowed. One glance up at the deck showed the same figures silhouetted against the night sky.

Nobody up there seemed interested in anything but the party, and for a moment I thought I was going to get away with my brazen move. Their voices rose and fell like lapping waves, while every fiber of my being focused on the smaller of the two boats tied on the east side of the jetty. My plan had a chance of working—if there was a key in the ignition.

284   *David Griffith*

If there wasn't, I would die. Even if I knew how to hotwire a boat, which I didn't, I would not have the time to make that happen.

Possibly, if I'd strolled briskly out onto the pier like a servant, I'd have made it farther before anyone noticed my presence. By the sound of the drunken laughter coming from the deck, they'd left it to the servants to fix the electrical problem. When I reached the dock, somebody on the deck yelled. I ignored him, but not for long. As well-oiled as they were, they soon figured out whoever scrambled for one of their boats was a stranger. The music started, but even injured and exhausted, I somehow stayed ahead of the bullets. My body had little tolerance for more holes that leaked blood. I just kept running at a one-legged lope toward the last boat in the line.

As I passed the front painter, I threw the loop off the cleat and scrambled for the back one. In the meantime, it seemed prudent to send three slugs from the Beretta onto the deck. That cooled the shooting party. I'd never been a great shot with a handgun, but it was good enough that shards of cocktail glass drove them under the table.

The back cleat had a couple of sailor hitches on it, which wouldn't have been a problem if I'd had two good hands. As it was, I lost precious seconds before I could get them loose and dive into the boat. I hoped one of the drunken idiots sitting on the deck owned the thing, and that he'd be proud enough of his boat he'd not want to shoot it full of holes. I was wrong. They perforated that hull until it looked like a garage sale dartboard. The only bonus was the key in the ignition. I cranked it to the right. Behind me, the distinctive purr

WITHOUT REDEMPTION 285

of the big inboard engine muffled the gunfire. I sent another round of lead toward the deck which sent the shooters back under the table. Their ammunition, and possibly their nerve was limited. They might be evil, but the majority of those cartel folk have a head for business. They're not real interested in prosecuting a shooting war. They have lesser men to face those dangers.

I grabbed at the throttle and jammed it backward. The boat responded beautifully, and when I cleared the dock, I cranked the wheel around and let that big engine do its thing. Once, I looked back. The small group of men peered over the railing, their faces lined up like heads on a spit. I fired the last two rounds. An instant spider-web appeared in the expansive glass panels behind them. They all popped out of sight, at least temporarily, enough for me to get out of pistol range. I'd have felt pretty good if it weren't for the rapidly rising water around my feet.

Chapter 39

The mainland was less than fifteen minutes away, but all those holes in the front of the hull sucked water like a giant sponge. Before long, the bow slumped forward like a square-ended barge, and no matter how far forward I pushed the throttle, it would no longer plane. That fancy boat was going to the bottom of the lake. It was only a question of how soon.

An island off to my right presented an option. Common sense told me I should head for it, but that wouldn't get me any closer to Clarissa, so I ignored it and stared straight ahead. Somehow, this tub had to make it. I peered over the side. The motor labored, and a foot of freeboard was all that stood between me and drowning. Lake water sloshed around my knees, but even if there had been a bailing bucket, my arms wouldn't have cooperated, so I drove her at full throttle.

She stayed afloat long enough that the mainland was well in sight before she went down. I'd not tried to reach the dock. I'd hoped to drive her up on the nearest beach, but that wasn't to be. A couple hundred yards from land, the intake sucked in a big gulp of lake water. The engine coughed, sputtered twice, and died. As she settled lower, I stepped onto the bow. Did I have the strength left to swim that far? It wasn't likely.

WITHOUT REDEMPTION

My body rebelled at anything resembling a leap forward into the water. I waited until I was waist deep in the water before I kicked away from the hull and struck out for shore. Weariness sent subliminal messages to every muscle. "No more work. You're so tired. It's useless to try." But before I gave up and sucked in the first big lungful of water, the gene that makes men protectors kicked in. Clarissa and Conor needed me, and so I forced my injured arms to flail at the water as I struck out for a shore I never expected to reach.

Trailing blood from the wound in my shoulder, with both arms full of pain and weary beyond anything I could have ever imagined, I paddled toward shore. Without knowing how it happened, I dragged myself onto the beach. The gravel bit into my face as I collapsed with the water still lapping about my legs. My mind told me to stand, to walk forward and look for a way to get to the marina where the boatman would have landed with Clarissa, but my body wouldn't obey, and in spite of my determination, oblivion made a mockery of my effort.

Sometime later, my eyelids cooperated enough to let in the glaring light of the early morning sun. I struggled to my feet. One painful step at a time, I staggered to the strip of grass at the top of the gravel. My right hand fumbled to the small of my back. The pistol had survived my swim, but my fingers were now even more stiffened and useless. I dropped to the paint-peeled seat of a dirty blue bench, unloaded the cylinder, wiped the excess water off as much as I could reach without proper cleaning accessories. In front of me, a paved strip of road ran south to the little marina where the boatman

288   *David Griffith*

had taken me to the island, and also where he must have docked with Clarissa and the tracker.

My shoulders slumped with the ignominy of defeat. Where would he have taken her? I fumbled the gun under my belt, covered it with my shirt and put one foot in front of the other. Occasionally, I passed family groups or young people lounging on the burnt grass. Some stared. None spoke. No one wanted any contact with someone as wild and unkempt as me.

Though it was only a few hundred yards to the marina, each step seemed more effort than I could muster. Eventually, the boat landing swam into view. As I'd expected, the weathered panga with the swanky outboard Mercury rested in its slip. I stumbled down the dock and stared into the fiberglass bottom. I knew they wouldn't be here, but the disappointment at not finding Clarissa and Conor was still keen. Before I turned away, a flash of morning sun on glass drew my eye. I stepped into the boat and clawed under the front bench seat at whatever lay there. Clumsily, I held the tiny bottle of Clarissa's perfume up to my face. Had she lost it? More likely, she had left it there purposely as a sign, knowing I'd come? The familiar scent was the catalyst I needed. My jaw clenched. It didn't matter where they'd gone. I would find her—and our son. Stiffly, I clambered back onto the short dock and limped toward the steep street that led up into town. They were probably long gone, but with a little luck I might find where the tracker had taken them.

There are three ways to get in or out of the remote village of San Carlos. A few take the ferry up the giant lake to Granada which takes nine hours. Most are forced to take the

WITHOUT REDEMPTION   289

cheapest option, the twelve-hour bus ride around the top of the lake to Managua. The quickest way out, if you have some coin, is one of the daily flights. I doubted the tracker would be hanging around waiting for either a bus or boat, so I hired a decrepit taxi and headed for the pint-sized airport terminal to the north of town.

The tarmac was cluttered with several single-engine planes. A small business jet sulked on its own apron to the south of the runway. I hobbled inside the terminal and surveyed the passengers. A counter stretched across one end where an agent worked through a line of waiting passengers. The one and only morning flight to Managua must be leaving soon. I glanced at the clock on the wall behind the counter. Eight-twenty. Clarissa wasn't here, and neither was the tracker. I limped through every square inch of that building which didn't take long, then trudged outside into the already scorching sun. A twin-engine Piper Apache touched down on the end of the runway, then taxied into the tie-down area reserved for private aircraft. They apparently didn't have American level jitters about terrorists bombing their planes out of the sky, because I walked through the scattered passengers and airport personnel and out onto the tarmac without a challenge of any kind. A young man with an airline logo stenciled across his shirt pocket stacked luggage onto a cart. I walked up to him and pointed to the twin Apache that had just shut down his engines." Does that man do charter flights?"

"*Si*, sometimes. I think Carlos did one very early this morning to Managua."

290   *David Griffith*

I began to get excited. Maybe . . . God in heaven, let this be right. Praying seemed the thing to do. Truth be told, I didn't have much for other choices.

It felt like a hundred miles across that parking area, but it couldn't have been far because the pilot still sat in the cockpit filling out his logbook when I arrived. I stood in front of the left wing and waited. He glanced at me and scowled, but then my filthy clothes and soot-blackened hat would hardly advertise me as a paying customer. Finally, he crawled out onto the tarmac.

I limped forward. "Good morning, sir. I wondered if I could hire you to fly me to Managua?"

"Tomorrow—at the earliest." His tone was surly and dismissive. "One trip up there is enough." He didn't even look at me as he fumbled for something from inside the cockpit.

"Oh, I didn't realize that you'd already been there . . . the story of my life. If I'd been here sooner, I might have caught a ride."

He pulled out a leather satchel. "Maybe. I did have an empty seat, but I don't think the last fare wanted company."

The pounding inside my chest picked up intensity. I turned away and stared out at the runway as a larger twin-engined prop-job taxied into the terminal. "So why was that?" I kept my voice calm, like I was only making idle conversation.

"Oh, the flight was for a couple. They squabbled, and the kid shrieked. It didn't make for a fun trip."

The serenity I'd feigned deserted me. I clutched at his arm. "Describe them to me—please!" He shrank away from my filthy, blood-stained hand, and I couldn't blame him for that.

WITHOUT REDEMPTION 291

"Listen bud, I don't talk about customers. When these people show up, I just do what I'm told. I don't ask questions—"

"You mean you've flown these folks before?" My heart hit my shoes. I'd been so sure . . . a couple, and a kid.

"No, not these exact people, but those drug cartel guys are all the same. It's not healthy to turn down their business—or talk about them after they leave."

He pointed at the loading area where the small prop-job from Managua unloaded passengers. "Hop on the commercial flight. It's a lot less than what I charge."

"One last question. Did the woman have sandy-blonde hair?"

"Yeah, I guess. I didn't really notice. She looked scared, and the guy threatened her."

"What did he say?" A twinge of anger shot down into my left hand as it balled into a fist.

"Oh, I don't know. Some domestic spat, I suppose. Some guys shouldn't . . . well, never mind. Anyway, I gotta go."

"How much did they pay you to take them to Managua?"

"My base rate is two hundred and eighty an hour. Takes two hours to get there and back, so it costs about six hundred."

I didn't even hesitate. "If you'll go right now, I'll double it."

His eyes widened, and probably a touch of wariness caused him to step back. He surveyed my filthy clothes. "Listen, I don't want to get in the middle of anything if you guys are having a war. I just try to run a business and—"

David Griffith

"You're already up to your eyebrows. When you gave that guy a ride, you took sides. He's a *sicario* for the Sinaloa cartel."

His voice pitched a half-octave higher. "And you're—"

"Never mind who I am." The numbing tiredness in my body crept closer. For now, he could presume I was Los Zetas, or anybody else for that matter. "Tell me about the kid. Did he have black hair?"

He shrugged and shook his head. "I don't know . . . yeah, I guess. I didn't really look at him. He hollered the whole way."

In spite of myself, I smiled. I'd just wanted to make sure. That was my boy.

The pilot turned away and spoke over his shoulder. "Be here at eight in the morning. I'll take you then, but not today."

"No." Like a razor-edged machete, my voice sliced across the space between us. Unfortunately, the single word didn't seem to affect his decision. I'd not wanted our conversation to come to this, but the time had come to be more persuasive.

Chapter 40

All the way to the mainland, the kid hadn't made a peep. Paolo had meant to chuck him overboard, but he'd been intent on watching for pursuit and had nearly forgotten about the little nit. Just as well. It would be an easier trip back to Mexico if the woman cooperated. If he had to rough her up, she'd not be much of a bonus for Chapo. Besides, there would be other opportunities to get rid of the kid. He scowled at the bundle she held in her arms. She must have seen him stare at the child because she held him closer as if to protect him.

He snickered as they pulled into the dock. "Keep him quiet. If he makes a sound . . ." He left the sentence for her to finish and again he scanned the lake for pursuit. She could figure out on her own what would happen if that kid squalled.

The woman hadn't spoken a word since he'd taken her, and her voice startled him. "You would hurt a child?"

"If he slows us, I will kill him like a pesky mosquito."

He felt her gray-green eyes on his back as he turned away. Something about her, like the Indian, was disturbing, only more so. Several times, he caught her staring at him with the same quizzical look. Once, her lips moved though no audible words escaped her lips. Was she casting a spell—or praying? The latter seemed reasonable in her circumstances, for

294 *David Griffith*

whatever good it would do her. He'd had victims before who muttered some mumbo-jumbo. Moments later, their brains were scattered on the pavement while their bodies twitched in the final throes of death. No God had reached down to save them. Still, the woman bothered him. Though she must know her coming fate, she wasn't afraid. He shrugged. Even if Chapo didn't want her, a dozen more would jump at the chance.

When he found a pilot to take them to Managua, he pushed her off to the side of the runway, then tapped the blanketed *niño* in her arms. "If you make any wrong move, your little one will die in front of your eyes. Do you understand?"

Momentary fear transfixed her features, and he laughed at his sudden success. But the horror on her face was immediately replaced by that same unearthly calm. When she spoke, her voice was quiet, devoid of any anger. "You can only do what God allows you to do." With that, she turned back to her child and ignored him.

His temper flared, and for a moment he thought to kill her. If he could draw the Indian some other way . . . no. Later, she would die but first he had other plans for her.

Paolo paced back and forth while the pilot readied the plane and scribbled in his log book. The woman sat on an overturned fuel drum and nursed her child. Her features softened as she talked quietly to him. Finally, Paolo could take it no longer. He had to know.

"Why are you not afraid? Don't you understand what is going to happen to you?"

She stroked the child's face. "Yes, I do."

WITHOUT REDEMPTION

"Then why do you say God will protect you?" he sneered. "He doesn't care. He never did, and He never will. Your fate is in *my* hands. I can do anything to you I wish."

Her slim hand smoothed the child's hair. She never spoke, and it was as if she'd forgotten his belligerent assertion.

He didn't need an answer, but he did expect fear or hate—some response. For her to show neither of those emotions irritated him.

The pilot finally signaled he was ready.

Paolo jerked his head at the plane. "Get in." He grabbed her arm when she stood and pulled her face close to his. "If anything goes wrong—I will shoot you. But remember; it will be the kid first." He shoved her roughly toward the back seat and scowled at the pilot, who quickly looked away.

The woman never spoke during the hour long flight, other than to the little brat who howled most of the way. How Paolo wished he'd dropped him in the lake. One thing was for sure; that kid wouldn't make Mazatlán. But if he eliminated the kid, the woman would cause trouble. He growled under his breath. Maybe he'd just have to plug his ears and put up with him. Surely he couldn't howl for five hours.

When they landed at the small airport north of Managua, the pilot parked in front of a dilapidated Quonset hangar. Paolo shoved a wad of bills in his hand. It was enough. Like the boatman, he should be paying the Sinaloa cartel for protection. The pilot scowled at being short-changed, but knew enough to keep his mouth shut. He beckoned Paolo to the hangar. Inside, he introduced him to a bearded man with dark, piercing eyes under the turned up brim of a jungle green army forage cap, clearly a Fidel Castro 'wannabe'. After a few minutes of negotiation, the man agreed to fly them to Mazatlán. However, no matter how much Paolo argued, the man refused to leave until evening. He claimed it would take him that long to obtain Mexican entry documents. Paolo swore viciously. The guy flew cocaine. Did he have paperwork for that? He briefly wondered whether this pilot might be on somebody else's payroll? The thought scared him. Unless he was very careful, he wouldn't survive until tonight. The man had promised an early evening departure. In the meantime, Paolo would stay here with the plane and the woman. To leave the hangar was too risky.

THERE WAS NO DOUBT in my mind who the pilot had taken to Managua on his early morning run. My family, along with the tracker, so I did what I reckon any man would do.

Necessity demanded that I keep the .45 clean and ready for action, so when the pilot refused my generous offer, it seemed an opportune time to take care of that chore. I peered down the barrel to check for general cleanliness, and of course it was disgracefully dirty. I should have been more careful. Unfortunately, the business end of the barrel pointed in his direction. The pilot backed up a step. He seemed nervous around guns. Come to think of it, I had forgotten to remove the cylinder, which is inexcusable for one of my experience with firearms. It's those kinds of safety violations that get people killed. The pilot made an instant decision that a trip to the capitol of Nicaragua had real merit, especially for the kind of money I'd offered.

WITHOUT REDEMPTION 297

We climbed into the sky a half-hour ahead of the commercial flight. He leveled off and pointed the nose northwest while I did my best not to let on how bad I was hurt. Both arms, swollen and stiff, were now completely useless. The gun had been pure bluff, a desperate last resort, but he didn't need to know that. Sixty minutes later, we touched down and taxied over to the parking area. I started dragging out cash. He took the money and counted it twice—twelve hundred American dollars.

After he'd tucked the bills into his shirt pocket, he met my gaze. "Thanks. Appreciate the extra. Please understand. I just want to run my business and stay on everybody's good side."

"That is not possible—not anymore. That woman and little boy are mine. You made a bad mistake."

His jaw hit his chest, and though his dark flight glasses hid most of his eyes, I saw the panic.

"I had no idea. Listen, I can tell you . . . the man wanted me to take them to Mexico City. That's where he's going."

"So why didn't you take him?"

"My Mexican insurance has expired and I don't have a permit to charter into Mexico. They're a lot stickier than they used to be, and I sure don't need my plane confiscated while I—"

"That isn't where they really wanted to go." My eyes never left his face, and I gave him my best Indian tough guy look which was usually pretty good, though the useless pair of hands in my lap didn't help the charade. "Did they mention anywhere else?"

298 David Griffith

"Yeah, he did. Listen, Mr. . . . if it wasn't your wife, there's no way I'd tell you, but they shouldn't terrorize women and kids."

"Where?" I lashed out. "What did he say?"

"He wanted me to fly them up the Pacific coast to Mazatlán, to a little airport on the edge of the city. He insisted we had to go in low enough to avoid any radar so we wouldn't have to clear Customs. He would have made me do it, but I don't have the fuel capacity. I gave him the name of a guy who specializes in that kind of stuff. He flies a lot of drugs and other contraband—for a price."

"So you dumped them at the international airport?"

He alternated between staring through the windscreen and his side window. "No. There is a small airport north of Managua at Los Brasiles. Digmar operates from there."

"Digmar?"

"Yes, Digmar Trotsky."

I raised an eyebrow at the name.

"He's a product of the revolution. Thirty years ago, there were lots of Russians in Nicaragua."

"How long does it take to drive to this airport from here?"

He scrunched up one side of his face in thought. "Probably an hour."

"How long to fly?"

He hesitated, knowing what I was going to ask.

"Never mind. I'm not getting out, so get this thing in the air."

He sighed, and started the engines. While he talked to the tower, I shuffled through some more bills until I'd added another three hundred to his pile.

Mazatlán needed no explanation. Right in the middle of Chapo's territory, it was a city large enough to bury Clarissa and Conor, where I'd never find them. My only hope was that if they did arrive there, I might finally have some help. What had happened to us over the last few days was inexcusable. We should have been whisked out of the country and back to the U.S. before we even got out of Costa Rica, and here we were still in Nicaragua, with no help, and Clarissa in the hands of a twisted, lethal enemy.

PAOLO STOOD IN THE doorway of the Quonset and stared out at the giant warehouses on the south side of the single runway. He had a clear field of fire for at least two hundred yards. The plane was parked right beside him, and only one door led into the hangar. The AK-47 would cover that quite well. If they had to wait, the setup couldn't get any better.

The pilot who owned this dump must have occasionally slept here. A greasy blanket covered an old army cot shoved against the far wall. Thankfully, the building was equipped with a bathroom, though it didn't appear to have been cleaned since the day it had been installed.

Shortly after they'd arrived, the kid went to sleep, a huge relief. Later, he heard the woman rummaging through the cupboard under the bathroom sink. He paced back and forth, occasionally peering out the open door at the pock-marked runway. Heat waves shimmered off the gray tarmac. Mourning doves cooed from scattered low bushes in a field to the south. Trucks slowed for a sharp corner on the busy highway to the west, their engine brakes annoyingly loud in the mid-morning stillness. An eastern breeze gusted fitfully, intermittently rattling a loose piece of tin on the roof. In the filthy bathroom, the sounds of scrubbing. Scrubbing? Why would the woman sanitize someone else's grungy facilities? He snickered. She was loonier than her man. What was wrong with these people? He propped the rifle against the fuselage of the plane and slipped toward the bathroom door. She was on her knees, scouring excrement and urine off the revolting toilet.

"Why are you doing this?"

The scrubbing instantly stopped. Slowly, she turned and stared at him. "Well, we're going to be here for a while, aren't we?"

"Yeah, so what? Can't you put up with a dirty toilet for a day?"

She wiped at her sweaty forehead with her forearm before answering. "Yes, I could."

"Then why are you doing it?"

Her eyes fell to the floor, and she started to turn back to the work she'd started. "You wouldn't understand."

His voice rose with sudden anger, his backhand blow loud in the confines of the hangar, "Why wouldn't I? You think I'm stupid?"

Her hand shot to her stinging cheek. "No, that's not what I—"

"Then what *did* you mean?"

WITHOUT REDEMPTION

She sat on the floor in front of the toilet with her knees together, the side of her face crimson, already starting to swell. Her hands dropped to her lap. They nervously worked at each other.

Paolo waited impatiently. He stepped forward to hit her again.

"It might be that God has ordained that I die. I would want to be more like his Son if my death is imminent."

A snicker turned into a full-fledged belly laugh. "And how's cleaning a toilet like your supposed Savior?"

She showed no reaction or emotion to his taunting. "Jesus washed the feet of his disciples. I think He would have me do this for you . . . or those who would abuse—"

"Listen!" White-hot anger seared whatever was left of his heart. "It doesn't work. There is no God! You will die, and probably your kid will die, and your weak-hearted man, and there is no one to save you . . . except me. You would do well to—"

The distinctive thrum of a twin-engine plane broke his train of thought. He whirled and scooped up his rifle before he peered through a crack by the door. The same plane that had delivered them earlier taxied off the runway. As it stopped in front of the building, he scrutinized the two people in the front seats. One was the pilot. The other? He peered intently through the slit beside the door. The man in the passenger seat looked like the Indian. He turned to the woman and smiled.

"Your God has once more delivered your man into my power. This time I'm afraid he will have to die."

Chapter 41

Fifteen minutes north of Managua, we taxied up to a ramshackle Quonset building at the edge of a small town. I wished mightily that I had some way to contact Frederick, but Clarissa still had my phone, and there didn't appear to be any working pay phones in the vicinity. Not that contacting him had done any good so far.

I peeled off an extra hundred, added it to the three, and thanked the pilot. We wouldn't be exchanging Christmas cards, but in my line of work one doesn't burn bridges, no matter how distant they might be. On the apron beside the building, the pilot pointed out a sleek yellow twin with a long, pointed nose and a million dollar look, one of several planes Digmar apparently owned. It had plenty of cargo space, and I had no trouble imagining it jammed full of cocaine. The pilot taxied to the front of the building, shut off the engines and dialed a number on his cellphone.

"Digmar?"

"Yeah." I could faintly hear the high, whisky-rasped voice on the other end.

"I thought you were taking those customers into Mexico this morning?"

"Tonight. Why, what's the problem?"

"Nothing. I have another fare for you. Can I just drop him at your building?" Seconds later, he snapped his phone

WITHOUT REDEMPTION

shut and turned to me. I had the door open and was ready to clamber to the ground.

"Where's he live?" I asked.

"Don't know, but he said he'd pick you up in an hour. Just wait in the hangar."

I stepped onto the tarmac. "Thanks, and don't worry; nothing's going to come back on you." I waved, but the pilot had already gunned the engines and was headed for the runway. An ominous disquiet settled over me, but my mind and body were too numb to make sense of anything. I trudged toward the rusty Quonset. A big roll-up door served to let aircraft in and out. A paint-peeled man door had been built next to the big overhead hangar doors. I shoved the man door inward with my shoulder, stepped inside, and instantly realized—we weren't ever going to make it home.

The tracker stood halfway across the hangar with that AK-47 pointed just above my belt buckle. Clarissa sat on a toolbox wedged against the far wall.

I tore my gaze away from the woman I loved, and focused on the evil man in front of me. Anger built like a raging forest fire, until it consumed every piece of good sense I'd ever possessed. A red haze dropped over my eyes. Whatever blood I had left pounded through my head as I stumbled toward the man who had followed me for way too long. I wanted to end this so badly. This time it was over. A high voice in the distance screamed a warning, but the words evaporated like droplets of rain on a red-hot skillet. This guy had my family. His gun was pointed at me. I had a revolver, but I couldn't remember where I'd left it.

304   *David Griffith*

Whether it was the delirium or just my hardheaded Indian obtuseness, I kept walking toward him. Somewhere in the distance, I heard the voice again, and this time it penetrated. "Lonnie—no!" I smiled at her as she ran forward. This guy had done more than enough damage to those most precious to me. My step may have slowed while I gazed at her. I hoped she understood how much I loved her and Conor, and that I would do anything to stop the pain for them. This man, the tracker, had caused it all. Now, he was going to turn my family loose.

The face in front of me dissolved into sneering laughter. "No, Indian, I'm not going to kill you." His gun muzzle dropped. The bullet tore into the top of the same leg that already had a bullet hole. My fingers flexed as I tried to walk forward, to reach for his throat, but my limbs didn't work anymore, and my face ground into the concrete. I felt no pain. As I lay there, the answer came to me. The tracker was desperate. He had earned Chapo's displeasure, probably because he hadn't been able to capture me. Now, his neck had been fitted for a noose. The only way he could safely walk into Sinaloa cartel headquarters was with me—preferably alive. Only a living victim to torture and kill would suffice to blunt Chapo's anger and resulting judgment.

I struggled to my feet and again limped toward the tracker. My eyes never left his face. Clarissa screamed my name, set Conor down and pushed between us. The tracker backed up a step.

I pushed her away and stumbled forward.

He retreated another step, his gun barrel zeroed in to the middle of my chest. I glanced over at Clarissa.

WITHOUT REDEMPTION 305

Wild, tortured anguish twisted her face into an unrecognizable mask. She shook her head violently. "No! I will not let you kill him." I glanced back. Tears cut little trails through the grime on her cheeks, but I continued shuffling toward the leering visage in front of me. His lips split into thin lines of desperation that should have hammered a message into my brain, only it would no longer process information. He kept backing away, his gun barrel now wavering between my head and chest. Would he shoot? I no longer cared.

Suddenly, he stepped back three paces until he stood over Conor. Instantly, I realized what he was doing. I lunged forward, but it was too late. Swiftly he turned the gun barrel toward Conor and held it a foot from his head. I froze, for even in my condition, I understood that now, everything had changed. I backed up a step. Clarissa's terrified eyes glazed over with something I'd never seen before. Her hand dropped toward her waist, then reappeared. Anguish contorted every muscle in her face as she ran toward the man who threatened her child.

A tortured cry escaped her lips. "Get away from him!"

The tracker laughed and moved the barrel closer to Conor's head.

As if from a far distance, there was a pop. The sound didn't seem loud enough for a gun, but a hole appeared in the middle of the tracker's forehead. His eyes held a momentary look of surprise. The rifle slipped from his hands and clattered to the concrete. He staggered backward, then crumpled, his head slamming into the hard surface with a sickening crunch.

My knees buckled, and though I tried to push off the floor, my arms and legs refused to support me. The oblivion that for days had threatened to pull me into a black tunnel from which I could not escape, finally triumphed.

Chapter 42

Unfamiliar voices dragged me back to some level of consciousness. The cool dampness of the concrete was a stark reminder of where I lay, but my eyes couldn't seem to focus on the camouflage-clad figures around me. A face blocked my view. That droopy handlebar mustache? I recognized it. Nobody in the world had one like it except . . . I couldn't remember his name. I just knew he was my friend, one of the good guys. Others milled around. They seemed to have a purpose, but when I tried to rise, the man with the mustache gently laid his hand on my chest and pushed me back to the floor.

Suddenly, Clarissa knelt over me, Conor held tightly to her body. Silent tears streamed down her face. I tried to reach for her, but my right arm refused to work. My voice wouldn't obey any better than my arms. Twice I tried to speak, to say something to comfort her, but all I could manage was gaze into her eyes and try to convey how much I loved her. Even that lasted only a few seconds before everything went black again.

When I next woke up, it was in some hospital. I'd seen and smelled enough of them over the years, I recognized my surroundings before I even opened my eyes. One glance told me the private room with a view was a tall cut above normal, the only good thing that happens when you acquire bullet

David Griffith

holes on company time. I turned my head toward the window. Clarissa sat in a rocker nursing Conor. She sang softly to him and stroked his hair. I was so thankful to be here, my eyes misted over, and I had to blink the wetness away. More than once, I'd thought we'd die in that Nicaraguan jungle. By God's grace we hadn't, and the twangy southwest accent of the two nurses who'd just passed in the hallway outside the door was proof enough we'd arrived back in America.

Clarissa glanced in my direction. Our eyes met across the room, and it was as if a knife sliced across my heart. Her eyes were haunted, yet devoid of any emotion. I didn't have to ask why, nor did I want to, at least not yet. "How's he doing?"

Her gaunt face creased into a tired smile. "Of the three of us, Conor's probably doing the best." Her hand dropped to cup his little head. With her other hand, she smoothed his soft, dark curls.

"Can I hold him for a while?"

"How are you going to do that?"

I looked down at my arms. The left had a new cast and a sling, and the right had bandages from top to bottom. I grinned ruefully. "Hmm, I guess I can't. Well, at least come sit over here so I can watch him—and you."

Clarissa eased out of the rocker and laid Conor on the bed beside me. He never stirred, and that only happened if his little tummy was full. For way too long, getting a decent meal hadn't happened, but it appeared he'd made up for it. Clarissa slipped over to the other side and lay down beside me, and for a long while we just held each other, thankful to be safe; far away from jungles and drug cartels. Afterward, she paced back and forth, her arms tightly folded against her

WITHOUT REDEMPTION 309

chest. I watched, worried at her drawn face and unnatural silence. Often, her eyes strayed to Conor's sleeping form beside me. Every time she did, I could hardly stand to look at her pale, hollowed out cheeks. Several times I thought to start the conversation we had to have, but any words that came to mind didn't seem appropriate.

Suddenly, her hands clenched at her side. She turned and stood in front of the window, but not before I saw the lone tear slip down her cheek. Her shoulders hunched forward, and I knew she was back at that potholed airstrip outside of Managua. For a long while, she stared outside the window, occasionally wiping at her eyes. If I could have gotten out of bed, I would have quietly held her, but no words I could say would make up for what had happened.

After a long time, Clarissa turned and shuffled toward the bed. Halfway there, she unfolded her arms and stared at the upturned palms of her hands. "I am a murderer! I killed that man."

"Sweetheart, you can't—"

"No . . . no, you can't make me feel better. I will never forget the feel of the trigger against my finger, the horror of seeing the black hole in that man's forehead." Her eyes appeared vacant as she stared at the far wall, reliving the horror. "Every time I try to sleep I see that man. It's never going to go away." Tears cascaded down her cheeks.

"Hon, you did what you had to do."

She shook her head violently back and forth. "How can you say that? There might have been another way."

"Sweetheart." I struggled to a sitting position. "There *wasn't* another way. He would have killed Conor."

310   *David Griffith*

"Maybe he wouldn't have. Lonnie, don't you see? Now, we'll never know."

Desperately, I tried to hold her, but she kept shaking her head, the horror in that faraway hangar mirrored in her eyes. I wanted so badly to relieve the anguish and torment, but that wasn' something I could do. In this, the worst time of her whole life, I couldn't make the bad stuff go away, so I did the only thing I figured would work. I prayed—for her, and for us. I told God he'd have to drive the demons away that tormented her.

Later, we talked, and I did what I often hadn't done well. I listened without answers to her heartbreak. Conor still lay beside me, oblivious to the pain his mother carried, as it should be. Clarissa sat on the end of the bed, her bare feet tucked up under her. Often during those hours, she wrapped her arms around herself and shivered.

"I never thought I would do anything like that. I've always felt killing another human being to be so wrong. Yet, when Conor's life was threatened, I didn't hesitate to pick up a gun and pull the trigger."

"Hon, you never should have been forced into that kind of decision. It's my fault that happened." She followed my eyes to Conor's sleeping form and stroked his little bare feet as more tears fell. All I could do was pray the tears would wash away the horror and guilt; a first step to healing.

Long stretches of silence left plenty of room for me to think, and I realized it might take a long time for her to process the visceral response that had caused her to point that gun at a man's head and pull the trigger. She shouldn't have had to deal with that. Back there on the trail, I should

WITHOUT REDEMPTION

have killed the tracker. If I'd done what I knew was necessary, Conor's life would never have been threatened and Clarissa would not be facing this agony. Laying in this bed, I couldn't come to terms with my decisions. How could I expect her to deal with hers?

I'd heard it said that God specializes in healing scars. I hoped that was right, because we both had plenty that needed attention.

Clarissa swung her feet off the bed at a soft knock on the outside door. Seconds later, a familiar bulky figure blocked the light from the hallway. After a quick glance at the figure who slipped into the room, Clarissa scooped up Conor and moved to the rocker beside the window.

Frederick murmured polite greetings to both of us. My eyes darted between him and the woman I loved. The tenseness in her shoulder and the flat-lipped, frozen expression shouted out her anger. Nevertheless, she returned his greeting with a tired, expressionless nod.

I wanted to let loose with a shotgun blast of my own fury, but when Frederick shuffled to the end of the bed, I only felt compassion. His face was as weary and haunted as Clarissa's, and his voice when he spoke was halting, nervous, something I'd not heard before.

"I—I am so sorry." He jammed his hands in his pockets, his eyes shooting to the corners of the room. "Never would I have thought this could have spun out of control as rapidly as . . . well," he swallowed and dug for a handkerchief. When he pulled one out, it seemed he'd forgotten why he'd wanted it. He wadded it from one hand to the other, then shoved it into the inside breast pocket of his blazer. "I know at this

312   *David Griffith*

point it probably means little, but the company would like to do what we can to make up for what happened. I'm aware that is hardly possible—but we'd like to try." He turned to Clarissa. "I cannot tell you how devastated we are to have put you in that kind of position. What you had to do is something no wife and mother should ever be faced with." He pulled the handkerchief back out and again seemed to forget why he had it in his hand. He peered at it, then wiped his forehead and shrugged. "Anyhow, we can talk about all that later. There is a secluded beachfront condo outside of Honolulu that is yours whenever you would like to use it, and for as long as you want. Plus," he hesitated before he again turned toward Clarissa. "I can only imagine what you are going through. If there's anything the company can provide as far as professional counseling or help while you're there—consider it done."

Clarissa's face remained frozen. Finally, she nodded slightly and whispered what might have been a polite thank you, at least I think that's what she said. She had her emotions on a tight rein. If one tiny trickle of passion reached the surface, it would instantly turn into a raging river of dammed up debris, an unstoppable torrent of anger and sorrow.

Frederick's level gaze settled on Clarissa for a moment. Perhaps he saw more than I gave him credit for because whatever he was going to say, he left unsaid. He turned back to me, the question mark I'd expected in his eyes. I knew what he wanted.

I turned to Clarissa. "Hon, could you grab my *mochila*?" She reached under the bed and set it beside me.

WITHOUT REDEMPTION 313

"There's a pocket inside with a hidden zipper. It's in there." Frederick pulled it over and rifled through it. He found the zipper and fumbled around in the pouch, the instant consternation on his face a mirror of his unsuccessful search.

"There is nothing there."

"There has to be. It was there before—"

His shoulders slumped at my instant panic. "Sometimes nothing goes right. It just happens."

It seemed he would bid us goodbye and leave. Instead, he stood in the middle of the room while he alternated between folding his arms and jamming his hands into the side pockets of his jacket. "I don't know what to say. We did everything wrong. I have absolutely no excuse for not being able to evacuate you. We underestimated the situation, and it was a series of mistakes from which we have learned a multitude of lessons. I cannot tell you the sleepless nights we went through at headquarters . . . well, never mind; it all sounds a bit mawkish."

I didn't even know what mawkish meant, and he didn't explain. He turned away, fumbled for the handkerchief again and blew his nose. I watched, incredulous. This man didn't resemble the Frederick I knew, and suddenly I understood better than I ever had before how important it was for him to protect us. For him, our ordeal had been a very personal and haunting failure. The papers, the mission, would always be secondary to that deep need to take care of his people.

Frederick took a deep breath and seemed to remember that he'd started to leave. He walked to the window and held one of Clarissa's hands in both of his as he knelt in front of

314   *David Griffith*

her. For a few moments, he talked to her. I didn't catch every word, but it seemed to be another attempt at an apology for what she'd gone through. I watched her face. She nodded several times and appeared to be making a valiant effort not to break down.

He left her, then paused by my bed and touched my shoulder. "We'll talk soon." I understood. There had to be some kind of debriefing, though it didn't seem like it would be of much value to rehash a multitude of mistakes. The papers missing from my *mochila* were a mystery. Until the time I'd walked into that hangar I'd never let it out of my sight, so where had they gone?

Frederick shuffled toward the door, but Clarissa's voice stopped him. "Mr. Roseman?"

He turned, a questioning look on his weary face as she laid Conor on the bed beside me. Clarissa reached in the closet beside the bed for the mud stained backpack, the one she'd stuffed full of diapers, food, and whatever else she carried to make Conor's life as normal as possible. She rummaged to the bottom. When her hand came out, it held a bedraggled envelope, the same one Chapo had handed me.

I shook my head. A slow smile broke through the weariness etched over her features. Despite the horror of what had happened, this woman had always been in control. I laughed, glad that she had the envelope, but more grateful this beautiful, tough woman was my wife. It would take time, but one day, she would be whole again.

"How did you get the envelope?"

"Never mind how. You haven't had it since the first night in the jungle. I decided if we were in this together, then we

WITHOUT REDEMPTION   315

might as well succeed. It was a lot safer in the bottom of a diaper bag than in the *mochila* you so obviously guarded with your life."

Frederick took the envelope from her hand and awkwardly hugged her. Then he stepped back, one hand still on her shoulder. "Clarissa, this side of Heaven, few will know how many lives you have saved with this." He waved the bedraggled envelope at both of us. "I am grateful. Someday, hundreds of others who were able to live because of what you did will be even more so."

Frederick tucked the envelope in the inside pocket of his tan sport jacket and turned to me, his face serious. "Oh, I almost forgot. Early this morning, Mexican Marines arrested Chapo at the Miramar Hotel in Mazatlán. You kept him in the jungle long enough he seems to have needed a rest. Satellite surveillance tracked his plane back into Mexico. Due to your efforts, they were able to follow him right to the hotel. And remember, those tickets for a *real* holiday are at headquarters, whenever you want them."

I waved him away. It was too early to talk about another "holiday." I should have been glad we'd had a part in El Chapo's capture, but we'd been through too much, we were too numb to think about anything beyond the moment.

After Frederick had departed, Clarissa sat on the bed again while she stared at the wall. When she spoke, her voice again carried that tortured guilt. "What bothers me is that I took away any further choice that man might have made toward salvation and possible redemption."

"Hon, you can't do that to yourself. He was a killer, a man intent on spreading evil. Conor would have died. He would have killed me—and you. What you did was necessary . . . and right."

She lay down beside me, and as much as my hurting wounded arms allowed, I held her close. Whatever it took, we would walk hand in hand through this valley of despair. Together, we would find deliverance from a drug cartel's hate and horror, a release we desperately needed, because without redemption—there could be no peace.

Epilogue

Los Angeles Times - Tracy Wilkinson, Don Bartletti and Richard A. Serrano MAZATLÁN, MÉXICO — Joaquín "El Chapo" Guzmán, one of the world's biggest drug traffickers and Mexico's most-wanted fugitive, was captured Saturday in a joint U.S.-Mexican operation after more than a decade on the run, officials of both countries announced. Guzmán was arrested by agents who burst into the seaside condominium in the Sinaloa resort of Mazatlán where he had moved just two days earlier.

The Guardian.com -Two Mexican federal judges ruled on Tuesday that Joaquín "El Chapo" Guzmán will face trial on drug trafficking and organized crime charges in Mexico . . . the Mexican government said there was no way Guzmán would repeat the 2001 escape that let him roam western Mexico for 13 years as he moved billions of dollars of cocaine, methamphetamine and heroin around the world. Mexican authorities say they want . . . to dismantle his Sinaloa Cartel, a multi-billion dollar enterprise that dominates drug trafficking in much of Mexico and stretches into 54 countries . . . .

(Reuters) - Mexican drug kingpin Joaquín "Shorty" Guzmán won a temporary injunction to block his extradition to the United States where he faces narcotics and arms

318 *David Griffith*

trafficking charges, a (Mexican) federal judge ruled on Tuesday.

(CNN) - Authorities are scrambling to find Joaquín "El Chapo" Guzmán after his stunning escape from a maximum-security prison west of Mexico City.

The leader of the Sinaloa cartel stepped into a shower Saturday night, crawled through a hole and vanished through a mile-long tunnel apparently built just for him.

Mexico's government is offering a reward of up to 60 million pesos ($3.8 million) for information leading to his capture.

(Fox News) The children of Mexican drug lord Joaquín "El Chapo" Guzmán are denying they had anything to do with a recent ambush on a military convoy that resulted in the death of five soldiers, Guzmán's lawyer said Monday.

(CNN) - Joaquín Archivaldo El Chapo Guzmán Loera was transferred from the maximum-security Altiplano lockup in central Mexico to a prison in Ciudad Juaréz, a senior Mexican law enforcement source told CNN.

"Due to the proximity (to the U.S.), it makes it easier to extradite him," the official said.

(AUTHOR NOTE) - Joaquín "El Chapo" Guzmán has spent the better part of three decades building a bulletproof network of informants, attorneys, judges and politicians. After his last daring prison escape from the high security Altiplano prison near Mexico City, he was recaptured by Mexican federal troops. Inexplainably, in May of 2016, he was moved from Altiplano, a short walk from the Texas border in Cuidad Juaréz. It is also the center of power for the Sinaloa cartel, and a short distance to the mountain villages that have

WITHOUT REDEMPTION

shielded him from the searching tentacles of Mexican law enforcement. El Chapo Guzmán is arguably the most powerful crime boss of our time, and the Sinaloa cartel is still immensely powerful. Theories abound as to why the Mexican government would move El Chapo so near to a city he still holds with an iron fist. The official line is that he is closer to the American border to make extradition easier. Time will tell, but it may be that the Cefereso prison where he is now held may prove as porous as the last two where he was incarcerated. If so, El Chapo will once again fade into the vast labyrinth of rugged mountains and vast canyons that make up the Sierra Madre of Mexico. the heart

March, 2018 – The Mexican drug wars continue to write new chapters. Juan Guzmán presently resides in the Metropolitan Correctional Center in Manhattan, New York. America won. El Chapo, the most powerful of the drug lords has been captured, extradited, and chained. Will he stay that way? The odds are against him, but only time will tell.

I hope you enjoyed *Without Redemption* as much as I did writing it. After researching the plot in Nicaragua and Costa Rica, I started the first draft. It's fiction of course, but too many of the details continue to resonate, because the Mexican drug cartels permeate society in every town and city in North America.

Thank you for reading another of the stories in The Border Series. If you enjoyed it, please consider posting a review on the book site of your choice.

Best Wishes,
David Griffith

Brothers of the Blood
Book 4 in The Border Series
Chapter 1

The ancient hunting rifle in my hand was not my choice in a firefight with a drug cartel. Though I was desperately low on ammunition, I made good use of it. A few of the Los Zetas troops below us were ex-military. They'd added a few of my contacts to their growing list of scalps, and if it weren't for Derek, they'd have taken mine. He'd appeared when I figured it was all over but the funeral. Now, he was holed up in the rocks to my right. Every time they tried to rush our position, he knocked them off like they were ten pins in a border town bowling alley. That worked until they figured out how to scale the near vertical cliff behind us. I shot a worried look at Derek. This wasn't good, and as near as I could tell, we would now both die in this drug-infested hole. Derek just grinned, then pulled out his canteen for a swallow of water, which made me angry. How could he be so blasé about the few minutes of life we had left?

We were most of a hundred feet apart, too far to talk normally, and if we'd yelled back and forth, they would hear every word. Neither of us wanted that, so we kept silent. Derek motioned me to work my way toward him. I raised my

David Griffith

eyebrows, held my open palms upward and violently shook my head. If I moved from behind this boulder, they'd pick me off like a gut-shot coyote. Whatever he had in mind was on the north side of stupid.

Derek ignored me, which is what he usually did in these situations. Mind you, there were times I ignored him too—like this one. There were too many bullets flying, and I wasn't moving. Even after all the times we'd worked together, we'd still never developed a leader-follower pattern. We both did whatever felt right, which is contrary to every Special Forces protocol in the world. Most times in shooting situations, I let Derek call the shots. This wasn't one of those times.

Five minutes later, Derek gave the same signal. I glanced at the cliff over our heads. If they were actually there, we had only minutes before the bullets would find us. Los Zetas had the best sniper rifles money could buy—and the best training. Some of their troops were defectors from the Mexican Special Forces. They knew how and when to shoot.

The heat was unbearable, and I leaned back against the rock and wiped the sweat off my forehead. A flash of movement up on the rim caught my eye. Two of them were already there, and suddenly whatever Derek had in mind didn't seem so crazy. We were trapped. Death was imminent, so I ran.

The first stretch was the most dangerous, because it was the farthest and completely exposed to the rifles below. I tucked the rifle into my chest and made like I was one of those big talented guys who run hundred yard dashes for a living. I didn't do too badly. Bullets are a great motivator. Olympic guys don't have to deal with bullets scuffling over

WITHOUT REDEMPTION

which would first penetrate their tender bodies. I did a first base slide behind Derek's rock, and then checked my body for leaks. No blood. Definitely a bonus. Derek turned and gave a non-committal nod, which was so like him. I'd risked my life to follow his instructions. His response? What took you so long?

I scowled. "You could have covered me better than that. I didn't hear you shoot more than a couple rounds."

"Bullets are expensive."

"Yeah, well my wife says I am too. I hope you have a plan after that little exercise."

"I do. You're taking my rifle and going up the cliff. Then you're going to cover me while I climb to the top."

I glanced over my shoulder. Instant vertigo made me grip the rifle in my hands. It was straight up for eighty feet. Even lying prone on the ground I broke out in a sweat. I could face bullets or a bar fight. Heights turned me into a sniveling coward. "I'm not doing that. What's the other option?"

Derek shrugged. "There ain't one. Besides, you're not going to climb it here. They'd pick you off before you even got started."

"Well thanks. I'm touched that you're concerned about my safety." I turned and stared at the ochre rock face behind us. It ran for a couple hundred yards to our left. To the right , it made an abrupt curve toward the north.

"Just around the corner, there's a chimney. It's not great protection, but it's better than that." Derek inclined his chin toward the wall behind us. "Besides, they won't even know you're gone" . . . suddenly Derek swiveled and pumped off

324   *David Griffith*

a couple of quick rounds at the top of the cliff face. "Go—now!"

The two Los Zetas troops on top of the rim scrambled for cover. As much as I wanted to argue, there wasn't time. We switched rifles and I skedaddled. It was only when I was around the corner and staring at the rock chimney in front of me that I thought about ammunition. I reckon Derek intended to pass me a couple of spare clips, but in the rush it hadn't happened. The rifle clip was half full, which meant I only had fifteen shots to protect him while he followed me. I stared at the narrow chimney. Like Jack's beanstalk, it spiraled toward the sky. I couldn't do it. I wiped my sweaty hands against my pants. If I even got halfway up and glanced at the ground, I would freeze, and then it would all be over. Derek knew I was deathly afraid of heights. I swore an oath that no matter what happened; if I didn't die while climbing this wall, he would pay more than he could have ever imagined.

The rifle he'd passed to me had a worn leather sling, unusual for an assault rifle unless you're in a real war. Most of my life I qualified for that, so I braced my feet on one side of the chimney, my back against the other, and started to crab my way upward. Fifteen feet up, I made the mistake of looking at the ground. Everything went topsy-turvy which is what I expected. I closed my eyes and sucked in deep, measured breaths of air. I had to do this—or die, and that didn't seem a good option.

I will never be able to explain how I made it to the top of that cliff. When I hoisted myself over the edge, I scrambled as far as I could from the cliff, then turned my face to

WITHOUT REDEMPTION 325

the ground. My trembling fingers clawed at the black dirt under my fingernails. Eventually, I regained control. I had to. The shooting below had intensified which likely meant that Derek was running for the chimney. I had to protect him, which meant I had to get out on the edge of the cliff, look down and fire with enough precision to hit something. Every instinct told me to get as far away from that rim as I could, but all my life I'd placed great store on loyalty. I'd counted on Derek more times than I could count. This time the tables were turned, and though I'd little stomach to accomplish what I was called to do, I crab-scuttled to the rim, swallowed my fear, and started shooting. It might not have been my best performance with a rifle, but it seemed likely that several of those below would need urgent medical care if not an undertaker.

Out of the corner of my eye, I watched Derek zigzag to the chute. My part was to keep those below from moving closer. Though I had only a few shots, I placed them well enough he made it to the top alive and with no extra holes in his body.

When Derek crawled over the rim, he lay for a moment on the ledge while he tried to catch his breath. I stayed vigilant. Where were the two on top?

Derek struggled to a sitting position and held out the old lever action rifle. "Give me my gun."

"No, you gave it to me. Shoot that one." I slid the rest of the 30:30 shells I'd carried in my pocket across to him.

He still held the gun with his right hand curled inside the lever action. Suddenly, he one-handed the lever and shot over my head. I dived for cover, rolled and came up firing.

326   *David Griffith*

There was no need. Derek had already fired a second time, and he was not a man who missed what he aimed for. Two shots—two bodies. There might be more of them on top of the rim, but the original pair were no longer a concern.

We had a long trail ahead of us if we were to escape. For eight more days we slogged through mountain passes where we froze at night and roasted during the day. As we made our way north to the small town of San Carlos, we avoided both cartel goons and the police. The Federales were the good guys, and though we had all the right clearances, to be picked up by Mexican federal police would have only complicated matters. It was best if we slipped out of the country unnoticed, and unseen.

On the fourth day the rain came, a bone-chilling drizzle that refused to stop. By the time we staggered into San Carlos, we were both close to pneumonia. I'd never been happier to feel the wheels of that company plane break contact with Mexican soil.

When we touched down in Albuquerque, I breathed a sigh of relief and swore I was done. This time had been too close. Mexico was a cartel cesspool, and my cover had been blown one too many times.

I ran a hand through my hair. At the end of every mission, when I looked into the mirror, I tried not to see the white hairs and deep worry lines. But they were there, and no matter how I wished it was otherwise, the stress of the job was taking its toll. I grabbed my *mochila*, the survival backpack I'd carried through a hundred missions and gingerly navigated the aluminum stairs to the tarmac. A mind-numbing weariness seeped through my body and rested in

WITHOUT REDEMPTION

327

my bones. I shrugged it off. A good night's sleep would put everything in perspective. Derek and I threw what gear we had in the back of a cab and headed for the hotel. We were safe. Tomorrow, I would be winging my way north to the woman I loved. Then, at the proper time I would hand in my resignation. I was no longer cut out for what Derek and I had endured.